BENEDIC

A CORPSE FROM THE PAST

IZZY PALMER BOOK TEN

Copyright

First edition July 2024

Cover design by **info@amapopico.com**

To my wife Marion,
my children Amelie and Osian,
and my accomplice Lucy.

This book and this whole series is also
dedicated to my brother Daniel,
who has laughed at me since I was a small
child and now laughs at my books instead.
I love you, Dan, and just like when we were
little, I believe you can do anything.

Reader's Note

This is the final book in a ten-book series (not including the five novellas), and it brings together a lot of characters and threads from previous stories. This means that it is full to the brim with spoilers, including the identity of killers from earlier books – in particular, A Corpse Called Bob, A Corpse in the Country, A Corpse in a Locked Room and… well, most of them really.

Many of the books in the series were written for casual readers to enjoy. This one is for the fans. Yes, all six of you! But even you might need a hand, so feel free to turn to the very back of the book where I have included a detailed character list which should help you remember who everyone is. I've still tried to write the story in a way that is easy to follow, but there are a lot of old faces who pop up in this one, so it might help!

And with that established, we can begin…

Chapter One

"Tell me, Izzy, what do you think it takes to be a successful killer?"

I believe this was the most nervous I had ever felt in my own living room. It wasn't that I'd never been interviewed before. In fact, I'd appeared in the Croydon Advertiser on five separate occasions, and only four of those were connected to the case of the missing squirrel. What scared me this time was that the frighteningly well-dressed young woman in front of me had been sent there to get to know "the real Izzy Palmer".

Ooh, tell her about the time you—

Nope!

"Perhaps I should rephrase the question." Janet Ellison regarded me as though I'd been staring gormlessly into space, probably because I'd been staring gormlessly into space. She looked more like a Bella or a Chloe than a Janet, and she reminded me of all the pretty, capable interns I used to work with who made me feel ugly and useless. "How is it that some killers, even in the age of high-tech forensics, literally get away with murder?"

I blew my fringe out of my eyes. Compared to the replies I'd provided to her previous questions, I felt this was a strong response. I'd already jabbered on about my family and talked of the time my first stepfather had chased me around the house with a broom. I doubted it could get much worse than that.

"I would imagine…" I tried again, "…that some people are… lucky." I was speaking so slowly that I might as well have replied in Morse code.

She raised her eyebrows as if to say, *Could you expand on that?*

"The way I see it, it is incredibly difficult for a murderer not to slip up at some point along the way." I smiled with relief that I'd managed to complete a whole sentence. I must have looked quite deranged. "In my experience, the ones who manage it can only do so because…" *Deep breath, Izzy!* "…because they don't let their emotions confuse their thinking."

She nodded approvingly, like a dog trainer when a chihuahua has finally learnt to use a litter box. "Of course, you're yet to leave a case unsolved. Isn't that correct?"

This is the perfect time to boast about your 100% case-closing record. Ooh, and your bowling average!

"That's correct, and I've learnt from the mistakes that each of the culprits I've identified has made. The fact is that murderers tend to be fairly desperate people, and desperate people do desperate things."

Pretty smooth, Iz. This isn't going nearly as badly as I'd expected.

I know, right? I sound all confident and knowledgeable all of a sudden.

Janet Ellison leaned her knitting-needle-esque legs around to the other side of her chair and smiled her sparkly smile. "Okay, Izzy. Let's move on to something more personal. Are you seeing anyone at the—"

"Hot chocolate!" I blurted so that she wouldn't finish that question. "I mean… I'm so sorry, I didn't offer you any hot chocolate."

"I'm more of a coffee—"

"Hot chocolate all around. What a good idea." I was up on my feet and halfway out of the room before she could disagree.

"I try not to consume dairy!" she called after me, but I was long gone.

I made it to the kitchen, which was unexpectedly occupied by half of the people I'd ever met.

"How's it going, Izzy?" my mother called from the breakfast table as soon as I set foot in the room. Like a queen in a Tudor court, she was flanked by various respected advisors. There was her hairdresser-turned-life-guru Fernando from Penge, her devilish rockabilly-esque talent manager, Eddie Vanguard, and Brian, the guy who collects trolleys in our local supermarket. As one of Britain's most beloved stage performers (and occasional guest on daytime chat shows), my mother had collected a large posse of such middle-aged men, many of whom were standing in my kitchen, eating my chocolate digestives. I couldn't understand how they'd got through the back door without me seeing them.

"It's going," I replied, no longer quite sure what I was doing in the kitchen.

Luckily, my supernaturally sensible (second) stepfather was on hand. He must have sensed that I had fled the interview to make hot chocolate, as he immediately set about heating milk.

"There's absolutely no need to panic," my best friend Ramesh insisted in a panic. "Think of your brand, Iz. Think of your brand!"

I was tempted to ask what my brand as a detective actually was, though I had the sneaking suspicion it was the kooky girl who breaks off an important interview in search of hot chocolate that no one needed. Instead, I plumped for a far more important question.

"Why are there so many people in my kitchen?"

"We're here for you, Izzy!" my childhood dentist insisted through a mouthful of somewhat hypocritical sweetened crumbs.

Holding his cats Kiki Dee and Tammy Wynette (his old cat Elton John had recently retired), Ramesh looked perplexed. "We knew you'd lose your head in the middle of the interview, and so I put out an alert and brought the gang together." He came to put his hand on my shoulder but, thanks to the aforementioned moggies, it proved rather difficult. "This is your first exposure in a national broadsheet newspaper that isn't linked to a squirrel, Izzy. The tabloids have been all over you for years, but this could take your career to a new, more sophisticated level."

"And that's what frightens me. The journalist's too classy. Her shoes look like they weren't bought at a supermarket."

Mother left her throne to console me. "We've talked about this, Izzy. It's just a puff piece, and there's nothing to worry about. You are a confident, successful young woman, and a major publication has taken an interest in you because of your myriad accomplishments." Somehow, her pep talk was actually working. "You're going to go back into that lounge, answer a few simple questions, and then we'll have lunch."

Ramesh had stacked the cats in one arm by this point and looked serious. "I have a hankering for Lebanese food. Surely that will motivate you."

Greg handed me the two mugs of hot chocolate. My biological father cheered from the background, and I finally felt ready for the challenge before me.

"So what you're saying," I began, finally putting the pieces together and finding a solution, "is that I should be myself?"

Approximately twenty-eight of the approximately twenty-nine people who were shoved into that room like anchovies in a can instantly broke eye contact and peered down at the floor.

"That's the spirit, my love," Dad said, and his belief made up for everyone else's doubt.

I walked back to the lounge, and it wasn't just the fact that the mugs were burning my hands that meant I had a spring in my step. I was eager to put the best side of myself forward.

The only problem was my interviewer. There was something deeply intimidating about Janet Ellison, and I'd almost melted when she'd turned up at my door. You know how everyone laughs at Barbies because of their humanly impossible waists and pointy feet? Well, Janet proved that the designers at Mattel knew what they were doing after all. With her glossy blonde hair, perky smile and perfect skin, she was like an after picture in the laboratory of a mad scientist who had developed a dollification ray. She was one of those people who you can't help hating, even as you dream of becoming her best friend. Or perhaps that's just me.

I'm sure if she had been a little less perfect, I would have managed the interview just fine but, when I sat back down on the sofa, I lost all willpower and sat there mumbling to myself. So it was lucky that I'd found that exceptional woman's kryptonite.

"Hot chocolate! Is there anything else like it?" she asked, her pretty smile now adorned with a perfect brown moustache. "It tastes better than I remembered. It's one of those things you give up when you reach adulthood for some reason."

"Oh, completely." I hugged the cup to make me all warm and cosy. "I really don't remember the last time I had some."

It was this morning.

Janet shuffled happily in her seat, which made her both more human and less frightening than before. "Now, let's get back to what I was saying. As you are aware, I've been sent here to get to know the side of Izzy Palmer that we don't normally get to see. So perhaps you could tell me about the string of eligible men you've been linked to?" She consulted the notepad on her lap then. "There was Edmund Porter, the new CEO of Porter & Porter, where you previously worked."

I'd never actually dated Edmund, but I wasn't about to contradict her when she was making me sound impressive.

"Then I believe you were also the childhood sweetheart of newly popular TV doctor – and every middle-aged mum's pinup – Dr Danny Fields. There was even talk that you might have had a dalliance with the world-renowned inventor and founder of X-Tec Spyware, Dean Shipman."

I had to interrupt her before she could mention the Father Christmas impersonator or the murderer I'd dated. "They were all very nice men, and I am lucky to know them."

She moved a little closer, as if she intended to whisper, then continued in her normal voice. "Oh, come on, Izzy. There's no need to be coy. Just between the two of us, what's your secret? What is it about you that has caught the eye of so many thoroughly tasty bachelors?"

I let out a squeal that I immediately regretted, but her question had made me laugh for three different reasons simultaneously.

That I might have the first idea how to attract a man.

That journalists still asked such slimy questions.

The fact she'd described my friend Dean as "tasty".

To cover this slip-up, I said the first thing that came to me. "Well… I am pretty good at bowling."

She shook her head in bemusement as she noted this down, and her reply, when it came, was one long laugh. "Oh, you're funny, you are. I like that." Her face suddenly turned very serious, and she continued scribbling down notes for some time. I felt like a patient, waiting to hear the bad news. "And what about now?"

"Now?" For a moment, I thought that she wished to know my lunch plans.

"In terms of hunks, I mean?" She appeared to have used this word unironically, and I struggled to think of a response.

Perhaps old-fashioned language is back, just like old names come in and out of popularity. Perhaps it's okay to say "hunks" and "tasty" now. You know, like it was in the 90s?

"I must admit that I am totally hunk-free going on a year. The last man I dated told me he wanted to be friends with benefits. That sounded alright in theory but, in practice, it meant that it was just as unsatisfying as any other bad relationship I'd had, and he didn't have to buy me a birthday present."

"That must have been really tough." That serious look was still on her face, and she bit the end of her pen as she spoke. I'd read somewhere that this was a sign of internalised stress, but it was hard to imagine Janet's life being anything but perfect. "Now, let's move on to your cases. You'll be happy to know that I'm not here to talk about the time you heroically located a lost squirrel for an old lady who paid you in cake. We know all the details of the case from the TV movie they made."

"Thank goodness." I took a sip of my drink and felt good about the world. "I have to admit that it gets a little boring to talk about it so often."

"Which is why I'd prefer to know about the aftermath of the case. Are you still friends with Mrs Langley, who was played on screen by Helen Mirren? Do you ever visit Squibbles?"

"I have investigated plenty of other, more serious cases, you know?" I could probably have phrased this more politely. "I've done more in my life than just finding a wild squirrel who wasn't actually lost so much as eating nuts in a neighbour's garden. I've solved loads of murders." I sounded like a little girl boasting about how many cuddly unicorns I had.

She apparently didn't notice, as she continued in quite the same tone as before. "Which is a real feather in your cap, especially when we consider that some of the victims were very well known. Mr Aldrich Porter, for one. You solved his murder before his son took over the business, and then there was that actor, Sammy Akerele. Would you say it's more difficult to solve a celebrity murder than that of a normie?"

"I… I approach all my cases in the same way."

It was hard to know what sort of person my questioner was. I had looked her up online as soon as she e-mailed my press manager, of course. There wasn't a great deal to go on, but her website revealed that she'd written one novel about the trials and tribulations of modern dating, which didn't get many reviews so probably wasn't a bestseller. From the fact that she only appeared to have published a few articles over the last year, I concluded she was one of those society girls who are too rich to need to work.

If I was too rich to need to work, do you know what I'd do?

No.

Not work.

You are very wise.

She'd studied at Oxford and then travelled all over the world, so she sounded like a serious sort of person, which made the questions she was asking all the odder. She veered between the banal, the perceptive and the entirely ridiculous, and I only realised that she'd been softening me up when a slightly evil glint flashed in her eyes, and she asked, "What do you say to the people who accuse you of being an amateur who plays at detective work the way that some people dabble in golf?"

I think I might have gasped then, though it was well disguised by a slurp on my drink. For all the insecurities I may have had over the years, for all the doubt I'd held onto, I'd recently come to realise that the only thing that actually matters is the way I view myself. I was working hard to ignore people's bad opinions – whether they were real or in my mind – and the thing that helped me to achieve this was the knowledge that I was actually a pretty good sleuth.

And a damn fine bowler!

"I would say—" I began, but there was no answer that wouldn't make me sound petty or self-important, and I think she knew it.

"And what about the fact that several of your cases have overstepped the line between investigation and what might be considered entrapment, leading to at least one murderer walking free?"

The old Izzy would have sat there, tongue tied as the smug young woman in my favourite armchair tried to spark a reaction. Fortunately, the new improved me was capable of constructing a half-decent sentence under pressure.

"You're making things up now." My voice rose with each word. "You might disapprove of the fact that I'm not what some people might consider a traditional detective, but I'm good at what I do. I've solved cases that confounded the police. I've saved lives and put terrible criminals behind bars."

"And what about the suggestion that you've hand-picked cases that resemble classic murder mysteries, as opposed to taking more problematic assignments, such as tackling the rise of gang violence in our country?"

She was a sly, contemptuous person who had come into my house under false pretences. Janet Ellison wasn't there to write a puff-piece.

She'd come for a hatchet job, and I'd welcomed her in and given her hot chocolate. I'd been a fool, but at least I'd cottoned on before it was too late.

"Why don't you tell my readers who you really are, Izzy?" There was a smile on her lips, and I think it gave her a small thrill to put me to the sword like that. I don't know whether she believed that her gotcha journalism would actually make a difference, or she only cared about what page of the newspaper her story would end up on, but I wouldn't take it anymore.

"Because I very much doubt you'd print the truth even if I told you." A surge of power rushed through me as I realised that I was more in control than I'd believed. "So why don't you get out of my house?"

She didn't need asking twice. "Of course, Miss Palmer. I won't hold you up any longer. It was a pleasure to meet you."

Up on her Manolo Bionics (is that a make of shoe?) Janet Ellison made it to the door just as swiftly as I'd escaped to the kitchen a few minutes earlier. I almost dashed after her to see her out, but my ingrained good manners were not quite so overwhelming that I couldn't resist. Instead, I sat and watched her wave to me through the window before she marched along the road towards the train station.

She'd turned so quickly from sweet to sanctimonious that I was stunned for a while. It was only as the clock in the hall struck eleven that I came back to myself and realised that she'd left something behind. Sadly, it was not her notebook, which I would have enjoyed burning, it was just that morning's paper.

Feeling indescribably weary, I got to my feet to fetch it. I was thinking that, if one of her articles was in it, I could have given it to Kiki, Tammy, and Elton (who had retired from public life, not died) to do as they fancied. Sadly, it was just a free London paper, and I was about to put it in the recycling when I noticed something on the cover. I don't know why I was so drawn to it. It was only a small story towards the bottom, but the name of my town must have caught my attention.

It said, "Police Draw Blank over Croydon Man Slain at Home" and just above, in a photograph the size of a postage stamp, was the likeness of Jack Campbell, the security guard at my old job. I had once suspected him of murder before he was sent to prison for dealing drugs, and now he was dead.

Chapter Two

"Who's my good boy?" Ramesh wasn't listening to me. "Bub bub, who's my good boy?" He was talking to his son in the ridiculous voice he reserved for babies. Its silliness was only matched by the matching onesies that the pair of them were wearing. Faux-zebra fur only looks good on faux-zebras.

"Ramesh, did you hear what I said?"

"You're a good boy, Pacino. You're Daddy's little superstar. You're the Emma Stone to my Taylor Swift, the 50 Cent to my Bette Midler, the… other celebrity bestie to my celebrity bestie."

His cats seemed to take exception to this. Kiki – accessorised with a black and white plush fabric collar – came to sit on my lap and cast angry glances across the room at her owner. I managed to avoid being quite so jealous, even though Ramesh had little time for anyone but his beautiful baby boy ever since he'd become a father.

We were sitting in my office-cum-creche in Leicester Square, and we were supposed to be having a meeting.

"You know that I'm happy for you to have Pacino here with us."

He finally looked at me side on. "Obviously you are. He's the greatest baby of his generation, which is why I called him Pacino in the first place."

"And I'm glad we both agree that Pacino is better than DeNiro."

He picked up his son from the baby bouncer and turned to look at me. "Hang on a second. Are we talking about babies or actors now?"

"I have no idea how good a baby Robert DeNiro was, but— Actually, we've gone off track. I'm trying to say that, even though I'm very happy for you to bring your son to work, I don't see why you have to take your cats everywhere you go."

Kiki did not seem too offended by my comment – proving that she doesn't understand a great deal of English, no matter what my friend has claimed since he watched 'World's Cleverest Pets' on Channel 5.

For his part, Ramesh looked thoroughly appalled. "My friend Wazza thought he was being nice buying us a triple pushchair so that we'd have more space for our stuff when we're out with Pacino. Imagine how stupid I would look if I was pushing it around everywhere with just one baby in it? Kiki and Tammy have done some real heavy lifting."

"I see. I should evidently never have mentioned it."

He was perched on my desk, dandling Pacino on his knee. I have to admit that my godson was the most handsome little creature I had ever had the fortune to adore. He had his mother's fine features, Ramesh's lovely dark skin, and a constant smile for his auntie Izzy.

Oh, yes he does!

I just want to eat him up. Yum yum yum.

"Izzy, now *you're* not listening to *me,* which I think we can agree may be more serious." Ramesh must have been talking while I was watching the little tyke watch me. "Are you going to tell me what I've done wrong or not?"

I cleared my throat, tried to look professional, gave up on that and began. "It's the newspapers. As part of your responsibilities as my long-serving assistant, you pledged to read them for me and inform me of anything relevant."

He became a little agitated then. "If this is still about the free Krispy Kreme donut promo you missed, how many times do you expect me to apologise?"

"Many, but that's not the problem. I'm talking about Jack."

"Which Jack? I know at least two."

"The moustachioed former drug dealer who was killed in his home, not your neighbour's twelve-year-old son." I picked up Kiki and got up from my chair. I would have put Ramesh's behaviour down to baby brain, but I think that's more common in new mothers than fathers. "You should have told me that he'd been killed. A week has passed since he was murdered, and I only found out by chance."

He opened his mouth as if to counter my complaint and then stopped himself and looked a little humble – it was a noteworthy moment. "You're right, I should have told you. I just didn't want you to go back to the dark days of our time at Porter & Porter. To be perfectly honest, I don't like to think of them myself."

I felt a bit guilty then. We'd both suffered bullies and bad times at the dull office job where we'd met, and I should probably have been more sympathetic. "It's fine, but please try to keep me abreast of such things in the future."

He shifted Pacino onto his hip and pretended to be a ventriloquist. "We're sorry, Auntie Izzy. Will you ever forgive us?"

I got distracted by the lovely little bub bub again and, when I came back round, Ramesh was saying, "… something something something why you called us here in the first place. Couldn't we have worked from home today?"

"No, we couldn't, my stripy friend. We had to come up to town because we have an appointment with—"

"D.I. Irons!" Our favourite police officer burst through the door at just the right moment. "I must admit, I've been listening outside for several minutes in the hope that you would say something like that."

She spoke in her typically flat tone even whilst confessing to this ridiculous behaviour. Perhaps aware that it was an odd thing to do, she shuffled gingerly into the room – this is what happens to ordinary, sane people who spend too long with us.

Under her arm was a manilla file that was fat with papers.

"You brought what I needed?" I asked and, though she wasn't one to smile, her cheeks became a touch less rigid than before.

"I certainly have." She placed the file down on the desk and Ramesh, Pacino, Tammy and I gathered around to look at it.

"Is this a police file?" Ramesh put to her, though I thought it went without saying.

"It certainly is," the salaried detective replied.

"Don't you keep everything on computers these days?"

"Ah." Irons scratched the short hair at the back of her head. "We normally do, but I thought I would have looked lazy if I'd rocked up here with a USB drive and plonked it down on the table.

"So you printed this stuff out for effect?" Ramesh still looked puzzled.

"That's right."

"I don't know if I've ever told you this, Inspector, but I like your style." He put his hand up for a high five, and Irons was only too happy to oblige.

I decided to take over as they would have talked nonsense together for some time otherwise. "Now that your prop has been used to full effect, perhaps you can give us a summary of what it says."

She gave a brisk nod and pulled up a chair. "I certainly can."

I'd met Irons on my very first case – excluding a youthful investigation of the theft of a frozen steak, at least. She'd been a great help throughout my career, but I'd never asked her to access police files for me before. Well, not that I can remember at least.

We waited as she gave a brief, dramatic cough. It was definitely a tension builder rather than a sign she had a cold. "Jack was murdered last Thursday night in his home in West Croydon."

Ramesh was quick to interrupt. "To be honest, I didn't even know he'd made it out of prison."

"Course he had." Irons closed her eyes as she spoke. "There's no money to run the places these days, so the government has decided to decriminalise everything but the really bad crimes… oh, and littering. Besides, Jack Campbell only sold a bit of weed."

"He was running a city-wide drugs racket," I had to remind her.

"As I said, he was selling a bit of weed."

"Fine, whatever." I tried to get us back to the matter at hand. "Do any details of the crime stand out to you?"

She thought for a moment. "Time of death was around midnight and the neighbours didn't hear anything. They told the investigating officers that he had been seeing a new woman, but no one could tell us her name. In fact, I get the impression from my colleagues' notes that old Jack was a bit of an old dog in that respect."

This was more than I needed to know. "Were there any fingerprints at the scene?"

"Nope."

"Any footage of the culprit escaping on people's doorbell cameras?"

"Nothing. Just a black Ford saloon that arrived at ten to midnight and left at five minutes past. It's too common a model to identify with any confidence, and we haven't been able to trace its path around the town after it left the road. As the newspapers reported just yesterday, there is a dearth of evidence, and people are upset at our lack of progress. That's the only reason the powers that be let me print out this file and take a folder to put it in. After all that trouble last month, we can't be too careful."

I was still wondering who might have wanted to kill Jack and didn't think about this comment too carefully.

"Have you been through Jack's finances to look for any explanation as to why someone would have wanted him dead?" I asked a little hopefully.

Irons raised her voice. "Of course we have, Miss Palmer. We're not absolute amateurs. Croydon isn't my patch anymore, so I can't vouch for the officers involved, but if they followed basic procedure, they should have sniffed out any unusual transactions."

"And there were no significant messages on Jack's phone or evidence of where he'd been that day?" I completely accepted her point but still had to ask.

"He'd been to the pub in his neighbourhood. The publican said that he was in fine spirits and even bought her a drink." One of the things I like most about D.I. Irons is that she uses words like publican. I believe that the world would be in better shape if more people used such pleasantly antiquated terms.

Ramesh had been flying Pacino around the room like an aeroplane for the past minute but took this opportunity to tune into the conversation. "Is it really so surprising he was killed? He was a drug dealer. Perhaps he crossed someone that he shouldn't have."

Irons turned her sardonic gaze on the poor, silly man. "Weren't you listening, sonny? He was hardly Pablo Escobar. He sold herbal marijuana, and his distributor was the Royal Mail. He was lucky to break even."

"He didn't cross anyone in prison who could have had a grudge against him?" I tried again. This conversation was certainly trying.

"That's a nice idea, but minimum-security prisons in Britain aren't like the animal factories in American movies. From what I've read, he spent most of his time learning to carve wood and bake bread. The warden says that Jack was a model inmate. I'm not saying it's a holiday park, but he wasn't fighting off assassination attempts or made to join a skinhead gang."

I stared at the thick file, wishing that it would flip open to reveal some secret that could explain what had really happened to poor Jack.

"It's terribly sad," Ramesh whispered when no one had said anything for some time. His little boy looked up at him as though he didn't recognise the melancholic tone in his voice. "Jack wasn't a bad guy. He certainly didn't deserve to die. He only sold a bit of weed."

"Which is a criminal offence in this country," Irons was quick to remind him, though he was only quoting her words back to her.

"So where does that leave us?" I knew the answer would do nothing to cheer anyone up.

As my friends avoided answering the question, I opened the file. There were pictures of Jack's body with a knife in his back. Most people would have looked away from such a violent image, whereas I thought, *Oh, come on, police photographer. You can do better than that. The lighting is all wrong, and you could have got down a bit lower to show the expression on the dead man's face.*

He was lying on his side with his head against the floor. It rather amused me – though that sounds terribly insensitive, so let's just say I observed the fact – that he was still wearing the only outfit I'd known him to possess. He had the same heavy black knitted jumper with the epaulettes on the shoulders that he'd worn to work. The only difference was that the breast was covered in what looked like badges. There were about six of them, and I couldn't make out what they said at first, but there was another photograph that showed a close-up. I saw Oxfam, Cancer Research, Marie Curie and the British Heart Foundation. They were the little stickers that charities give you when you make a donation. I flicked through a few more pages, but nothing else stood out to me.

"It's a tricky one," Irons muttered, still scratching her head. "No one has the first idea of what could have happened. If it weren't for that black car that drove straight up to Jack's house and didn't stop anywhere else, I'd assume it was a random killing. A robbery gone wrong or something along those lines, but that doesn't seem possible."

"Could we go there to look around?"

She thought for a moment. "Not unless you have a key. I'm not even allowed to leave these papers anywhere without supervision."

It was a bit early in a murder investigation to be glum, but that's how I felt.

"I have a key," Ramesh suddenly declared, and I half expected him to make a joke. Instead, he gathered up his brood and took the three of them out to our reception where he was supposed to sit welcoming people but rarely did. He returned a moment later with the triple pushchair, which he tried very hard to fit through the door. He ended up having to tilt it forward on two wheels and then sidling into the room. “My key!”

“No matter how cute they are,” I replied as I took in the three pairs of innocent eyes staring up at me, “I’m not sure that they’ll get us into a house that has been sealed by the police.”

“Not the scene of the crime, then, but what about our old office? Perhaps someone there knows what happened to Jack. It was the last place he worked before he went inside, and a few of our colleagues knew him well.”

“Porter & Porter?” The sensation that had risen up within me suggested that I feared the old place more than Ramesh did.

“That’s right.” He looked quite stoic as he rolled the buggy over to me. “It’s time we went back.”

It was a touching moment and the perfect place to end a scene in a book or movie or what have you, but after a few moments of intensely emotional silence, D.I. Irons said, “Would you mind if I used your toilet? I’ve drunk far too much tea this morning.”

Chapter Three

The next morning, Ramesh and I were standing in front of the No. 1 building in East Croydon. The white tower block stretched up into the sky above us with all its 1970s charm, like a satanic wedding cake. I didn't want to walk inside. I didn't want to take the noisy lift up four floors to Porter & Porter, and I certainly didn't want to see half of the people who worked there – the same lot who had thought me a murderer and called me a freak when I'd innocently walked in one morning and found my old boss dead. I didn't want to be anywhere near that place, but there was no backing out now.

"Why don't I just wait outside?" I mean, I still tried to *evit*[1] the inevitable, but it wouldn't work. "Surely you've picked up enough from me over our numerous murder and missing-pet investigations to know what to do?"

"Goodness me, no," Ramesh replied. "I haven't been paying anywhere near enough attention for that." He started to laugh, which made Pacino, who was dangling from his chest in a baby harness, laugh too. He was a surprisingly empathetic person for one so young. And, yes, I'd made Ramesh leave the cats at home.

"You haven't been paying attention for the last four years? Two of which I've paid you a salary to do just that?"

"In my defence, I've had a lot of other things to think about. It took me at least that long to choose what to call my firstborn."

I was still relieved that Ramesh and his wife hadn't had a baby girl. I don't know how I would feel about a child named Cher-oncé, though that was already an improvement on Gaga-riah and Brit-donna. I suggested that they opt for just one diva's moniker, as opposed to a portmanteau, at which point Ramesh turned very sullen and wouldn't make eye contact until he was distracted by something shiny and forgot my terrible offence.

"Fine, I'll come in with you." I looked one last time at the octagonal tower looming over us and wished that I hadn't. For a moment, I remembered just how it had felt to enter the building every Monday

---

1 This isn't a word, though evite apparently is. And, yes, the best jokes are the ones you have to explain.

morning with the knowledge that my boss Bob would be up there waiting to insult and denigrate anyone who showed the faintest sign of weakness. My gut still hurt just thinking about it.

Ramesh had made it through the sliding doors, and so I hurried to catch up. The place wasn't as grim as I'd remembered. Perhaps it had been redecorated since I'd last been there, but it was far more generic than I'd previously pictured. In my head, there had been blood dripping down the walls and the odd human bone left about the place, but it was just an ordinary entrance hall that you would find in any office block.

The lift was still oddly noisy. It wasn't just the bings of the speaker system as we passed each floor, there was a space-age buzzing that got louder as we rose. As if I wasn't nervous enough already, this certainly did the trick.

"It'll be alright," my friend told me, and his son offered a friendly wink. Oh, okay, that never happened, but Pacino was just so jolly that it was hard to be gloomy around him.

The lift binged for the fourth time. The doors opened, and we got out at the Croydon office of Porter & Porter. It's weird when you've done something hundreds of times and then stop altogether. I still occasionally wake up feeling dread at the thought of going to work before remembering I have a different life now. It must be how ex-smokers feel when they reach into their pocket for a cigarette and find that there's nothing there.

As I walked along the corridor to the glass doors with the big P ampersand P on them, some sort of muscle memory kicked in. I knew how many steps I would need to take. I knew the patterns of light on the carpet from the overhead lighting, and I knew that the door would stick a little bit to begin with and then go swinging open too fast when I applied more pressure.

Inside, there was the same tappy tap tapping of fingers on keyboards, the same continuous background whir of a photocopier which, by 2024, you would have thought would be relegated to history. The place even smelt the same, and fragments of memories came back to me as I glanced about the foyer. The cubbyhole where Jack used to sit was now empty, and there was no sign of the young guy who had come along after him. The door to Bob's office stood ajar, and I had to wonder who was unlucky enough to occupy the room where he'd been murdered. It was all so familiar, and yet one thing was dramatically different.

Looking about the open-plan office, I realised that most of the faces looking back at me (or otherwise) were new. There was no sign of the previously ubiquitous Pauline from accounts – her regular porcine grunting now absent from the Porter & Porter soundscape. My old desk mate Suzie wasn't where I'd expected her to be. The receptionists had all changed, and I didn't recognise a single face from the consulting team – which wasn't a bad thing, as those guys were bottom-feeders of the lowest standing.

Just like when I'd returned to my old high school and expected everything and everyone to have stayed the same, it appeared that Porter & Porter had moved on. To my surprise, this didn't mean that no one knew me.

"That's Izzy Palmer!" a voice yelled out, and a woman in the middle of the immense space rose to point across at me. She was sitting right where I had, and she probably did the same nothing job that I'd done. She was young and tall and skinny, so essentially my replacement, and she seemed to be something of a fan. "That's Izzy Palmer!" she said again. "I can't believe she's really here."

The volume rose by twenty decibels (if that is the amount I think it is) as the young woman's colleagues spotted me and rushed forward from their desks. I could already tell how disappointed Ramesh was that no one had noticed his adorable son, or the fact he was dressed a bit like a daddy kangaroo.

Izzy 2.0 was the first to reach us. "We never stop talking about you around here, Miss Palmer. The people who used to work with you have got so many great tales. I could listen all day."

A guy in a skinny suit with sharp cheekbones and a floppy blonde fringe came to stand next to her. He looked a little shy but was moved to make a confession. "I'm sorry, but I have to tell you that I've read every newspaper article about you and follow all your cases." By the look of him, his name was Chad.

As the bustle and chatter continued, I noticed a few people whose faces were at least half familiar, having worked alongside them for several years.

"Ramesh!" a middle-aged woman in an almost quintessentially middle-aged outfit bellowed over the heads of the crowd, and everyone finally noticed the man dressed from head-to-toe in taupe with a human strapped to his front.

"What an adorable baby," another of the admirers sang. "He looks just like you."

"Such flattery will get you everywhere." Ramesh pretended to blush as the talk turned to the tales of my hilariously over-the-top sidekick, and everyone realised who the real star was. I can't say I minded being shoved from the limelight. While they were busy fawning over him, I realised what I'd really come there for. I glanced across at the far corner of the room where my former boyfriend had once had his office. Staring at the door just a fraction too nostalgically, despite the fact that my former boss-friend David had been convicted of murder and eventually cut off all contact with me from prison, I wished that he would walk through it.

I think I might have gasped and somehow choked on the air at the same time as, in the next moment, the door opened and right there, in the very same room as me, was…

…another person altogether. "Izzy Palmer, as I live and breathe." Amara emerged and walked across to us. She had taken charge of the company after Bob's boss killed him, before *his* boss was then murdered by his own daughter; you know, the usual story.

"It's so nice to see you, Amara," I actually meant this as Amara has the warmth and authenticity of a really good children's TV presenter.

Just behind her was what I took to be the new management team. There was Will Gibbons from consulting, my friend silent Suzie Hawkes and (less happily) another of my old enemies, Wendy… I don't remember her surname. Even though I had no interest in seeing the woman who had called for my head after Bob was murdered, I must admit I was glad that some people from my time there remained. It felt right that there would still be a few suspects knocking about the place.

"Here she is," fake-Izzy exclaimed, and all the young people seemed very excited by the presence of (one of) my former nemeses. "Hey, Wend. I was just saying that you always talk about Izzy."

From the way the new generation of staff there looked at her, it was almost as if… I don't quite know how to say this, but it was almost as if they liked her.

"Hello, Izzy!" Wendy still had that same gravelly voice and coffee-stained teeth, but there was something different about her. She was… *smiling.* "It seems like only yesterday that we were all working happily together." She turned to my friend then. "And Ramesh, you're also here."

Wendy had all the makings of a good cat lady, minus the cats. She wore heavily embroidered skirts, smelt strongly of something I can only describe as general mustiness, and her hair looked as if it had been transplanted on to the top of her head from the hide of a long-deceased cow. Apart from that (and her personality) she was lovely.

"What funny stories have you been telling about us, Wend?" Ramesh asked.

Wendy pretended not to hear him and joined the line of people who were trying to make Pacino smile. "Look at that little fellow. What a beaut."

There was plenty more of this sort of thing, and I stood feeling uncertain how to proceed. I felt how noted local celebrity "man from a once popular yogurt advert" had surely felt on coming to open our staff morale-building day – in that I wasn't entirely sure why I'd thought it was a good idea to go there. Bad memories were firing in my head like guns at a rifle range. Just beside the water cooler was where my colleagues had straddled my supine body to keep me in place until the police arrived on the morning I found Bob's body. In the centre of the office was where that vile bully turned corpse had mocked Ramesh so mercilessly through countless impromptu announcements. It was not a happy place to go back to.

At least Suzie squeaked her pleasure that I had come. Will looked a little shy around me, as he had ever since I'd discovered his secret life and forced him to stop being such a monster in the office, and eventually Amara got to the heart of the matter.

"Have you come to talk about Jack?"

"No, don't be silly." I quashed the idea with a laugh before remembering that this was the very reason we'd come and changing my answer. "Or rather, yes, that's exactly it. Would it be possible to have a word with you?"

Three minutes later, we were convened in the room where I had outed my boyfriend as a murderer, thus putting to an end my chance of happiness with a kind, loving, slightly stabby man. The whole management team had come with us, which included a guy called Tom who didn't have anything to add to what the others said, as he'd only met Jack once. He was the new head of accounting and presumably didn't want to be left out.

"It was terrible news about Jack," Amara said on behalf of the whole Porter & Porter corporation. "He had made some mistakes in his life, of course he had. But he had served his time and returned to the outside world as a rehabilitated member of society."

I immediately found myself thinking, *Ahh, isn't Amara nice?* But something in her words caught my attention. "Is there any reason that you phrased it in that particular way? Do you know what he's been doing since he got out of prison?"

It was Will who would reply. "He came to visit us." He had always had a slightly lupine appearance, but in the years since I'd worked there, he'd turned into a cowering pup. "He sat right where you are now and begged us to make use of him."

I saw a flicker of panic on mousy Suzie's face, but she said nothing. Gosh, I've only just realised that I viewed all my colleagues as different types of animals. Jack had been a trusty old fox, Amara the mother bear, and Wendy… well she was evidently some kind of rabid stoat. Even as we spoke, she gnashed her teeth down the table at me, so I had to assume that her transformation to everyone's favourite fun co-worker was only superficial.

"Make use of him?" Although Ramesh was showing Pacino the view through the window, he was apparently still listening.

"I'm sure there's a more diplomatic way of saying it," Amara clarified, "but that was the upshot. He came here to ask whether he could be of any use to Porter & Porter. He even offered to take up his old post without pay."

Suzie might well have wanted to speak, but her timidity meant that, even one-on-one, she struggled. It was amazing she'd made it out of the pool of employees in the main office to climb the corporate ladder.

"I think he must have had a hard time in prison," Will attested. "He wasn't the same man I remembered. He was slow and nervous. It was sad to see."

I smiled at him, pleased to confirm that at least one of my colleagues' conversions had been genuine.

"Did the police come to talk to you?" I asked, and it was naturally the senior member of staff who answered.

"No, but Jack stopped working here even before you did. It's been four whole years."

"Did any of you see him outside work?" Ramesh was surprisingly engaged, even as he made a cooing noise to entertain his son.

I made sure to watch their reactions. Amara was either the best actress I'd ever met or just as calm, confident and sympathetic as ever. Wendy grimaced again and looked across at Suzie. Suzie herself gripped hold of her seat, and Will's sad expression didn't change. Oh, and Tom (the unnecessary extra) just shrugged. Body language isn't the perfect barometer that many fictional detectives like to claim, but this was good enough for me.

"I don't think so," Amara glanced about at her colleagues. "If I remember correctly, he kept to himself even when he worked here."

"When you consider that he was an international drugs dealer," Wendy finally contributed with a growl, "it's hardly surprising."

"Regional drug dealer," I responded with petty indignation on his behalf. "He tried to be environmentally friendly and only despatched to London addresses." I was surprised to hear myself parroting his justification to them.

"Have it your way!" The woman did not enjoy being contradicted, and it really was too funny that she'd been pretending we were besties. I suppose that, with the changing of the guard that had occurred after Bob's ghost had been exorcised, and so many of her contemporaries moving on, she'd had to do something to keep in with the young'uns.

"Can any of you think of anything which might give us some clue as to why he was killed?" This was a terribly vague question, and I didn't hold out much hope.

"What about his daughter?" Amara always knows how to make people feel better and smiled across at me as she spoke.

"Oh, that's right," Will said, remembering the situation. "She was an intern here. What was her name?"

“Pippa,” I said in a rather abrupt snap of a reply. “I suppose I could try contacting her.”

“That might be a good idea, Izzy.” Amara looked at her colleagues one last time to ensure that there was nothing she was forgetting. “We would have liked to help Jack, but we couldn’t be seen to associate with a man who had been running an illegal business from the premises. I was sorry to say no, but that was the last we heard from him.”

No one had anything more to add, and so I wheeled my chair back, nodded to Will, Suzie and Tom, and then followed lovely Amara from the room. I caused an even bigger stir as I crossed the office (hopefully) one last time. Fake-Izzy had apparently organised a leaving committee by the door and insisted on giving me a hug. I’m not necessarily the cuddliest person, but this was the warm farewell I’d dreamed of when I’d finished working there, and I did not refuse. Ramesh insisted on shaking hands with everyone, mainly so each of them would tweak Pacino’s cheek and say how adorable he was, and then it was time to leave.

Wendy, of all people, had the final word. “It really was nice to see you, Izzy.” She almost sounded sincere, and I wasn’t sure how to respond. Even Ramesh stayed silent, and he was known for his stinging comebacks.

“You too, Wend,” I mumbled, and I put my hand on Ramesh’s shoulder to steer him out of the office as if I was his mother.

We’d only made it to the downstairs lobby when someone came after us.

“Iz!” a mouse called, and it was barely loud enough to hear over the sound of the lift doors opening. “Ra!”

I eventually identified the sound of Suzie squeaking, and we stopped by the exit to wait for her. “Sorry, is this about the stapler I took when I left all those years ago?”

She looked at us each in turn (including Pacino) and then forced herself to do something that really wasn’t in her nature. She spoke in full sentences.

“It’s Jack. … don’t know how to… You see, Jack and I were…” Well, they were almost full sentences, and we could practically follow what she was saying. “We started writing to one another when he was inside and I… it might sound a bit… we fell in love.”

"You were together?" Ramesh asked, so that I didn't have to, and Pacino dangled there in amazement.

She nodded in that quick, nervous manner of hers. "He was a lovely man… so much heartache in his…" It wasn't that she didn't pronounce the missing words, it was just that the volume of her voice would peak and fall through the course of whatever she was saying. "I just wanted you to… he was making a huge effort to be a better…"

Ramesh seized her by the shoulders at this moment. "A better what? A better dancer? A better lover? What was he trying to be—"

"A better person, Ra," I told him. "That's why Jack came here. He was trying to make up for the mistakes he'd made."

Suzie silently confirmed my interpretation, and it seemed to give her the confidence she needed to keep talking. "Even Pippa forgave him. They were closer after he came out of… She lives in Edinburgh now, but she rang him every… We went up to see her on a mini-break before…"

The poor creature started crying then. I really must stop referring to people as animals. It's incredibly patronising. She held the back of her hand to her eye to stem the tears, but there was no hiding her sorrow. She was a shy, skittish person, and I was both happy that she'd found someone to share her life with and upset that he'd been taken away from her.

"Is there anything more you know that might explain what happened?" I asked, to echo my equally vague question from up in the conference room.

She breathed in for courage and did her best to answer. "I've racked my brain, and I can't think why anyone would have wanted to hurt him."

"What about the people he met in prison?" Ramesh asked. "Couldn't that explain it?"

She looked about the wide lobby and back towards the lift before answering. "We talked about his time there, and… of course, but it made him determined to never return. He didn't fall into a gang… what you're thinking. He decided that he was going to… he was supposed to be. And that's exactly what he did."

I didn't say anything for a moment as her words needed that long to sink in. "Can I ask you something else, Suzie? Can you tell me how he felt about me for getting him arrested in the first place."

I don't know why I thought to ask such a question but, in reply, she looked a little sorry for me. "You needn't worry about that. Jack knew he'd broken the law. It wasn't your fault that … only doing your job, after all."

The truth is that I'd always felt bad for what happened to him. I know what he did was wrong, but it's not as if there are any Christie novels in which Poirot doggedly pursues a lonely middle-aged man who sold herbal marijuana. I don't think she'd have become quite so famous if she'd focussed on such crimes.

As the time had come to leave, Suzie offered a few parting words. "He told me once… happier after he was arrested than before." She blushed and glanced down at the floor as she said this. I had no doubt that she was one of the reasons that Jack had felt so positive about his life after prison. "He was a good man, and he didn't deserve… So, please, Izzy. Please find the person who…" Her words faded out, and she squeezed my hand and turned to flee.

Chapter Four

"Isn't it possible that Suzie killed Jack herself?"

"How can you say such a thing about that sweet, kind, broken-hearted lady?" I looked at my monstrous friend across a table at our favourite Tapas restaurant in South Croydon. El Burro Caliente was quiet on a Wednesday lunchtime, but the food would be no less delicious.

"Because you told me to!" Ramesh explained. "You have specifically told me on any number of occasions that, in a murder investigation, we must doubt every alibi, consider every person a potential maniac, and drink as much hot chocolate as the fillings in our teeth will allow."

"You have been listening!" I beamed.

"Some of the time," he confessed. "Though if you'd returned the favour, I would have told you my killer theory by now. Imagine that Suzie and Wendy were having a secret affair and—"

"Nope! Stop. That's enough." I dropped my voice to a whisper. "Ramesh, what if your son is absorbing everything you say, and he grows up thinking that everyone he meets is having a secret affair?"

"Then he'll turn out just as well adjusted as I am." Before he could go any deeper into his conspiracy theories, our friends arrived. We were on a triple date with Danny and Shandy and Dean and Fiona. I say "triple date" but obviously I was sitting with a happily married man and his baby son.

In case anyone was wondering, yes, I had gone on a few dates since I'd broken up with Danny however many decades earlier. And, yes, the majority of the men I'd met had turned out to be certifiably bananas. I've sadly come to accept that, now that I am thirty-three, my chance of meeting a suitable man without a clown fetish or a criminal record was practically nil.

"It's so nice to see you," all six of us said in slightly different ways, and Pacino implied as much with his soulful brown eyes.

"We have an announcement to make," Danny declared as soon as we were all sitting down.

"And so do we," Dean added. I'd never seen him look so shy in all the time I'd known him. The fact that I'd managed to get him to a restaurant that didn't serve burgers was the first miracle of the day, and the second was about to arrive.

"We're getting married," Fiona and Shandy said at the same time.

"Wait, who's marrying whom?" Ramesh was presumably suspecting secret affairs again, which made Dean's jaw fall open in bemusement before he explained.

"I'm marrying my fiancée, and Danny's marrying his."

"Congratulations to you all," I said about fifteen seconds too late. "That's fantastic news."

This greatly increases the chances that we will now die alone.

Oh, come on, brain. We'll always have each other.

Yes, but Danny was our fallback, and Dean was the fallback to the fallback if Danny got married!

As my inner monologue quietly fumed, I continued being happy for them. "Have you decided on a date?"

"August!" Fiona (Dean's lawyer girlfriend with the hair of fire) and Shandy (my old school friend) said at the exact same moment.

"Wait, is it a double wedding?" Ramesh still hadn't got his head around the idea. "Are you secret Moonies?"

"No, Ramesh. The ceremonies will be on different days," Danny explained for the simpleton.

"And I'd like you to be my maid of honour, Iz." Shandy was almost bursting with excitement. Danny put his arm around her to prevent any such outcome.

Dean clicked his fingers and pointed across the table before saying. "You'll be my best woman. I know it's a bit weird because it's typically a man, but I don't have many friends."

Always the best woman, never the bride! Do you think they're doing this to rub it in?

"It is perfectly normal to have a best woman," Ramesh intervened before I could agree to the request. "All the best people do."

"I'd love to be your maid of honour, Shandy, and your best woman, Dean. And I would like to say how happy I am for all four of you. Dean and Danny, you are both very lucky men. Fiona and Shandy, you've played the hand you were dealt."

Dean's smart, funny and beautiful girlfriend nodded at this. In her lovely, lilting (fine, I might have had the tiniest girl-crush on her) Irish voice, she declared, “That sounds about right.”

Dean rolled his eyes, but Danny was grinning with all of his usual puppy-dog energy.

His bride-to-be still hadn’t come back down to earth. “I can’t believe that I’m going to marry my very own Danny.” She shook her head in amazement, then shot a lustful look in her fiancé’s direction.

Ramesh was equally shocked. “Not just any Danny, but the man Closer magazine named Britain’s sexiest new TV doctor of 2023. It’s incredible to think that an everyday ordinary woman from Bromley could marry a real-life celebrity!” His eyes bulged in his head as he said this word. “Fairy tales really can come true.”

This was too much for Shandy and she launched herself at her man so that they were soon sprawled out on the bench beside Dean. He did not look particularly comfortable.

“Murder!” I said in the hope it would stop them doing all that mushy stuff.

“Weddings,” Dean tried for presumably the same reason.

“Awww,” Ramesh reminisced, “do you remember when someone got murdered at my wedding? Happy days.”

When none of this had the desired effect, I clapped my hands several times. “I need your help with the case I’m not being paid to work on.”

His face covered in Shandy, Danny managed to right himself. “Okay, yes. Good. Tell us all about it.”

His fiancée was still mouthing declarations of love at him, but I had five out of seven pairs of eyes on me (as Pacino was distracted by the electric fan that was spinning overhead), so I began what I had to say.

“It happened last week, but I only found out yesterday that the security guard at the office where Ra and I used to work was murdered.”

“Murdered!” Fiona said, her voice gripped with fear, but she couldn’t hold a straight face and soon started laughing. “I’m sorry. I’m so sorry. But what else would you expect to happen around you? When I told my mother that the man I’m about to marry is your friend, she suggested we elope to the Bahamas. She says that we’re more likely to make it through the vows without anyone dying if Izzy doesn’t come.”

“Ha! That is so funny.” Ramesh enjoyed this a little too much. “Just like at my wedding, when the bridesmaid was killed with a samurai sword, and we even considered that my wife was to blame. Good times!" He had to shake his head as the memory came back to him. "Still… poor Cindy."

"So about this new case," Dean said, as he is a smidge saner than most of my friends. "Do you think it's got something to do with your boss's murder?"

"Sorry," Fiona interrupted. "Which boss are we talking about? Bob? The one who killed Bob? Or the rich one who was then killed?"

"Bob," her beloved replied, and Ramesh continued laughing about his disastrous, though elegant, wedding.

Shandy ignored all this and had another suggestion. "Perhaps one of the original suspects was the real killer, and you got the wrong man." She had not been in my social circle at the time, so it was impressive she could follow this much.

Danny looked uncomfortable on my behalf. "I'm not sure that Izzy wants to talk about all this."

"No, it's fine," I replied. "You can talk about the time the love of my life was convicted of murder. No offence, Danny."

He was making eyes at Shandy again, apparently not bothered that I had downgraded him to merely the second greatest love of my life.

"I've basically forgotten all about him," I continued. "David who?"

They all dropped eye contact at this moment and pretended to be busy with other things. Fiona cooed at little Pacino. Shandy went back to her romantic adoration, and Dean stared at the menu rather than having to respond.

I decided to return us to the burgeoning investigation. "Back on topic, Jack was killed in his own home. There's no evidence pointing towards a particular suspect, and nothing to say that he had crossed swords with anyone. It really makes me think that this is more than just a robbery gone wrong."

Fiona was sceptical. "Croydon does have the worst record for knife crime out of all the London boroughs last year."

Dean had evidently read the same article. "Including statistics for knife possession, not just violent assaults."

"It's certainly a mixed picture. Croydon is the 27th safest city in Britain, excluding Scotland," Ramesh of all people added, so I guess he did glance at the newspaper occasionally.

“That’s right.” It was Shandy’s turn next. “Bicycle crime is at an all-time low.”

I had to wonder whether some people stay up to date with crime statistics the way that others follow football results. I wasn’t the only one to be surprised by this. Danny was regarding our friends through scrunched up eyes with his head to one side and his tongue hanging out. Fine, that last part wasn’t true, but he was a very good boy and deserved a treat.

“Perhaps we should order,” he said, and we waited to discover what Ramesh had a hankering for.

“I fancy some Fabada Asturiana. It’s a stew made with meat and beans.” He kissed his fingers like the great chef that he occasionally was when he took the time to watch cooking tutorials on YouTube.

Food is one area where I have no need to doubt my eccentric sidekick, and so I ordered the same as him, along with a selection of goodies for the table.

There had better be enough jamón ibérico for us, or I will not stay quiet all night.

“Perhaps we should get an extra plate of ham, just in case,” I told the waiter, and then we were all set for a cheerful conversation about weddings and romance and undying—

“Let’s go back to talking about how master detective Izzy Palmer got something wrong,” Ramesh suggested. “I was really enjoying that.”

I would have kicked him under the table, but he had moved to sit next to me when our friends arrived and so I had to give him a dead arm instead.

“I don’t think that Izzy is wrong,” Danny kindly rushed to my defence, and I loved him all over again.

“Were you not listening?” Dean had turned grumpy on the matter… well, grumpier than normal. “Jack Campbell was murdered in London’s crime capital. He probably didn’t have the right change for the newspaper, and so his newsagent tracked him down and did him in. It happens all the time.”

“No, Dean,” his fiancée told him. “It really doesn’t.”

“Why do you believe me?” I had to ask my ex. “I have no evidence or even a hypothesis, and it’s just about the flimsiest hunch I can remember."

He gave me a daffy smile. "Yeah, but Jack's not the first of your former suspects who's been murdered recently, is he?"

"Isn't he?"

The chattering dimwits had all fallen silent and Danny wore a proud smile as he explained what none of them had realised. "Surely you know what happened to the Italian politician we met in Ramesh's uncle's hotel on the Spanish coast?" We evidently didn't and so he had to explain. "Marco Romanelli was murdered last month."

There was an uncomfortable silence as reality sank in around the table.

"Oh, come on, guys," Ramesh threw his hands in the air to disguise his own mistake, and Pacino looked a little alarmed. "Why does no one tell Izzy anything that's happening in the news?"

Chapter Five

Just in case your memory doesn't go back that far, let me fill you in on Marco Romanelli. He was a popular guru in Italy who had thrown his hat into the political ring only for his violent, pseudo-Nazi movement to falter when it turned out that his wife had murdered her way to fame and success. I may have put her in jail and spoilt all their dreams. Whoopsie!

What most surprised me about him was not that he was now dead, but where, as Danny soon informed me, his murder had taken place. Southorpe-on-Sea was a nothing town on the English coast, and it just happened to be the place where I'd gone to university.

Ramesh and I dropped Pacino at home for a feed – he'd been out for long enough that morning and was starting to be teary. Ramesh, that is; Pacino was surprisingly cheerful. So, after my friend had a cuddle with his wife and promised to be home before bed, we zoomed down to Southorpe to find out what had happened.

I say "zoomed" but I was still driving my mother's ancient yellow Vauxhall Corsa, and I was worried that the engine would fall out if I drove over fifty miles an hour.

Ramesh didn't seem to mind, as he was already singing along to a French Celine Dion song on the radio. "Bonjour, croissant fromage." He didn't know the real words, but he got the tune and mannerisms just perfectly. "Croissant fromage, bonjour."

After that, he had a go at Cliff Richard's "Summer Holiday", which was entirely inappropriate as I could barely see through the windscreen for the rain, and we were driving to the coast to investigate the murder of a noted fascist.

"Do you have any police contacts down here from the last case we investigated?" he asked when the song finished.

"I do but, as I put the man's son in prison, I don't think he'd be too keen for us to call by. I'm relying on the fact that the town itself will speak to me the way it did last time."

He looked wistful for a moment, just as he had on stage as *Bobby Number Three* in the Croydon Amateur Players' production of 'Jack the Ripper: The Musical'. "The seaside is a dangerous place; if all the murders that go on there aren't bad enough, you could easily get kicked by a donkey."

He perked up again and I can only imagine that he was considering the possibility that he might get to ride a donkey.

By the time we'd parked on the seafront, the rain had just about stopped, but it was so grey and gloomy outside that we stayed in the car to kill time before my appointment. I'd rung ahead to the bar where Romanelli had been killed, and a well-spoken man called Skunk would be expecting us at six sharp.

"It says here that Romanelli was in town for a talk he was giving. How the mighty have fallen, eh?" Ramesh peered out of the window at the pub we'd parked in front of. The Shank and Garrotte Tavern did not look like the kind of place you'd take your granny for Sunday lunch.

"I looked him up online while you were giving Pacino back to his mummy. It turns out that, after we upset his plans in Spain—"

"You mean when his murderous wife was locked up because of all the murder she got up to?"

"Exactly. Well, after that, he tried to save his career by claiming that the whole thing was a conspiracy that had been designed to destroy him. The worst thing is that, thanks to the ridiculous world we now live in, plenty of people were willing to go along with his excuse and he actually continued to be popular across Europe. The TV stations he appeared on weren't quite so prominent as they had been, but he was still selling his philosophy to the masses."

"Until someone killed him."

"Right again. But it's odd that he'd come to a place like this. Don't you think?"

He gazed along the promenade, which had always looked a little lonely when I was at university and was now a slightly gentrified version of the same thing. "It isn't the obvious stopping-off point for a celebrity politician."

"I remember all the tough kids hanging out here when I lived in Southorpe. Thursday night was rock night, and let me tell you, you did not want to walk past when they were about."

"Why? Were they violent?"

"No, they'd make nasty faces at us and go 'Boo!'. We took to staying in and watching movies instead."

I glanced at the digital clock on my dashboard, which was possibly the most modern gadget my inherited car possessed. It said 4:47, but as it was an hour and twelve minutes slow, I knew it was time to brave the elements.

"Are you ready for answers?" I asked my Man Friday, and he smiled back at me.

"I'm ready for an ice cream, but answers will do for now."

I grabbed my coat from the back seat and held it over my head as we dashed from the car. To be fair to The Shank and Garotte, it was uglier inside than out, so that was good. It was a large black room with a bar at one end, stickers all over the walls for punk and heavy metal bands and… well, that was pretty much it. I eventually spotted a small black stage that blended in to its surroundings, and there was a boy of about fifteen with unfortunate skin and greasy hair bringing out musical equipment from a back room.

"Can I help you?" the Viking behind the bar enquired. "We're not actually open for another hour. I need to change the barrels and the beer is warm at the best of times, but I can get you a couple of lemonades if you're desperate."

I was pretending to be a tough, confident detective in the mould of Philip Marlowe or Sam Spade. So instead of answering his question, I asked one of my own. "Are you Skunk?"

He looked behind him in a comical fashion. "I don't see anyone else here. You're the detectives, are you?" His voice was terribly plummy. I genuinely don't think I've ever met such a posh metaller.

Ramesh made sure to swiftly undermine my act. "I prefer to think of myself as an associate facilitator. Izzy does most of the brain work, whereas I try to convince her to wear more daring clothes." Skunk stared back as though he'd said something incomprehensible, and so Ramesh amended his position. "Or rather, yes, we're the detectives."

"I don't know what sense there was in coming all this way," Skunk told us as he polished pint glasses with a dirty rag. "I already told the police that the Italian guy was only here for a short time. He was not happy when he arrived."

"Why? Didn't he like the colour scheme?" Can anyone tell me why I let Ramesh talk? Or come with me on my cases, for that matter?

Skunk had a long scraggly beard that he pulled as he replied. "Actually, that *was* one of the things he mentioned. He told me that he'd spoken at the Royal Albert Hall before and called this place a dive, which I didn't think was very nice at all." The big, bearded barman had a surprisingly sensitive nature. "But his biggest issue was that only three people came to hear him speak."

This rather cheered me up. "Perhaps Southorpe rejected his virulent ideology."

Skunk continued to pull on his beard. "That could be why, or it could be because the organiser did nothing to promote it. The fellows who turned up were three regulars who had seen the date listed on our website."

"Who was the organiser?" Ramesh had asked a sensible question for once.

"I don't know."

He took on a sly tone. "You don't know, or you're not willing to tell us?"

Skunk smiled. "I don't know."

"Oh, okay. Thanks for clearing that up." Ramesh seemed happy with this and wore an expression which said, *This man has told us all he knows. Our work here is done.*

"How did they pay to rent the venue if you never met them?" I asked instead.

"That's the funny thing. A person calling himself Ernie Bath sent me his credit card details, but when the police looked into it, the card wasn't linked to a bank account. It was one of those pre-paid cards that you can top-up with cash at the post office."

"There's no way to trace it?" This seemed like a highly dubious invention if it enables people to hide their identities, but I suppose there were times when such a thing could be used for legitimate purposes.

"Not from what they told me. The card was registered to an E. Bath, but there's nothing to say that was really the owner. It had all been set up online."

I was fairly certain that whoever had organised the event had used a false name.

"So what else did Marco Romanelli do here?" I asked to keep the interview going.

"When it turned out that there was no dressing room for him, I had to calm him down with free lemonades. I did offer beer, but he described British beer as tasting like 'warm cat's urine'." Skunk said these last three words in a rather prudish whisper, as though he didn't want the beer to hear.

"How dare he insult our nation's greatest drink!" Ramesh complained, though I rarely saw him drink anything but fruity cocktails. "I don't go to Italy and insult their incredible food and fantastic wine!"

I spoke again before he could get a hankering for Italian food, or my brain became too patriotic.

We didn't fight two world wars so that—

And… shhhh!

"Did Romanelli actually give a speech in the end?"

Skunk stopped his beard bothering and took another glass to polish/smear. "He got up on stage, looked perplexed and then decided to sit down to talk to Stunk, Digger and Paul instead."

"Wait," Ramesh said, and we did just this. I was sure he was about to say something irrelevant, and he didn't let me down. "Are you saying that your name is Skunk and that one of your regulars is called Stunk?"

"That's right. He's my brother, though his real name is actually Tarquin."

Ramesh evidently found this charming. "How did you get your nicknames?"

Skunk's whole beard shifted higher on his face, which I took to be a sign of happiness. "It's actually a very funny story. We were both studying economics. He was at Cambridge; I was at Oxford and—" He must have noticed that I wasn't impressed with the interruption as he cut himself short and returned to the previous discussion. "I will admit that Romanelli was a smooth chap. His tiny audience had only come to protest against his presence in this lovely town of ours, but he was a very persuasive speaker. He said that if he could change just one mind, it would have been worth coming all that way to a dive bar at the arse-end of nowhere."

"Why did Stunk, Digger and Paul come to protest?" I asked.

"They're card-carrying centrists. I know for a fact that they reject the division that modern populist leaders sow."

I didn't know what more to say after this. Metalheads were clearly more politically conscious than I'd given them credit for.

"How long did he stay?" Ramesh asked, as I'd fallen silent.

"Just one drink. Paul had to shoot off early as his mother-in-law was coming for the week, and he was supposed to make a lasagne. It's his signature dish. Stunk and Digger enjoyed a brief chat with Romanelli, but he was all mouth. His big, pretty ideas didn't sound so impressive when they were delivered around a table with graffiti all over it."

I found my voice again. "And then he left, too?"

"That's right. He had calmed down by then. He even apologised for not being more polite. He had an incredible smile, and the way he looked into my eyes was quite magnetic. I understood in an instant why so many people followed him." Skunk was evidently a thoughtful chap.

"How long after that did you find out he was dead?"

"I'd say it was about an hour before I found the body. I'd gone to throw out a box of empties in the alley, and there he was."

"How was he killed?" Ramesh shouted over from the display of stickers he was inspecting.

"He had his throat cut. The police tried to work out how he ended up there, but there's no CCTV immediately outside the pub. They figure someone was waiting for him, and they persuaded him into the alley somehow." Skunk leaned closer over the bar. "If you ask me, the killer put a knife to his throat and forced him back there."

I considered his point for a moment, and it made a certain sense. "Did the police manage to identify any suspects?"

"No, but they gave poor Paul a talking-to. They said it was suspicious that he'd gone home early and believed that he was the one lurking in the shadows outside. He had the perfect alibi, though."

"Lasagne?" I suggested.

"Precisely. He'd already made the ragù by the time Romanelli was dead. And there were several witnesses to the fact."

I felt a bit deflated by this. It was not just because I was hungry and wished that Paul would bring me some of his home-baked speciality.

For a moment, I'd had the sense that we were getting somewhere, but we'd reached another dead end.

"I suppose we should look at the alley at least," I mumbled to myself as much as him. "Is there a door that leads to it from in here?"

Skunk was all smiles as he pointed us through the back of the bar towards the narrow alley where the man once described as Italy's next leader had met his fate. As we examined the dark, dingy space, I remembered the first time I'd met Romanelli. It was much as Skunk had said; the man had a sort of magnetism that was hard to resist. He had charmed people so effortlessly and attracted a wide range of followers. You only had to look at the list of suspects in the murder he was tangled up in to see the appeal he had. But now he was more than a spent force, he was gone entirely. I doubt that he'd even graduated to the status of a footnote to history.

I hadn't asked exactly where he'd been murdered, but there was a spot between a large wheelie bin and a metal crate full of folded-up cardboard that made me stop and look. I could almost see his crumpled body there and had to wonder about the gall of the killer. Okay, it had only been a Wednesday night and that part of the promenade was fairly dead even during term time, but they could easily have been caught. If Romanelli had screamed out as the knife flashed across his throat, a passing pedestrian might have rushed over. Or if things had unfolded a little differently, Skunk could have dumped his empties and come face to face with the assailant.

Ramesh cut through my gloomy thoughts with a sudden gasp. "You'd better have a look at this."

His words pulled me away from that sad spot, and I walked to the far end of the alley where a brick wall was splashed over with scars of red and blue paint. One graffitied phrase stood out in white on top of all the others. It said, "Izzy must die."

Chapter Six

"It's all too dark," Ramesh told me when we got back to the car, but I thought he was talking about the street and didn't answer.

I'd just noticed that the donkey stand on the beach was still open, at seven in the evening and in such bad weather. There was someone standing just in front of it under a tarpaulin. I was fairly sure it was a woman. She was holding the reins of a donkey and looking up at the sky as if she could will the clouds to roll away and the sun to come out. I waved at her, but she either didn't see or didn't wish to acknowledge me, as she turned and walked deeper under cover.

"Oh, I do like to be beside the seaside," Ramesh whispered in a voice so melancholic that he might as well have been delivering a Shakespearean soliloquy. "Oh, I do like to be beside the sea." He sighed, and it made me want to cry. "Oh, I do like to stroll along the Prom, prom, prom. Where the brass bands play, 'Tiddely-om-pom-pom!'"

I pressed the clicker for the car before remembering that it didn't work and inserting the key in the lock. This seemed to make my friend even sadder, and he hunched his shoulders and said, "I miss my family. Let's go home."

I started the car, and my thoughts poured out of me.

"Did you recognise the name on the credit card of the person who paid to reserve the bar?" I didn't wait for his answer. "Ernie Bath was my P.E. teacher at secondary school. He was murdered when we went to the reunion last year."

I expected an, *Aww, happy days* but Ramesh looked just as gloomy as before.

I pressed on regardless. "I've no idea who's responsible for the killings, but it's clear that they don't like me. The way I see it, the person claiming to be Mr Bath hired the bar and contracted Romanelli in order to get him alone and kill him. Then they slipped away and, almost exactly two weeks later, killed poor Jack."

Ramesh held his hand to his head, clearly not approving of the topic. "Sorry, Izzy. I know you're all about violent murder investigations, but can we talk about something else for a while? I'm just not up to it tonight."

This certainly put a dampener on our journey back to West Wickham. Even Ramesh's 'Guaranteed Fun-Time Playlist' couldn't lift our mood. Have you ever noticed how there's a rather depressive undertone to the Pharrell Williams song 'Happy'? No, neither had I until he pointed it out.

"Face the facts, Iz. No man who is really that happy needs to tell everyone so often. He's trying to convince himself that life is great because he can't face reality anymore. When he says nothing can bring him down, what he really means is that he's on antidepressants and his mood is being chemically controlled. The whole song is a cry for help!"

"Are you acting this way because you couldn't go on a donkey again?"

"Of course not." He looked truly offended. "Or maybe partly. But more importantly, I don't want to face a world without you."

I was actually quite moved by the sentiment. "That is really very sweet, Ra. But you mustn't worry."

He glanced down at his hands and took a deep breath. "It's been years since anyone's tried to kill you, and it feels wrong. What could the killer not like about my lovely Izzy?"

I considered pointing out that my early stories (I mean cases!) were surprisingly divisive. My reviews on rate-a-detective.com criticised everything from my excessively long wrap-ups when I identified the culprit to my consumption of carrots.

"Let's not be sad before we need to be," I tried to reassure him instead. "Everything will work out alright in the end."

It was a shame that he was so needy at that moment, as I could have used the support myself. My brain was not taking the announcement of our forthcoming demise well.

The end is nigh! Trust no one! Izzy, why is that truck driving so close behind us? Is this it? Is he about to drive us off the road like in that movie?

I would have asked what movie he, she or it (I've never quite decided) was referring to, but I knew that if I suggested 'Duel' it would turn out to be Disney's 'Cars'.

"Perhaps you're right." At least Ramesh was a bit chirpier. "I'll put another song on. That's bound to cheer us up."

'Don't Worry, Be Happy' by Bobby McFerrin not exactly blasted out of the tinny speakers, and Ramesh bopped his head and swayed side to side until the first line of the song, at which point my designated passenger's face turned sour.

"That's easy for you to say, Bobby. A madman with the power to evade video cameras isn't trying to kill your best friend." A similar reaction was triggered by 'Oh, Happy Day', 'Shiny Happy People' and even "If You're Happy and You Know It, (Clap Your Hands)!'

"What we need," I interrupted to stop him from ruining any more classic songs, "is a plan."

"Yes, a plan!" He clapped his hands. "Wait, we could take Pacino to one of those photo studios where they dress you up like people from the past! I could be a cowboy. Pacino could be a little lord, and you could be our servant."

I ignored this and continued what I was saying. "Someone clearly has it in for me. In order to work out who that is, we have to go back through my life and identify the potential suspects."

"What about your childhood? Could it be something to do with school? The killer did use your teacher's name after all."

I briefly considered the possibility. "I don't think so. Not only has one of my high school classmates already turned out to be a psychotic killer – which surely reduces the chances of us finding a second one – when we went back there last year, everyone was surprisingly nice."

This was the first thing that had made him smile in an hour. "Oh yeah. I love those guys. You know I still hang out with Bobby, Micky and Timbo sometimes. And that Barry Travers is a goofball. Talk about a good bunch of lads."

"I bet they are." They'd been nice at our school reunion when I'd saved them from certain death, but that didn't mean I had forgotten my miserable teenage years. "I thought that someone from Porter & Porter was to blame when Jack was killed, but now this second death has thrown that out of the window."

"Unless that was the very reason Marco Romanelli was murdered. Perhaps the culprit wanted to mess with your thinking."

"It's possible." I bit my nail as I took the Croydon exit off the motorway. "But that graffiti makes it less likely. It's either me they're after, or it isn't." This kind of observation would get us literally nowhere, and I regretted making it.

It didn't really matter, as Ramesh was already thinking about something else.

"You've worked on about fifteen murder investigations by now. If there were approximately five people per case who you accused of being a killer, that would give us a grand total of seventy-five suspects. Why don't we just throw a party and invite them all?"

"I'm bad enough at parties at the best of times. I certainly wouldn't want to be the centre of attention if everyone there hates me."

Ramesh was suddenly more enthusiastic. "This is it, Izzy. The solution to all your problems."

"Is it?"

"Trust me. What doesn't a party fix?"

I could have given him about sixteen thousand possible answers, but I preferred this version of him to the guy who'd been sitting in that seat a few minutes earlier.

"We'll invite all the suspects you can think of who aren't dead or in jail, and we'll make a real shindig out of it."

"And why exactly would the killer come?"

"Weren't you listening? We'll make a real shindig out of it." He spoke as if he was the voice of reason, and I was the thick one. "I don't just mean a few finger sandwiches in the back room of a pub. We'll go all out. Oh, and Pacino can come. It'll be his first proper party." He evidently started thinking about his little boy then, as he fell quiet and eventually whispered, "I love my baby so much."

"I don't want to ruin your plans—"

"Then please don't."

"I don't want to ruin your plans, but I can't see that any killer would just come to us on command. What good would it do them?"

"What don't you understand about 'a real shindig'?" He spoke through gritted teeth. "There'll be balloons and a DJ!"

I considered what other solutions there might be. It was annoying that the killer had picked targets so far apart across the country. I prefer cases where everyone knows one another, and the victims are picked off in the nice, manageable confines of a village or perhaps a large house. That is what I like to call a considerate murderer.

"It feels like the killer is too clever for us. He (or whatever) hasn't left any forensic evidence at either of the crime scenes. She (or, you know) has avoided leaving any trail to follow, and if there's any link between Jack Campbell and Marco Romanelli, I can't imagine what it is."

"So what you're saying is that you would like me to organise a party?" His eyes grew so wide then that he looked just like his son. If his lip had started wobbling, I would have had to pull the car over to rock him to sleep.

"Oh, fine. But I'm choosing the refreshments, and I want Jammie Dodgers!"

"Yes!" He made a fist and pulled it down through the air in celebration. "You won't regret this."

Chapter Seven

"I am already regretting this," I said as I stood on the stage of Croydon's Grand Sapphire Hotel and Banqueting Hall in front of a gigantic sign made out of flowers. It said Mr and Mrs but instead of a plus or an ampersand, there was a massive neon heart in between the two words.

"Stop being a muddy stick, Izzy," Mother complained. "Everyone's having a wonderful time."

Wait just a moment. I should probably explain the big sign before we go any further. Ramesh had managed to get a cheap rate on renting the grand ballroom, but only because there'd been a Sikh wedding in there that afternoon, and he'd told them that they didn't have to clear up until we'd gone. The floor was strewn with petals, which may or may not have come from one of the eleven extremely realistic-looking, life-size cherry trees. The ceiling dripped with crystal chandeliers, and I had to keep squinting because, almost everywhere I looked, there were flashing disco lights.

"Yes, Mother, but our guests having a wonderful time is not my main objective. I've organised this party to find a killer."

"Well, I think that's a very selfish attitude, Isobel. I would expect better from a daughter of mine."

"Then you should adjust your expectations," I was quick to respond. "You only have one daughter, and she is me."

Mother wasn't listening but danced away with her fists twirling around one another in the air like those spiny metal balls at the top of a steam engine.

They're called centrifugal governors. Don't be so dim.

How do you *know* that?

My brain did not respond, as it was singing along to Sister Sledge's 'We are Family'. My father and second stepfather were dancing with Dean a few feet away. It's hard to describe the three-person routine they'd fallen into, but it featured both imaginary lassos and fishing lines. Danny and Shandy were doing a grinding, nineties-style R'n'B dance move at the side of the stage – it was not a pretty sight. Ramesh and his wife were boogying Pacino about between them, and my friend Lady Penelope was leading the singing. Thank goodness she didn't have a microphone.

You have to hand it to Sister Sledge. They know how to get a party started.

Of course, it wasn't my friends who concerned me; I was examining the crowd for the psycho killer who wanted me dead. Internationally adored film stars Beth Chaplin and Andrew Winterton were tucking into some mini pork pies (my choice) at the buffet. A small delegation from the picturesque (read: crime-infested) village of Shackleford Rise had formed a circle around Kebe Akerele, the grand dame of the British stage, and several of my high school teachers were leading a conga line. There were senior police officers, three priests and a selection of part-time elves. And yet, not one of them was holding a sign which said, "It's me, Izzy. I'm the one who's plotting to kill you."

Ramesh spotted me standing on my own in front of the throbbing neon sign. When the song was over, he handed his pride and joy to his wife, Patricia, and came to try to convince me to dance.

"Not a chance. I'm working."

"So am I." He pulled his head into his neck in disgust. "Or are you saying that dance is just a fun activity that anyone can do? I'll have you know, Isobel Salome Palmer, that I work relentlessly to bust these moves, and I do not appreciate such comments." To prove this, he shook an imaginary cocktail shaker very hard indeed in my direction.

"Calm down, you lunatic. I just mean that I'm trying to work out who amongst all these people might want to kill me."

"Ohhhh, I see. Why didn't you say so?" He came to stand next to me but performed the moonwalk on the spot while we talked. "Have you had any luck?"

"Not yet. From what I can tell, only the nice people are here."

He did the mashed potato and looked confused. "How do you mean?"

"Well, I've come to notice over the years that, on my cases, there are people who seem nasty at first and turn out to be nice. People who seem nice and turn out to be nasty and people who are nice all the way through. It's mainly that last group who turned up today."

"Were there any who started nasty and continued being nasty?"

It took me a moment to decide. "There were a few, but half of them ended up in jail, some were murdered, and the others haven't come."

He inspected the nearest group of suspects, but it didn't seem to help. "I give up."

It was a strange feeling to be in a room with so many people I knew. A triple date already felt like a big crowd to me, and I was not in my element. "This reminds me of a poster from the Simpsons that Danny had on his wall when we were kids. You know the one with about three hundred characters on it? I kind of expect each of them to step forward and say their catchphrases."

"I don't think that's very likely, Izzy," Ramesh replied as if everything he'd ever said was entirely normal. "Wait! What's my catchphrase? I don't have a catchphrase!"

"Calm down," I told him. "Practically everything you say is quotable."

"Yes, but I don't have one sentence that defines me. How am I ever going to become famous for doing very little if I don't have a catchphrase?" He delivered this tragic lament whilst twisting down to the floor and back. "I'm going to get some food and have a serious think about this. I have a hankering for cheese and pineapple chunks on a stick."

DJ Coolpants was behind me on the stage, and he gave me a wink as he picked up the mic from between his wheels of steel. "This song goes out to the birthday girl."

"It's not my birthday," I called, but he couldn't hear me because the music had changed. Chris de Burgh's 'Lady in Red' blasted out of the speakers, and several terrified gentlemen fled the dancefloor like rats… rats escaping from Chris de Burgh.

"It's only six thirty in the evening," Dean complained as he evaded his fiancée's grasp and made it to the stage. "What is that DJ thinking?" I suppose I must have been looking at him in a suspicious manner, as he frowned and asked. "Izzy, did you just consider my potential as a killer?"

"What, no?" I was surprised by his reaction for about half a second. "Though, to be honest, my resting face greatly resembles the dubious look emoji."

"Well, I'm not… the killer, I mean."

"Of course you're not." I couldn't help imagining the possibility now, and he clearly knew it.

"We're friends, Izzy. Best friends, I might even say." He looked more offended than the time I'd accused him of threatening to withhold my alibi for Bob's murder if I didn't go on a second date with him. "How could you imagine it even for a second?"

"You thought I was a killer when we met."

"Yeah, but that was..." He must have realised he was on shaky ground, as he changed the topic. "Fine, but as we've already established, I'm not to blame."

In my defence, he'd put the idea in my head and a list of potential evidence presented itself to me. "You must admit that you have certain traits that, from a particular angle, might appear a little... evil. That doesn't mean that you would murder two complete strangers, but I would be a nice parallel if my story of becoming a heroic detective mirrored your own supervillain origin tale."

He didn't reply to this but jutted his chin out indignantly.

"Oh, don't act like that," I said to defend myself. "You're suspiciously rich. You always walk about with a lot of gadgets, and you have a soundproofed basement."

"No, I don't."

"I might have made up that last bit, but I'm hardly a million miles off."

He frowned and swayed in time with the music for a few seconds before saying, "You've got me. I have all the trappings of an evil mastermind except for the predilection to kill. To be honest, I get Fiona to remove insects from the bathroom. I just don't have it in me to swat them... or pick them up, for that matter."

I held out my hand to him to shake. "Very well, I officially rule you out of the enquiry. Now I don't suppose you have any idea how I might slim down this crowd to the most likely four or five names?"

He took out a pair of glasses from his pocket, unfolded them and placed them carefully on the bridge of his nose. "It's funny you should ask, as I've been working on an AI that carries out just such tasks."

"Seriously?" My voice turned all squeaky in surprise.

"No, Izzy." He scanned the dancing throng before shrugging again. "But if you ask me, the only person here who stands out as a guaranteed criminal is Ramesh. The leopard-print tuxedos he and his son are wearing must be illegal on grounds of taste alone."

I smiled at him and, as the music had changed, his fiancée came to tempt him back to the dance floor. Certain people I won't mention have told me over the last couple of years that I lack character progression, but it was nice to see how far my friends had come in that time. I mean, I had gone from a mind-numbing office job to becoming Britain's most successful private detective. I'd built a business on the back of my own hard work, learnt to drive, saved up for a house, and my streak on Duolingo French is really something to boast about, but whatever… The point is that Dean was unrecognisable compared to the rude, nerdy weirdo I'd first been on a date with years earlier, and it made me happy to see how happy he could be.

I think what people mean when they say that your life has stood still, Izzy, is that you're still a lonely singleton with no hope of—

And that's enough out of you.

I saw someone in the middle of the crowd at this bittersweet moment and thought that I might have a dance partner after all.

"Edmund!" I said to the smartly dressed young man with slicked back hair and blue-grey eyes. "Edmund Porter," I tried again when he showed no sign of recognising me. I don't know why I thought that saying *his* name would fix this situation, but that's what I did.

"I'm sorry, do I know you?" he replied, and I felt like a real idiot.

Of course he doesn't recognise you, Izzy. You're no one. You're nothing – except all that stuff you talked about a minute ago, and have we mentioned your bowling average yet?

"I'm Izzy Palmer," I explained, hating myself as I did so. "I solved your bazillionaire father's murder?" When that didn't work, I tried, "I got two of your relatives sent to prison?"

"Izzy?" he said, and I remembered just how impossibly smooth he was. "Izzy, I'm joking. As much as I love Croydon and its wonderful banqueting facilities, I came here to see you."

I tittered like a prize idiot. "No, you didn't, you silver-tongued devil. Be away with you!"

Ooh, talking like you're from the Victorian age. You certainly know how to charm a man.

He didn't seem to notice, or at least, he wasn't put off, as he danced up closer to me and performed a slightly theatrical swaying of the hips. In case this wasn't clear enough, he whispered in my ear a moment later.

"You know, your invitation arrived at just the right time for me. I've just got out of an intensely messy relationship. Happy birthday, by the way."

He danced around me, and I realised that I'd been standing rooted to the spot this whole time without even any arm dancing – my usual speciality, which involves no movement from the waist down.

"It's not actually my—" I began, but the music was so loud, and he'd moved away from me to wheel his arms through the air.

"Have you ever noticed, Izzy, that almost every other human on earth is quite mad?"

"I have!" I replied enthusiastically. "It amazes me on a daily basis that I am generally the sanest person I know. At least animals behave according to type. People veer between one ridiculous act and another. It's impossible to know what anyone will do."

He took a sip of the luminous drink in his hand, which he'd almost splashed over my one nice cousin's head during the arm wheeling. "I was this close to getting married, Izzy. I'd never been so in love my whole life, but it turned out…" He stopped to laugh then. "It turned out that the woman I was about to devote my life to wasn't the person I thought she was. She seemed so perfect, but it all fell apart and now here I am dancing with you."

I don't think he meant this to sound as offensive as it did, but it did. "Thanks, Edmund."

He moved in closer again. "So, how about it? You and me, Friday night, in Croydon's premiere dining venue."

"*Le Sheek,*" I whispered, as though it were a mythical, mystical place. I'd been once, but didn't get around to eating anything, so the idea of having dinner there with a charming man like Edmund was quite attractive.

Do it, Izzy. He has all of his own teeth and, as far as we know, no criminal record. Say you'll go.

"I'd love to," I responded, my whole body suddenly smiling. "But not until I work out who's trying to kill me."

His dancing became more restrained – which is odd, as DJ Coolpants was playing the theme from 'Men in Black'. He clicked his fingers as though to say, *I respect your decision, Izzy.*

"I don't suppose your sister could be behind it?" I said without thinking this scenario through. "I mean, I know she's in prison but, with all the money your family has, is it possible that she could pull strings from inside?"

"Well, she certainly isn't your biggest fan," he shouted as the chorus of the song had just started and everyone was singing along. "I would not put it past her to plot some terrible scheme to bring about your demise."

"Great. Thanks." This was not the reassuring message I'd hoped to hear. "Do you have any idea how I might find out whether she was actually involved?"

"You could try visiting her in prison. She's always asking me to go, but I rarely bother. You know, I lost my affection somewhat when I discovered she'd murdered our father. Even if the old man was a monster, Audrey is worse."

"I know what you mean." I couldn't shake the feeling that Edmund was a much deeper person than his lothario image suggested. "I can't tell you how many people have tried to convince me that they were justified in murdering someone, but I've yet to agree."

He threw his head about for a moment. I'm fairly certain he was drunk and entirely unaware of the music that was playing. "Perhaps my family screwed me up so much that I'm only attracted to terrible women now."

I once more had to hope this didn't reflect badly on me. Either way, he clearly had his own stuff going on, and he stopped dancing at this point to break down in tears.

"I'm sorry, Izzy. I really am. It's been a very difficult year for me." And with that, my prince charming ran from the dancefloor to cry in the corner. He must have been worse for wear not to notice Danny and Shandy making out a few feet away.

I stood in the middle of the ballroom as everyone had a great time. I watched the people from entirely separate cases interacting with one another and wondered if one of them had it in for me. Countless ideas zipped through my brain. Possibilities, hypotheses and solutions bounced about like atoms, and just when I thought I had an idea of how everything that had happened that week would tie together, Ramesh grabbed me, and I was suddenly the head of a conga line.

Chapter Eight

I still remembered my last visit to a correctional facility but wished that I couldn't. It had been a men's prison that time, but now I was at HMP Bronzefield to see a woman who had a fairly good reason not to like me. When I'd first met Audrey Porter, I thought she was incredible. She was as beautiful as her film-star namesake, as smart as the woman on that quiz show who's good at checking words in the dictionary, and as charming as… well, her brother, I suppose.

Audrey Porter (and Hepburn, for that matter) was everything I dreamed of being but would never become. She was also a convicted murderer, so whatever my current issues might have been, my life was a fair bit rosier than hers.

I took a seat in a large hall with tables and chairs scattered around it. Apart from that, the place bore no similarity to the room where I'd visited David almost four years earlier. For one thing, there was a large area with slides, tricycles and games for children. The chairs were actually quite comfy, the tables low, and there was even a kiosk selling chocolates, snacks and refreshments.

I could get used to this place.

Please don't.

What united the two prisons was the look on the faces of people anxiously awaiting their loved ones. A little boy at the table next to mine stayed close to his father and gazed about the room as if the rest of us couldn't be trusted. A young man sitting alone by the wall wouldn't raise his eyes, even when his wife, girlfriend or perhaps sister was brought to him. I felt fortunate not to be so invested in the situation this time, and I sat mulling over a list of doubts as I waited for my convict to appear.

Audrey was born into a family of millionaires, and I had to wonder whether being rich is all it's cracked up to be. My mother had a cousin who inherited a grand estate but hated her own family so much that she killed herself in an attempt to shift the blame onto her children. Society teaches us that money is the balm that can soothe all ills, but it didn't seem that way to me. I'm not saying that I don't like the idea of buying the biggest bag of Maltesers in the supermarket without looking at the price tag and thinking, *Bloomin' heck! They've gone up in price.* But as the Beatles famously said… Urmmm… I can't actually think of a relevant quote at the moment.

"Hello, Izzy," a voice said to break through my daydreaming, and I was surprised to see that Audrey was not how I normally pictured her.

It wasn't just that she lacked the black and white striped t-shirt, which all prisoners wear in my very limited mind. She was a faded version of her old self. She sported a baggy blue tracksuit which I was sure she would never have worn outside of her home gym before she was imprisoned. Her hair looked frayed and unkempt, piled on top of her head and secured with a simple elastic band.

"Hello, Audrey. Thank you for seeing me today." I hadn't picked the right register, so I tried again. "Or rather, thank you for agreeing to let me visit."

I was searching for signs of her true feelings and thought I noticed the hint of a snarl as she replied. "I didn't have much else on today. Time goes very slowly in here."

"That's nice," I said without thinking. "I mean, it's not nice that your time is not your own. I just—"

"It's fine. Calm down." She had that same sense of authority as when I'd known her. She was both confident and sympathetic, and that was an alarming combination. It had come through in her trial, too. If the evidence against her hadn't been so strong, I'm certain she could have convinced the jury of her innocence. "Are you going to tell me why you're here?"

"I saw Edmund," I said because I had to start somewhere.

"That poor man. You do know that he's in a very fragile state at the moment?"

I hesitated this time but couldn't see that I had much left still to conceal. "I did get that impression."

She turned to look across the hall. "I'll never forgive that woman for what she did. I've never met her, of course – people don't tend to bring their fiancées to meet their jailbird sisters – but she sounded like a real horror."

I wanted to ask her how she knew so much about what had happened if Edmund hadn't visited her recently, but I was just as tongue tied as when we'd first met on her family estate.

"Daisy," she said, and it took me a moment to understand what she meant. "It's my sister Daisy who tells me everything. My brothers aren't interested in me anymore, and Beatrix moved abroad." She could anticipate my every question and soon said, "America, if you were curious. Anyway, Daisy was the one who told me about Edmund's engagement, and she was the one who told me that he'd found the courage to call it off."

Though she still possessed an impressive degree of self-assurance, one big difference I'd noticed was that she had lost her urgency. I hadn't explained the purpose of my visit yet, and she was in no hurry to hear it. "As I was saying, I didn't trust his fiancée for one second. Her father owns the Jameson media empire, and she'd followed him into the family business. You know the type – tons of money, but not a scruple between them." She made it sound as if this was a great failing, but the criticism could be applied to at least half of her family. "What really set the alarm bells ringing was when she moved into his apartment in London after they'd only known one another for a few weeks. I thought, *Something is wrong here,* and I was right."

As if she were an elderly relative who I'd decided to humour, I found myself falling into the conversation that she'd engineered. "Why? What did she do to him?"

She held in her answer for a moment, as if debating whether to share her secrets. "She did him over good and proper. She made him believe that he was worthless, and she was doing my poor brother a favour by having anything to do with him. You hear this kind of thing about men often enough, but plenty of women are capable of coercive control and some men are weak enough to be manipulated." She no longer sounded quite so sympathetic as she had, though the fact that a murderer had felt it necessary to remind me that women can also be nasty did not pass me by.

"It's terrible," I said, to hide my real feelings.

"Dear little Edmund. He never has had much luck in love. It was a horribly messy break-up. The girl turned into a real viper, and now he's fallen to pieces. Daisy told me that he looked quite wild the last time they met. She was afraid he would do something terrible, and now here you are." She managed to hint for the first time that my presence was less than ideal.

"I'm sorry for your brother. I've always thought he's a nicer person than his reputation suggests, but he's not the one I've come here to discuss."

She sat back in her chair and examined me as she threaded her fingers together. "Oh, really. So what service can I provide for you today, Miss Palmer?"

Is it just me, or did she sound like the villain in a Bond film?

"I believe that someone's trying to kill me… or at least mess with my life, or…" I couldn't decide what I thought.

"Oh, dear. That must be terrifying. And you've come to the conclusion I'm to blame?" She held my gaze for five ticks of the cheery yellow clock on the wall, and when the time was up, she released a hollow laugh. "Izzy, you are funny. I always did like you. *Did* being the operative word in that sentence, of course. I still haven't forgiven you for sending three people I love to prison."

It took me a moment to work out who she meant.

Her brother, her butler and…

She's talking about herself!

I was no longer intimidated by her. My response when it came was stern and direct. "I didn't force you to kill your father, Audrey. That was your doing. You were also the one who invited me to your house to investigate the crime you were so confident of pinning on someone else."

This clearly piqued her even more. "It was not my intention to pin anything on anyone, I had hoped to—" She interrupted herself to say something in an even more furious voice. "The point is that my father was a brute and deserved— In fact, do you know what?"

I doubt she was expecting an answer, but I shrugged anyway.

"I'm not interested in your moralising. Just say what you've come here to say and get lost."

Her outburst had caught the attention of the nearest guard. Though the room was disguised as a play centre, the inmates were being watched just as closely as in any other prison, and the line of burly men and women in black and white uniforms looked just as tough.

"I've come here because two suspects from my previous cases have been murdered."

"And what's that got to do with me?" She delivered her response in a grim whisper.

"To begin with, if the killer is going through my investigations one by one, they'll eventually get to yours. Every last suspect on that case was someone you love, and the only ones who aren't in prison are your siblings. Surely it would be in your best interest to help me."

She considered this for a few seconds, and she could apparently see my point. "Very well. What do you want to know?"

"If you aren't responsible for the killings, you might at least understand how the culprit feels. Why do you think someone would go after me?"

She looked perplexed that I would even ask. "So you're saying you'd like me to be your Hannibal Lecter? You want me to give you a peek inside the mind of a killer?"

"Not quite, but I've surrounded myself with violence for years. I thought that I understood why people come to think that murder is the only solution. But now that I could end up being the victim, I've started to question the whole thing."

I imagined that she would maintain her antagonistic tone, but she apparently took pity on me. "I can't answer your questions, Izzy. I really can't. You know why I did what I did. My father psychologically abused my siblings and me. He brought me up to be a monster and so that's what I became. But I can't tell you why anyone else might hold a grudge against you. All I can say is that there are sure to be plenty of candidates."

Something in her tone disturbed me once more and, instead of thanking her and making my way back home, I lashed out. "You really believe that you did the right thing, don't you?"

"I'm amazed that comes as a surprise, especially when not every person found guilty of murder is treated the same."

I should have formed a response, but all I could do was stare back in bemusement.

"Oh, come along, Miss Palmer. Don't play the innocent. Whatever excuses you might have invented to explain it, you know that your boyfriend's crime was just as bad as mine."

"I beg your pardon?" I'm not sure if I said these words or merely thought them.

"David Hughes walked free because he looks good in a suit and convinced the parole board that he killed Bob to protect society. No judge would hold me to the same standards because the man I killed was considered a pillar of the business community. If they'd seen what Daddy was really like, I'd have been given a medal."

I don't know how much of what she'd said made sense to me just then. My brain was a mess of thoughts, though at least it wasn't singing the theme tune from an obscure TV show for once.

My voice, when I finally managed to speak, was small and far away. "What did you say?"

A smile reshaped her pretty face, and she leaned closer to me across the table. "My goodness. You didn't know!" She breathed in then in sheer amazement. "David was released from prison, Izzy. He's as free as you are."

Chapter Nine

Some points of order…

Yes, I was suddenly aware that both that nasty journalist and D.I. Irons had mentioned that there'd been a problem with one of my previous cases and, no, I hadn't thought anything of it before because I am a free-spirited butterfly who only lives for the moment (i.e. I didn't pay enough attention).

I'm also mindful of the fact that I had gone to accuse Audrey Porter of murdering Jack Campbell and Marco Romanelli only to chicken out and ask for some nice general advice, like an overly polite Clarice Starling.

And finally, I know that this is the second reference to 'The Silence of the Lambs' and, if you haven't seen the film or read the book – as I haven't because they would probably give me nightmares – it may be rather confusing.

After Audrey had delivered her gleeful revelation, I sat back in my chair and tried to put the world into some kind of order. I didn't manage it but stared into space until she eventually left.

"It was genuinely lovely to see you, Miss Palmer," she told me, and her voice was so sincere I almost believed her. "If you could do me one small favour, I would greatly appreciate it."

I looked up at her but said nothing.

"Be careful with Edmund…" She was short of words herself for a moment. "He's been through a terribly trying time, and I don't think it would be the best thing for either of you to become too close now. You must know…"

I'd never seen her look so hesitant. It was clear she still cared for her brother a great deal, even if he rarely came to visit.

"You must know how strongly he feels about you," she continued. "I wasn't there to see it, of course, but he'd only got over your rejection when he met the woman he was supposed to marry." Her face had become quite serious, but then she brightened up again. "Or at least, that's what Daisy says, and she normally tells the truth."

She put her feet together and stood up straighter, much as she would have when saying farewell to an important client at her father's company – before she conspired to stab him to death.

"Goodbye, Audrey," I finally uttered, feeling a touch of sympathy for her after all. "I hope life in here treats you kindly."

She opened her mouth to say something, and I willed her to tell me that it really wasn't too bad. I half hoped that she spent all her time making marmalade with a posse of colourful friends, but sadly 'Paddington 2' isn't the most accurate depiction of prison life committed to celluloid. In the end, she kept her thoughts to herself, but nodded as she turned to walk away.

Izzy?

Yes, brain?

Are you alright?

Why wouldn't I be?

Perhaps I'm being silly, but since you discovered that the murderer you've never really stopped loving is now a free man, and then found out that a perfectly nice guy you dismissed as a playboy was actually in love with you, you've sat right where you are in a prison visitors' hall staring at the wall for fifteen minutes.

I looked at my watch and realised that my brain was right. A chunk of time had disappeared, and I don't even know what I'd been thinking about. I moved to collect my things, before realising I didn't have anything to collect. Instead, I made my way to the desk where visitors had to sign out. I went through the terrestrial equivalent of an airlock on a spaceship, and then to a second building where I had to sign my name again.

I was in such a daze that I didn't notice the woman in front of me and, when she finished what she was doing and turned around, I believe we both got a shock.

"Izzy," Janet the journalist said with a look of something approaching guilt. "I didn't expect to see you here."

My emotions still weren't connecting with my mouth, so instead of shrugging moodily after the terrible way she'd treated me in my own living room, I said, "It's lovely to see you again."

In the end, this turned out to be the best option, as she took a step backwards and, presumably unnerved by my carefree attitude – I am such a butterfly, after all – she stuttered as she spoke. "The article will be coming out this week… I… I'm here to see a friend of yours."

"I just spoke to Audrey myself." My tone of voice remained surprisingly upbeat.

"Audrey Porter?" She looked a touch confused. "I didn't know she was in here. No, I've come to see your old school friend. Lorna Inglis is serving a life sentence for the murders at your high school. They say she's unlikely to ever be released."

She spoke gravely, as if she wanted the seriousness of the crimes I'd investigated at my high school reunion to intimidate me somehow.

"Say hello to her from me," I murmured and was about to leave when the human-Barbie hybrid found her confidence again.

"I hope you like the article when you get a chance to read it, Izzy." She was clearly looking forward to my public savaging. "I think it will be the first accurate portrayal of you in the press yet."

I smiled and crumpled my eyebrows as if she'd said something ever so sweet. "I can't wait."

I signed the form to leave the building, attempted once again to gather belongings I hadn't brought with me and walked outside to something approaching freedom. I felt as though I'd served a long sentence, and the cold air on my face did me a world of good. I mean, I still collapsed onto the bench at the bus stop to cry, but I felt a lot fresher than I had in that stuffy reception.

"I don't understand," I told Ramesh at his house that afternoon, and I realised that this had been a common refrain for the last week or so. "Why didn't you tell me David was free?"

Pacino looked sad on his father's behalf as he patted a very patient Elton, who was curled up on the golden cat throne that Ramesh had made him.

"You see, the thing is…" This was as far as my favourite idiot got before he became stuck.

"I think what Ramesh is trying to say," his far more sensible wife Patricia attempted, but she didn't fare much better.

"It's like this…" he began again. "I didn't tell you that David had been released from jail because…"

I wasn't the only one who was tired of unfinished sentences. Kiki hissed at her master and went to fall asleep on the windowsill. She was a true diva.

"I'm not going to punch you or stop being your friend." I channelled that fearsome feline's energy. "I just want to know how this happened."

The lovely, if complicated, couple looked at one another. I have no idea why Patricia had taken any blame on herself. This was all laughing-boy's fault.

"Perhaps it would be best if I answer in the form of a song," he suggested and immediately burst into a verse to the tune of his classic non-hit 'I Like Cake'.

"I can only say I'm sorry.
That I made such a mistake.
Will you ever forgive me?
Tell me, Iz, what will it take?"

I think he got a bit carried away at this point as instead of adapting the song for the chorus, he started singing, "I like cake… Yeah, yeah, yeah.
I like cake… woah, woah, woah."

"Ramesh, that's enough!" I really shouted these words, and he looked a little scared. "I need to know why you ever thought it was a good idea to keep this from me."

He took a deep breath and, with Patricia's hand on his shoulder, finally explained. "There were a number of reasons, really. For one, it was just before Christmas when we found out about the hearing, and I didn't want to spoil the festive season."

"Bad reason!" I barked. "Next!"

Pacino really laughed at this.

"Fine. David wasn't just released because the review board understood that the man he killed was a would-be killer, a sexual abuser and a horrendous bully, but because the British prison service is overwhelmed, and they were trying to free up space. I didn't want you having a bad impression of our hard-working government, and so I—"

"That's a lie, Ramesh. Next!"

He looked one last time at Patricia for support. "Oh, very well. I didn't tell you because David wrote and asked me not to."

My insides fell out then. Well, that's not true, of course, but it certainly felt as though they had. To make sure that I didn't mislay any organs, I lay down on the carpet in front of the sofa and made a sad purring noise. Tammy Wynette could evidently understand whatever it was I was saying as she came to sit on the back of my legs.

"Don't be like that, Izzy," lovely, sympathetic Patricia begged. I don't know whether I've said this before, but she is far too good for Ramesh. She didn't even murder anyone at her own wedding! "Ramesh was looking out for your best interests. He could barely sleep for weeks thinking about it."

"It's true, Izzy." He slid off the sofa to sit cross-legged beside me. "I wanted to tell you, but David swore me to secrecy. He knew that I read the papers for you, and it's not as if it was front-page news, so we were fairly confident you wouldn't find out."

"Why?" I whispered.

"Because you don't follow the news too closely, I would have thought that was—"

"No, I mean, why didn't he want me to know?"

The room fell silent. Even the cats seemed to hold their breath. They were surely thinking, *That poor pathetic girl. She basically put her life on hold – except for those other men she dated – for a man who doesn't want her.*

Pacino hiccupped, and the room came back to life.

"I don't know, Izzy," Ramesh told me, and he placed his hand on my back. I would probably have rolled over to look at him, but Tammy was perfectly happy where she was, and I didn't want to bother her. "He told me that it was for your sake, and I believed him."

Kiki wandered over to lick my hair just then. She was by far the most maternal of Ramesh's moggies, and it was just what I needed at that moment.

When I didn't reply, Patricia joined us on the floor. "I know it must seem like we were conspiring against you, but we really weren't."

Ramesh had to correct her. I think it's a common trend for married couples. "Speaking literally, that's not true. Everyone in your family and all your friends knew about it and we did in fact conspire to keep the information from you, but— Ow!" He stopped talking because his wife had just clapped him around the back of the head.

I didn't pay much attention. I just lay on my tummy, wishing that time would go faster, so that I wouldn't have to feel so completely awful any longer.

A sad, small question emerged from me, but I knew that no one there could answer. "What do I do now?"

Chapter Ten

To say that I regressed to an earlier stage of being would be an understatement. Rather than investigate the appealingly complex crimes that had been laid out before me, I lay on the sofa in my living room, watched bad cookery shows on TV, ate frozen pizzas – I did cook them first, at least – and drank pitchers of supermarket-brand, pre-mixed cocktails. None of this made me feel any better about thc world.

On Thursday that week, Janet Ellison's exposé of the unforgivably human Izzy Palmer appeared in the paper. I wouldn't normally have known anything about it, but since the David fiasco (and the Jack and Marco fiascos before that) I'd taken out a subscription to every major broadsheet in the land, though admittedly, I didn't look at The Scotsman quite as much as the London papers.

The vast majority of articles that morning weren't about me, but Janet's editorial made up for this with its lashings of vitriol.

"Great Detective or Cunning Self-Publicist?" the headline asked, with a terrible picture of me dressed in a truly unflattering puffy dress my mother made me wear to my cousin's wedding. I could only assume they'd got the picture from my slimy Uncle Bradley, which made me like him even less. And yet, the photo was the best thing on that page.

The journalist had painted a picture of a sly, egotistical woman who was so precious about her image that her only employee was a press officer whose job it was to cultivate the picture of Izzy Palmer as a master sleuth – of course, if she'd been there with me, I would have argued that Ramesh is also in charge of buying biscuits, enforcing *Dress-down Fridays* and staff bonding activities. I might have been able to cope with this mangling of the truth if she hadn't linked it to larger issues that would presumably help the people of Britain believe her constructed narrative.

"It will come as no surprise to readers of this paper that at least one conviction Palmer supposedly secured was later scaled back. Not only did David Hughes, former managing director of the Porter & Porter Corporation, have his sentence greatly reduced, at his appeal, Palmer's involvement in the police investigation

was brought into question, and Hughes's solicitor implied that the very much amateur detective may have interfered with evidence to catch the man responsible for middle-manager Robert H. Thomas's death.

"What is perhaps more predictable at this point in the story is the fact that, not only was the victim Izzy Palmer's former boss, but the killer was also her boyfriend at the time. It would be difficult not to conclude that some element of collusion was at play. Hughes served not quite four years for a cold-blooded murder. Perhaps he knew in advance that he would get off with nothing more than a slap on the wrist thanks to his girlfriend's manipulation."

I gasped instinctively (yet theatrically) after each sentence. It was nasty stuff, but at least I was so shocked by the thought of being ripped to shreds in print that I briefly detached from my body and read the article as if it was written about someone else. The real kicker came when she moved on to talk about the recent killings.

"It would be beyond me as a serious journalist to blame the self-appointed sleuth for any of the crimes she has investigated. The truth is that Izzy Palmer has put some deranged people behind bars. On visiting the West Wickham High Killer, Lorna Inglis, in prison at the weekend, she told me that she was glad that Izzy had put an end to her spate of killings, and nothing I said could convince her to say a bad word about her former schoolmate."

Ahh, that's nice. I always liked Lorna.

Don't be so gullible! She's building up to the big revelation.

"However, in the space of the last few weeks, two of Palmer's former suspects have been murdered. This is surely too much of a coincidence to ignore and prompts the question of what a private detective like Izzy Palmer would do to stay in the public eye. Izzy's big case finding that squirrel was some time ago now. The TV movie adaptation only received middling reviews, and I felt that the actress who played her, the excellent Gwendoline Richie on fiery form, showed up the real Palmer as a rather drab and unimpressive individual.

"I'm in no way saying that Palmer is a killer herself but, should she amaze her public by solving this string of terrible crimes, it won't be a surprise to me at all. What better way of getting back

into the national conversation than to solve a crime that very much resembles one of the cases from her beloved Agatha Christie?"

I wanted to scream but I couldn't.

In an instant, I wished that I wasn't alone. I kept hoping that Mother would pop up into my kitchen with her posse of followers. I held my breath for a moment to listen, but there was no one there and, for the first time since I'd left home a year earlier, I realised just how alone in the world I'd become.

I'm sorry. I don't mean to sound sorry for myself, but I was feeling rather sorry for myself. My friends were either getting married or having babies. Mother had a surplus of husbands. Ramesh had plans to watch every recorded Cher concert in a two-day marathon. Dean had his sound-proofed dungeon. What did I have?

I had a phone call, that's what.

I didn't recognise the number but swiped up to accept it all the same.

"Who's that?" I asked, and the fuzzy sound at the end of the line suggested that whoever was calling me was outside somewhere.

"Izzy? Have you been crying?"

"Hello Irons," I replied, as I'd never got used to calling my police collaborator by her Christian name. "How can I help you today?"

"You can come to central London. There's a car on its way to you right now."

"Why, what's happened?"

"We've found another body. It's someone you know."

Even as she said this, I saw a panda car pull up outside my house and so, instead of staying on the line to find out who was dead, I ran to my room to shed my fluffy second skin – and, no, I'm not going to apologise for wearing a Slanket; they are by far the most comfortable item of clothing imaginable.

By the time the officer tasked with collecting me had half banged the door down, I was looking more human in a smart black jumper – with very few daiquiri stains – and matching black trousers. Admittedly, I looked as though I might burst into mime at any moment, but I felt that D.I. Irons would have looked down on my previous attire.

It was nice of her to send a car, but the traffic in London meant that it would probably have been quicker to take the train into town, change to the tube and then walk to the office near Leicester Square. I recognised the building immediately. I had been there when investigating the death of the film star Sammy Akerele, who had collapsed in the street, not far from the premises of Vanguard and Associates.

Irons was waiting for me on the street outside the tall Victorian tenement. "The body's not here, but there's something I want you to see."

She didn't say hello or shake my hand. She just turned on her heel and walked through the door behind her that a young constable was guarding.

"Is it Eddie?" I asked, and Irons turned round to issue a silent nod.

Walking into the brightly lit reception, I came face to face with a giant photograph of Eddie Vanguard himself. The man was a legendary talent agent who represented stars of screen, stage and cruise ships. Images of his clients lined the walls. He'd worked with everyone from Dame Judi Dench to *boy on YouTube who fell into a large jelly.* One of the photos, of course, was that other viral sensation turned international star: my mother, Bu-Bu La Mer.

"When were you last here?" Irons asked, and though I couldn't imagine why she needed to know, I told her anyway.

"About three years ago. I only came to talk to him when his client was murdered."

She paused at the internal door to Eddie's office. "But you have seen him since then?"

"Of course I have. He was round my house last week when my mother amassed a group of men in my kitchen for—" I realised at this point that there was no explaining my mother's behaviour. "He came to my house for tea."

"It's a puzzle," my friend said with a puff of her expressionless lips.

We walked through the door to see not a body, but an empty room with a small pile of letters on the desk. Each had been cut neatly open and, sitting on a leather sofa in the corner of the room was a woman I sort of possibly half remembered as being the receptionist there. She was in floods of tears.

"Thank you so much for coming, Izzy," she told me. "I can't tell you how highly Eddie thought of you. He was always saying that if you had any talent as an actor, singer or dancer, he would have signed you up in an instant."

It was hard to take this as a compliment, but I tried my best. "Thank you, that's so kind." There was a junior officer there to comfort her, and so I turned to Irons instead. "What am I doing here? Shouldn't you keep your distance from me after David's sentence was cut short?"

"Oh, you heard about that, did you?" Irons' already flat voice fell quieter. "That may be true, but it turns out you're rather important to this case. Miss Bowen over there came in this morning and opened her boss's post as always. The first letter she read was for you."

I felt myself drifting over to the desk without knowing that I'd told my legs to move. In the centre was a typed letter that had been folded in three but now sat face up for us to read.

Izzy Palmer,

Vanguard had to die because of you. That's three murders now that are on your head, not to mention all the harm you've done in the past. Your time is coming, but until then, I hope you feel guilt for your crimes.

With all my loathing,

The one who will kill you.

It was a jolly little missive and made me feel so much better about life.

"You'd better tell me exactly what's been happening," I said in little more than a soft croak. Of course, the bad thing about feeling sorry for myself is that, when something really bad happens, there's nowhere left to go. I felt bad for Eddie, but I stayed at pretty much the same low ebb as before.

"A dogwalker discover a body lying on the bank of the Thames at Richmond early this morning. We've been through Eddie's phone and computer and found that he was contacted by someone claiming to represent an up-and-coming American singer. They arranged to meet last night, at which point the killer struck. The real singer didn't know anything about Eddie Vanguard or the man who contacted him. My officers are trying to work out if there is a digital trail they can follow to identify whoever sent the e-mail, but there's no trace of a talent manager called Ian Dennison, so the name is—"

"Definitely fake," I interrupted. "Ian Dennison was a man I met on the case I investigate in Spain. He was pushed to his death from the top of a cliff."

"Of course he was." She made her eyes really big as she processed the news. "If there's anything else you can think of that might point to the killer, I am all ears."

"Eddie was badly beaten once," I said, casting my mind back to yet another case. "The man who did it was sent to prison, is there any way that—"

"Not a chance. I remembered what happened to him from the media coverage of the murders you investigated in that 'quaint English village'." She made air quotes as she said this, but I hadn't a clue what she was referring to. "The man who attacked Vanguard and murdered two people was called Nate Hammer, and he's only eighteen months into a life sentence in jail."

The possibility that one of Hammer's friends was responsible for the murders briefly flickered through my brain.

"I have to conclude," Irons said as she perched on the corner of the desk, "that this is more about you than Eddie Vanguard or any of your other associates. After all, he is the third of your former suspects to be murdered." She'd evidently read the paper that morning. "Do you have any idea who you've angered?"

I was struggling to remember who I was or what we were doing there just then. The idea I might be able to solve a complicated string of murders was laughable.

"Izzy, why are you laughing?"

Oops, that was supposed to be between us. Sorry!

"I'm laughing because this is insane. Someone is blaming me for their actions, and I can't bear it. None of the men who've been killed were perfectly innocent. Jack Campbell was a drug dealer. Marco Romanelli was accused of inciting various violent acts, and Vanguard was an unscrupulous shark. Maybe that's why they were chosen."

"Maybe…" Irons did not sound convinced. "I suppose you've been through all the people who you've crossed over the years. You must have tried to work out who's responsible."

I didn't answer at first. I was attempting to look at everything from a different perspective. "There is no shortage of candidates. From the tone of the article in this morning's newspaper, half the people in Britain must have a bad opinion of me."

She looked rather philosophical for a moment before declaring, "That's the price of fame. Perhaps you could talk to your high-flying friends in the celebrity world to see if they've any insight into what's happening."

I assumed she was talking about Princess Penelope, though I had once been in the same room as Julie Andrews. "It won't hurt to try." My tone suggested that the opposite were true.

"Do what you can, Izzy. I'll keep you abreast of any changes."

"Is it worth me going to the site of the murder?" I put to her with little enthusiasm.

"Nah. There's a forensic team down in Richmond, but they don't hold out much hope. All we know is that he went for a drink alone in one of the riverside pubs. Then, at ten on the dot, he finished his pint and walked away along the bank. His e-mail correspondence suggests that he met the killer in a secluded spot away from the town. I don't know what he thought he would gain from such a clandestine meeting, but he didn't achieve his goal."

Each word she said weighed more heavily upon me, and I felt as though someone had hammered me into the ground like a tent peg.

Irons must have noticed, as she did something that was greatly out of character. She smiled. "Try not to be too upset. If the full force of the Metropolitan Police can't get to the bottom of this, then I'm certain that you will. Would you like a lift home?"

Chapter Eleven

I should probably have accepted her offer, and perhaps even asked for an officer to be stationed outside my house, but it was hard to see myself as the potential victim. This wasn't the first time someone had wanted me dead, and yet I had played the part of a detective for several years now, and I struggled to shift my point of view.

Taking the train home gave me the opportunity to think through my problems. There was something about the motion of the carriages as they raced along the tracks that helped my mind wander. I traced a thread through my whole life. I started with primary school, as I didn't remember much from before then, and travelled on through my adolescence, lonely sports summer camps, and a job in fast-food restaurant where the shapeless uniform made the guy I fancied think I was a boy. From there I jumped to university and on to my time at Porter & Porter before I'd established the Private I Detective Agency and investigated all those cases which had now come back to haunt me.

It felt throughout as if one piece of the puzzle should have been plain to see, but it kept evading me. I don't remember changing trains or getting squashed when everyone piled into the carriages in search of a seat, but I know the exact route that my thoughts took. And still, at the end of it all, I was no closer to the truth than I had been on my sofa in my Slanket that morning.

There's something missing, I told myself once more, and my brain finally worked out the problem.

Flip pads and pens!

I messaged my parents and, by the time I was back home, a group of key helpers had assembled in the front lounge of my childhood home. Sadly, they weren't the only people who were there to welcome me.

"Martin Overton, Daily Mail," a man stepped out from the bushes in front of my mother's house to wave a mobile phone in my face. "What response do you have to the allegations that you have interfered with more police investigations than you've aided?"

"My response is that it isn't true. My work has led to the conviction of numerous violent criminals." I was frankly amazed by how confident I sounded.

He didn't respond but looked disappointed as another journalist pushed past him with a question. "Peter Walker, The Times. Do you have any thoughts on the killer who appears to be targeting suspects from your past cases? And, I have a follow-up question; are you to blame?"

"No, of course I'm not!"

"Jennifer Coleridge, Daily Telegraph." The third and final hack stepped closer with a determined gleam in her eye. "Is there any truth to the rumour that you are in a polyamorous relationship with a murderer and a TV doctor?"

We wish!

"No, I… urmmm…." Why was this the question that stumped me? Where had my composure gone? I mumbled the first sentence that came into my head which sounded vaguely connected to what she'd asked me and then fell through my mother's front door. "I prefer cookery programmes."

Inside my childhood home, things were no less hectic. My fathers were setting things up in the lounge, my mother had descended the stairs in a feather and chiffon gown, and from the smell of things, I could only imagine that Danny was out in the garden, huddled around a campfire, making lunch.

"I think this is a wonderful idea, darling," Mother told me, as she sat in a chair in the middle of the lounge for Fernando to thread silver bells into her hair. To be fair to my exceedingly enthusiastic mother, I could tell she'd been crying over the death of her manager. Though Vanguard was a bit slimy for my tastes, the two had worked well together, and I Mum was doing what she could to hide her pain. Her next headline tour wasn't starting for over a week, so I could think of no other explanation for the flamboyant hairdo than her desire to distract herself.

My two most significant fathers, meanwhile, were limbering up in preparation for what we were about to do.

"Have we got enough red pens, Greg?" Real Dad enquired of his replacement.

"Plenty," my stepfather replied as he positioned two easels in front of the fireplace. "And black and blue, too, for that matter. Let's make this one to remember."

Right there on the sofa was one of the most helpful people who had offered their opinions on my cases over the years. I was happy to see that Mother had invited the elderly aunt of my ex-boyfriend/reformed murderer, David. Sitting next to Sir Hugalot, the oversized teddy I'd won in the school raffle when I was seven, Auntie Val was one of the very best minds I could hope to tap if we were to work out the killer's game. Oh, and Ramesh was there too.

"I think we should all take roles and act out what we believe happened," he insisted as he showed his son the giant teddy. "I'll go first." He cleared his throat and put on a Texan accent. "Hey, y'all, my name is Frank Cooper and I'm the long-lost brother of Izzy Palmer. When I discovered that my real parents had given me up for adoption… on a ranch, I decided that I had to track down that heinous hussy who enjoyed all the benefits that I was denied. I'm comin' for ya, Izzy. You see if I ain't!"

"Thank you, Ra," I said most sincerely, "for ruling out that possibility. It was incredibly helpful."

He pulled on his imaginary Stetson in acknowledgement and went back to chewing on an invisible piece of straw.

"Okay, Dads. Pens at the ready?" I asked. "Let's go." When nothing happened, I had to help them along. "What's the matter?"

Greg looked at my father and my father looked at Greg as if debating who should tell me a secret. My stepfather was the man to get things started. "It just doesn't seem very fair," he explained, before Dad took up their cause.

"Yes. It's hardly right that Ramesh should get the chance to make up a character if we don't."

I could see that it would be quicker to humour them than complain, so I took a deep breath and sought a compromise. "I'll tell you what, Daddies. When we finish what I've brought you all here to do, you can pretend away to your hearts' content, but can we do the first bit first?"

They seemed happier now and nodded in unison. "Very well, Izzy," Greg announced in a formal voice. "You may begin."

Dad took his black pen and wrote "People Who Hate Izzy" on his pad, as Greg took a blue one and put "People Who don't Seem to Hate Izzy" on his.

That neatly sums up everyone we've ever met.

"I've got a suggestion," Fernando announced as he stood back to admire his handiwork with my mother's sparkly hairdo. "Rather than picking names from the air willy nilly, why don't we go from the very beginning of Izzy's life and think through everyone who has ever taken against her chronologically."

"We could be here for a very long time," Ramesh said under his breath and, if Sir Hugalot had been a bit closer, I would have made him hit that cruelly honest man.

"Well, I can cover the first few years," my mother replied and cleared her throat to get to work. "At nursery school, Izzy was not what we might call a popular child. She would sit in the corner reading picture books as the other children ran about the place and had fun."

"Picture books *are* fun!" I reacted rather than replied, but I knew she wouldn't listen.

"Her teacher told me that very first year how she worried that my dear Isobel wouldn't integrate socially."

"This explains a lot." Ramesh nodded seriously, as though he were my therapist. "Tell me more."

Luckily, Auntie Val was on hand to rein in the madness. "Has Izzy had any contact with that teacher or any of the children from her nursery since?"

"Well, no, but you can never rule out long-standing grudges," Mother replied. "Look at Paris Hilton and Lindsay Lohan."

To my surprise, Ramesh didn't recite a list of other celebrity feuds, though he did mime a round of applause.

My father looked very confused indeed. "Are you saying we should put Miss Hilton and Miss Lohan up on the board?"

I nipped that in the bud. "Let's move on to my school days, shall we? It is my belief that anyone who might have hated me from that period of my life is either dead, in prison, or no longer interested in me. Can we all agree on that?"

There was some mumbling around the room, and without prompting, Greg wrote a name on his pad. "Gary Flint, Izzy. What do you say to Gary Flint?"

"Was that the one who she told everyone in school that his boxers had rather a lot of room in them?" Mother put most euphemistically.

"Nope, no chance." Ramesh of all people came to my rescue. "We met him last year, and he had practically forgotten the whole thing."

He clapped his hands, though there was no music playing. "I've got it: Izzy's first stepdad. What was his name?"

"Arthur," I and three members of my family said at the same time.

"That's a thought!" Mother seemed quite pleased with the idea that her ex-husband was responsible for a string of murders with the end goal of killing her daughter. "He certainly never approved of you, darling. He really wasn't the most patient chap and blamed you for everything." She must have realised that this didn't sound particularly nice and added a caveat. "So I really should thank you for helping me to find my true love." She stared amorously at her third husband.

"I never did like that man," my biological father exclaimed and uncapped his pen with some force. "I'll put him at the top of the list."

"Boyfriends!" Fernando declared. "There must be one of them who blames her for the breakup."

I buried my head in my hands and considered having a lie down on the carpet. "Why did I ever think this would be a good idea?"

Ramesh held up his son and pretended to make him talk. "What about the one whose mother Izzy flirted with?"

"I wasn't actually flirting with her."

*No, you **were** actually flirting with her. That simply wasn't your intention.*

"Nigel!" Mother was having a whale of a time. If nothing else, I had provided a distraction from her pain.

"No, that wasn't Nigel," Ramesh clarified. "He was the one who liked wearing Izzy's shoes. The one whose mum Izzy fancied—"

"I didn't fancy her."

"Then why were you flirting with her?" Even Auntie Val had been sucked into the nonsense.

"Because I'd just tried to convince his father that I was an expert on football, even though I don't know anything about it. I had to do something to change the—" I finally remembered to stop talking. "You know what? It's irrelevant because I haven't seen Paul from Caterham since that night, and I'm fairly certain that, if he does remember me at all, it's because of the brilliant anecdote I gave him."

They seemed to accept this, but Greg wrote his name up on the maybes list all the same. I might have accepted that Nigel the shoe guy deserved a place up there too, but the last time I'd seen him, he had a ridiculously pretty girlfriend and a good job. I had once thrown a potato at him, but I doubted that was enough to trigger such a bloody revenge plot.

"I admit that I've dated some unusual men, but I don't think any of them would murder another person."

"Except for the one who murdered another person," my stepfather muttered, which made me feel bad for poor Auntie Val, whose own nephew was being discussed.

I turned to apologise, only to find her looking back at me with great sympathy on her face. "Let's think about your cases, instead," she suggested and, as she was the smartest octogenarian I'd ever met, she already had some interesting thoughts on the matter. "Of all the investigations that I've heard about, I think that the most likely to have sparked a vendetta against you is—"

"Squibbles the squirrel!" baby Pacino declared in a conspiratorial whisper. Fine, it wasn't really him speaking, and Auntie Val soon shut up his silly father.

"No, of course not, Ramesh. I'm talking about the cases to which Izzy was personally connected. The most obvious is the one at her work."

"With Bob the corpse?" Fernando said as he filled the air with awful choking hairspray and spun my mother around on her chair.

"That's the one. But we must also consider the family reunion, and the school reunion, and the university reunion," Val continued though, for the sake of accuracy, only one of them was an official reunion. "Even if it seems that the ends were all tied up, it's possible that the arrest of each killer triggered some unforeseen circumstance."

"That is an excellent point, Valerie." Greg pointed across the room at her with one of the pens and then nudged my father to start writing.

"Bob's family," he in turn suggested. "And that woman with hair like a badger's."

"Wendy," I replied.

"And then there are your rich cousins Tedwin and Noémi," Mother put in. "She was a particularly nasty sort."

"I suppose it's possible," I reluctantly agreed. "But I'm not sure any of these people have suffered so greatly because of me."

"Then perhaps we should move on to university?" Greg asked.

It was hard not to get a little sensitive over the matter. "Do you really think I've collected enemies wherever I've been?" No one answered, so I fessed up. "Fine, there was one girl who I never got on with. Her name was Eilish Hart, but I've already accused her of being a criminal on at least two occasions. If I did it again, and I was wrong, I think I'd have to retire from my profession."

"Donkey girl!" Ramesh replied in his own voice. "She works just in front of the place where Marco Romanelli was killed."

There was an intake of breath across the room, but I wasn't convinced. "Listen, all of you. Eilish Hart is one of the worst people I've ever known."

"She really is awful," my friend concurred, and he'd only met her briefly.

"But the fact that Romanelli was murdered in the town where we were at university together, if anything, makes it less likely that she's the killer. Why would she incriminate herself like that?" Again, they remained silent, and so I put forward another point. "It's far more likely that the killer chose Southorpe-on-Sea because of my connection to the place."

There was some mumbling at this moment, just as one of the journalists pressed his face up against the window.

"Izzy, is it true that you have a bowling average of 210, are a skilled accordionist and fluent in Spanish?"

Claro que sí!

Good old Dad was quick to shut the curtain and the intrusion out of our lives.

Open it again, Ted. He was finally asking the right questions.

"So then who are we left with?" Mother's words emerged in a quiet, fragile tone. She was someone who liked to hide her sadness, but I could tell she wasn't herself that day.

We all glanced at the flip pads where a few measly names had been scrawled. Not one of them offered much hope that we'd identified the killer. We were just guessing – nothing more. Perhaps that was all we'd done since my very first case.

The others burst into discussion, and my mother seemed to be suggesting that my boss Bob had faked his own death and was manipulating us from beyond the fake grave. Ramesh made the more plausible and thus frightening contribution that we had got the wrong killer on a previous case and then, thank goodness, Danny came in from the garden to announce that the food was ready.

"Come on, you lot. There's enough Potjiekos for everyone!"

They rushed out en masse, but I stayed where I was. I wasn't thinking, so much as letting time pass until I had the strength to do so. After perhaps a minute of silence, I realised that I wasn't alone.

"I'm sorry, Auntie Val," I told the dear old lady, who was still squished up to Sir Hugalot on the sofa. "I'm really not the best company today."

"That's alright, my love. I'm not being funny, but I didn't get the impression you were in the mood to natter, and so I kept shtum." She fell quiet again, and I thought that would be the end of it, but then she leaned forward to talk to me. "There is something I'd like to say though, cariad, but I don't know if you want to hear it."

I'd never noticed her looking anything but jolly and relaxed, and it was a little frightening to see the frown that formed on her lips just then. "The thing is… You see, the thing is, I know what you must be thinking. About David, I mean. I know you must feel hurt that we didn't tell you he was free, and I'm sure it's difficult to understand why he hasn't been in touch himself, but he's gone back home to live with his parents and…" That was the moment that it all got too much for her and she couldn't continue.

She was such a strong, resolute person, and I wanted to help her, but I didn't know how. So, after an awkward moment or two, I went to take her hand. It was clear that the only thing I could do was tell the truth.

"You're right, of course. I don't understand any of it. I can't begin to imagine why David doesn't want to see me. Or rather, I can begin to imagine, and everything I come up with reflects badly on me. I feel like I let him down – that I abandoned him – even if he was the one who broke off contact. I feel like I don't deserve him, and he wouldn't want me even if I did, but—"

"That's it," she said, and her eyes sparkled just a little in the overhead lights. "That's exactly what you mustn't think, because it's not true. David hasn't contacted you as he doesn't want to cause you more pain. He's a good man. I knew it when he was a little boy, and

I knew it when he was found guilty of murder. He's only looking out for you."

I had started to cry without realising it. My cheeks were running with tears and yet I didn't make a sound. It was almost as if she'd sliced open an onion in front of me and it was an involuntary reaction. The actual pain – the sheer emotion of what she was saying – hadn't reached me yet.

It took me so long to reply that Val ended up putting her ever so delicate hand on my shoulder for comfort. "You'll be okay, Izzy. I promise you will."

I wiped my eyes and considered her words. "Oh, maybe I will. But I want you to do something for me all the same. The next time you talk to your nephew, I want you to tell him that he's wrong. He's been wrong since the last time we spoke. He's wrong because he thinks I need protecting, but I don't."

Chapter Twelve

The press didn't leave me alone for the whole of the next week. In fact, it only got worse. Other newspapers picked up the scoop on my inadequate detective work, manipulative ways and potentially homicidal habits, and it was soon the hottest topic of conversation across the land. Teenagers on Tik Tok and other apps that I don't understand the attraction of announced how they'd never thought I was that great in the first place and they'd been waiting for me to be shown up for years.

How dare they! My brain complained whenever such stories got back to us. I say got back to us; what I really mean is that Ramesh kept sending us outraged commentaries on the offensive videos he was watching, and my brain was just as indignant. *How dare they, Izzy? We've done plenty of stupid things before and no one was bothered. What's the big deal now?*

The upshot of all this was that I managed to find an even less-developed state to inhabit. Having become a total slob, I now… what's the opposite of graduated? I now regressed to a childlike existence, spending most of my time locked in my mother's spare bedroom, reading as many Agatha Christie novels as I could and eating whatever food my stepdad was kind enough to make for me. It was a bleak existence.

I suppose that's why I didn't think twice when the card arrived. I knew it was dangerous and foolhardy and just about the stupidest thing I'd done in my life, but I needed to break free, and this was my chance. There was another reason too, of course, but we'll get to that later.

"Izzy, darling," my mother cooed as she came into the box room where my Uncle Bradley sleeps on the odd occasion we allow him to visit. "Don't you think it would be a good idea to get out of bed today?"

The look I gave her in reply said, *No, Mother. No, it wouldn't. I'm halfway through The ABC Murders and I might watch a few hours of Cupcake Calamities on TV later.* She didn't exactly show it, but I know she understood every word.

"Very well, but if you haven't had a shower by the time I come back from rehearsals this afternoon, I will call Dean and Ramesh around to remove you by force."

"That is a very strong argument," I said with more than just my eyes this time. "You are a persuasive woman."

She set something down beside the door, and then lingered for a moment to look at me. "Have a nice day, daughter dear. Bu-Bu La Mer is off to the final dress rehearsal for the greatest theatrical spectacular the world has seen since the one I did last year." She released a wicked cackle and disappeared through the door without saying why she'd come in or what she'd brought me. She was cunning like that.

"Mummy!" I yelled in the hope she would show some pity and return. "I can't reach it!"

No matter how hard I tried to reach, I couldn't make up the three-metre gap, and so I reluctantly rolled out of bed and crawled across the floor. The fun thing about lying in bed for days is that your muscles atrophy far quicker than you might expect. If I'd stayed there much longer, I would have had the muscle density of a young snail.

On the stool in the corner of the plain yellow room, she had placed a small pile of letters. I could guess what most of them were just by looking. There was a plain, formal-looking envelope that was bound to be one of the slightly more reasonable newspapers trying to buy an interview with me – the less reasonable ones tended to send overweight men with greasy hair to shout through my letter box. There was also a letter sealed with a heart-shaped stamp on red paper, which might have been from a fan who wanted to marry me to help me through my difficult time but was equally likely to be someone offering to buy my hair. Yep, detectives get freaky stalkers just like everyone else these days.

There were a few adverts for local takeaways, so that was a nice change, and then, at the bottom of the pile, there was something unusual. It was a circular envelope made of black paper, which I had to rip to get inside.

If you want to know how this story ends, you'll get in your car this morning and drive to the Bron-Yr-Aur Hotel in Mid-Wales. I will be waiting for you there with some of your old friends.

If you tell the police, more people will die.

It's been too long, Izzy. The time has come to kill you in person.

It was tempting to believe that it was just a hoax. I'd received plenty of dodgy letters over the years from time wasters and attention seekers. What I found different about this one was that it was so short and to the point. It also helped that, together in the envelope, was a photograph of the graffiti in the alley where Romanelli's body had been found, a pamphlet from a Croydon-based charity – that I could imagine the killer had used to access Jack's house – and a beer mat from the pub where Eddie Vanguard had been before he was killed. I doubted that the police had released any of this information to the public, and so I knew that this was another message from the killer.

I considered the risk, of course. I'm not stupid… I mean, I'm not totally stupid. But people kept getting murdered, presumably for the sole reason that they'd crossed paths with me, and I figured that I should at least try to stop anyone else from dying. The address that I was supposed to drive to was written on the back of the photo. I looked it up online and it was a mere four and a half hours in light traffic. I would have a leisurely drive around London, take the M4 all the way to Swansea and then turn north, up into the Brecon Beacons. Allowing for a stop or two, I figured I could comfortably make it there in my little yellow Corsa by Tuesday two weeks later.

I didn't tell my parents where I was going or even call Ramesh. I packed a bunch of incongruous clothes into a bag, spent ten minutes looking for my car keys, and then sneaked out the back door to run along the alley to my car. Even the pesky paps didn't have a clue that I'd escaped, and I felt terribly proud of myself until I got to the M25 and realised I would be spending most of the day staring at the back of a selection of slow-moving trucks as the traffic crawled along.

This is our summer holiday! My brain sang as, for licensing reasons, we couldn't use a more famous song with a similar theme.

We're heading off today!
Everyone knows that it's going to be great.
Even if it's raining and we're going to be late.

This went on for the first half of the journey and, let me tell you, the lines did not always rhyme.

This is our summer holiday!
We're going to have a lot of fun.
Say goodbye to our troubles and goodbye to our woes.
Say hello to the sunshine and… and the… ice cream and things.

By the time we reached Swansea, I was fed up with being on the motorway, and so I took the exit for "the Barcelona of South Wales", drove to the centre of town, parked my car in front of my ex-boyfriend's parent's house and walked straight up to the front door determined to tell David Hughes what I thought of him. I had it all planned, and when he came out and his face turned grey at the sight of me, I opened my mouth to deliver my cutting diatribe, but I couldn't make a sound.

Instead of telling him what a coward and a swine and a meanie he was – I didn't say it was a particularly sophisticated diatribe – I fainted in his front garden like some Regency heroine who'd been caught in a rain shower.

Chapter Thirteen

"Izzy?" a distant voice called, and I wondered if it was an angel, beckoning me towards the light. I was fairly sure that I'd suffered some kind of attack from which I would never wake up again… until I woke up again a few moments later. "Izzy, it's me. Are you alright?"

I opened one eye and there were doilies as far as the eye could see, which wasn't very far as I was in a small living room. From the side tables to the backs of the armchairs, almost every surface was covered with crocheted white fabric. I had collected any number of questions to put to David since I'd spoken to him three years and nine months earlier, but "Does your mother crochet?" was not one of them.

The serious look on his face instantly disappeared and there was that winning smile that I'd fallen in love with. "Funnily enough, it's Dad. He says it relaxes him."

"Oh, how nice." Of all the great conversations throughout history, this was not one of them.

The doilies had really thrown me, and I didn't know what to say now, so it was lucky that he continued talking. "Are you feeling alright?"

I pushed myself up on the sofa and felt my head to check for gaping wounds. My brains didn't seem to be exposed.

Phew.

And I found myself smiling back at him. "I think so. How did I not bang my head as I fell?"

He looked a little coy, and I fell in love all over again. "I caught you just before you made contact with the garden wall. But if you plan to repeat the feat any time soon, please let me know so that I can be more prepared. I'll put some of those big ice hockey goalkeeping gloves on."

"I'll be sure to let you know."

We fell quiet then, and I found myself studying him to look for any changes since the last time we'd been together. There was a dash of grey in his hair on either side of his head, but that just made him more handsome, as though he'd expressly ordered an intriguing highlight from his barber. I can't say that prison had made him look any older. His skin had its usual clarity, and he was cleanly shaven with no sign of any impromptu tattoos. But the thing I noticed first and most and for the longest time were his bright blue eyes. Seeing them again made me feel that nothing had changed, though I knew that was wishful thinking.

"Are you feeling alright?" he asked again and let out a soft huff of laughter as he realised he'd repeated himself.

"I'm fine." I swung my legs off the sofa, almost bashing him in the process. This was an accident. I had not gone there to attack him. "I don't know what came over me. I only stopped by to tell you that you're an idiot, and now I can be on my way again."

"Are you going to the Bron-Yr-Aur Hotel?" he asked, and it knocked me back onto the sofa.

"How did you… Did you get a card too?"

He took his time answering and I felt that he was probably studying me too. "I got a strange letter suggesting that I'd been headhunted for a new job. The thing is, the Bron-Yr-Aur has been closed for thirty years, and it's not the kind of place to conduct an interview."

"So then you're not going," I needlessly concluded.

He'd been crouching on the carpet in front of me but moved away to sit in a chair. "Of course I'm not. It's just some idiot playing a trick. You'd better get back in your car and drive home to London."

This was the third time his words had caused a physical impact upon me. I felt as if he had pressed pause, and I couldn't talk again until it had passed. "Do you know what's been happening?"

He stood up to peer down at me and I remembered for the first time in a long time that he was almost as tall as I am, which is rare for the men I've dated. Why this was what I focussed on at that moment, I can't say.

"Auntie Val told me about the killings, and I read the paper, obviously."

"Obviously." I tried to sound serious. "Who doesn't?"

He gazed out of the window as if he was expecting someone. "I'm telling you, Izzy, I had a bad feeling as soon as I received that letter. They made up a fictitious company and mentioned a high salary in order to get me there. Whatever they've done to tempt you, they can't be trusted."

"I've no other choice; people could die if I don't go."

"So you think that the killer himself wrote the letter?" He clearly wanted to shout and tell me how foolish I was being, but he managed to control his temper. "Then you could die if you do go."

"I didn't come here to persuade you. I'm going and that's final." I should have left it at that, but a previously unspoken truth popped from my mouth against my will. "I need to know the end of the story."

"This isn't a book, Izzy. This isn't one of your whodunits."

Ha! That shows how little he knows!

He released a long, slow breath. "What if the story finishes with you being trapped and killed? What if there isn't the just and fair ending that you've come to expect?"

I rose a little unsteadily and had to keep hold of the armrest for support. "That can't happen..." I had to take a deep breath then. "It can't happen again. That's why I have to see this through." This was all so vague and abstract that I sounded like a dim-witted beauty queen or a character in a bad soap opera. I moved to leave, and my head swum, but I wouldn't stop.

"You should at least call the police," he told me because he's a normal functioning human... more or less.

"The killer told me not to."

"Listen to yourself, Izzy." He ran around me to block the door. "You're speaking like a crazy person."

"I appreciate that." I don't know why I said this, and it certainly didn't contradict his assertion. "But you don't understand. My whole life, I've been unable to resist a final chapter. I'd stay up all night to finish books. I'd catch snatches of a conversation on a bus and get off at the same stop as the people talking to hear the rest. The killer must know this about me, just as they know that you would be interested in a high-paying job."

He'd been holding his arms out in front of him, but they went oddly limp at this point. Don't worry, it wasn't his turn for a fainting spell. He'd just given up on trying to change my mind. Before he could say anything else, we heard the sound of the front door opening and his parents came into the house.

"Izzy, my dear," his father said in his beautifully resonant Welsh voice. I think it must have hit him at this moment that, as pleased as he evidently was to see me, it was not the most natural thing for me to be there. He shook his head and regained his composure. "Are you here for a singalong? I have Tom Jones' Greatest Hits on CD."

"Leave her alone, Mal," his wife told him, before pulling me in for a much-appreciated *cwtch*. "Come here, pet. We've missed you, we have. It's great to see you, but you don't want us stepping on your toes, so we'll leave you in peace. This way, Malcolm."

She turned her husband around and pushed him from the room. I was sorry they'd gone, not just because they were as fun and friendly as I'd remembered, but because I'd appreciated the interruption.

Silence returned, and I didn't know what to say. My fantasies about this reunion had all gone out of the window. I looked at David, and he looked at me, but we weren't about to rush towards one another to passionately embrace.

Boooooo!

All that counted at that moment was where I would go next, and so that's what I told him. "I've said what I came to say. I can go now."

I admit that I was disappointed when he stood aside to let me pass. I didn't show it, but I felt a chemical sting deep inside my stomach, as if I'd swallowed a shot of acid.

"You're not thinking straight. I thought better of you." He spoke as though he were generations older than me, rather than just six and a half years.

I didn't want to look at him anymore and walked out into the hall. "Maybe I've changed." This didn't come out as I'd hoped.

He followed me along the narrow corridor to the front door, and I knew that he wanted to say something more, but nothing else came.

"Have a nice life, David," I told him, turning back to look at the pebble-dash house where he'd grown up.

"Just be careful, Izzy." He didn't smile. We had reached an impasse and there's was no way around it – no way back.

"I'll do my best," I said, though we both knew this wasn't even close to true. I was a stubborn fool. I'd driven half an hour out of my way to see him and we hadn't spoken about anything that mattered. That didn't stop me getting in my car and starting the engine, though. It did just about keep me there for a minute longer as I desperately wished that he would run over to confess his undying love/offer to be my sidekick on my imminent adventure in the Welsh mountains.

It didn't happen, and I eventually drove away, cursing myself and wishing I was a different person altogether.

Of course, if you were a different person, you would never have left university with an English degree that wasn't very helpful for getting a job, taken the first thing that came along, in a financial services company that you despised, fallen in love with David and—

Yes, thank you. I get the message. What should we do now?

You drive. I'll sing the theme tune from 'Sesame Street'.

That'll do.

We… sorry, *I* left Swansea on an A-road that quickly became an approximately D-road as it reached the countryside and then climbed up into the hills. It took an hour before I reached the area I was looking for, and though the sat-nav on my phone insisted that it was the quickest route, I ended up taking a lot of muddy paths. I drove through a tiny village called Pen— something I couldn't pronounce, and then it would have been handy to have a rocket as the mountain shot straight upwards all the way to the Bron-Yr-Aur Hotel. It was hard to imagine why anyone ever decided to build a house up there, and easy to imagine why it had failed as a resort for tourists. Though the views were exquisite, with glacial lakes tucked away in bright green valleys, and regular stopping points where I could see across the endless patchwork landscape, it was in the middle of nowhere.

Had I not been summoned there by a lunatic, I might have appreciated the solitude, but with every mile that ticked over on the counter on my dashboard, the fear inside me grew. It didn't help that I could see black – that's not an exaggeration – actual black clouds on the horizon. I could make out shafts of rain in the distance, which were only made more dramatic by the beams of light that cut through the clouds here and there, but by the time I reached the immense gothic mansion near the top of the mountain, the storm was about to arrive, and the sky had been recoloured, as if someone had taken a photocopy of it on a darker setting.

I pulled up at the gates of Bron-Yr-Aur and waited for them to open. That didn't happen, so I got out as it began to spit with rain. There was no intercom or button to press, no bell or even a knocker, but the gate itself was ajar, so I pulled it wider and drove onto the grounds.

The house rose up before me, and I wished that I'd told D.I. Irons, or my family, or even just Ramesh where I was going.

Chapter Fourteen

I parked my car in a long line of bays, and the one positive was that I wasn't alone there. In the colours of a French flag, there were three other cars of red, white and blue alongside my yellow monstrosity. This might have meant that the killer was there with me, but, in fact, there was a nondescript black saloon parked under a tree I'd just driven past. It perfectly matched the description of the car that was seen near Jack Campbell's house.

I took my phone out and was about to ring Irons when I remembered the killer's condition. Ramesh wouldn't be much help now, and my parents would only worry. Dean might have been able to hack into somewhere to get the information I needed, but I didn't want him getting arrested before his wedding. That might be the kind of thing that best men often get up to, but I took my role as his best woman seriously. This left me with only one option. So it was lucky I had her number saved on my phone.

"I need your help," I said when she picked up. The line was terrible and cut in and out, so that I wasn't sure at first whether she would hear me. "I can't tell you why, but you're the only person I can turn to."

"Why should I help you?" the journalist who had attempted to destroy my career replied.

"Because, Janet," I sighed a long, sorrowful sigh and realised how tired I already was, "I don't care what you wrote about me. I don't even care that you seemed to take a real thrill in coming to my house to insult me. If you answer a few simple questions, then I'll make sure you get the full story of what I'm up to today in a frankly terrifying mansion on the top of a Welsh mountain."

She considered her options for approximately four seconds before agreeing. "It's a deal, Miss Palmer. What do you want to know?"

The line dropped out for a second and there were more pops and crackles than a kid's breakfast cereal, but we just about managed to hear one another.

"First, I need to know who owns the former Bron-Yr-Aur hotel ten miles from Llangadog."

"I can do that." I think I heard her scribbling something down, but it could have just been the rustle of the wind.

"And then I need you to search for a car for me. It's a black Ford. Number plate AD10 LHJ."

This clearly needed more consideration as the snaps and whispers on the line were joined by a contemplative hum. "That will require me to call in a favour with my contacts in the police. This story had better be worth it."

"It will be," I replied, with a bit more confidence than I'd been feeling for some time. "I'm going to catch the killer who's been killing my old acquaintances."

I could practically hear her smiling down the phone. "That sounds very interesting indeed. I'll get you that information as soon as I can. Oh, and by the way, Izzy…"

"Yes, Janet?"

"No hard feelings, eh? I've got nothing against you. I'm just trying to make a name for myself here at the office."

The tinny line crackled, and I let her wait for a few moments before saying anything. "I bet you did."

Like a person in a movie, she hung up without saying goodbye.

Ahhhh! Who even does that? It's so unrealistic.

Yeah, but also kind of cool.

It took another five minutes to convince myself to get out of the car, and the rain was falling more heavily by the time I managed it. I ran from the shade of a metal awning I'd parked under and, despite realising I'd left my bag in the car, I bolted for the grand porch at the front of the building.

There was something very school-of-wizardry about the place, and though the clouds were already closing in around them, I could see that the two main towers were topped with fairy-tale-esque turrets in weathered green copper. The brick beneath looked as though it could do with a good clean, and each pointed corner of the immensely tall edifice was decorated with stone gargoyles. Water spouted from them, so it looked as though they were having a rather extreme reaction to my presence.

I didn't stick around out there for long. I only had to run fifty metres across the wide courtyard and past the circular fountain, but by the time I got there, my apparently not-so-very-waterproof raincoat was soaked through. I shook off my clothes as I stepped inside the unlocked porch, feeling like a dog who'd gone for a quick dip.

My first surprise was that the house was unexpectedly warm. Its exterior had suggested that it would be a cold, unforgiving sort of place, but a wave of warm air hit me as I approached the main door and instantly felt brighter. The chatter of voices helped perk things up too. I could hear laughter and even music playing, and I stumbled through the long hallway towards a flickering light.

A voice carried out to me from what I assumed would be a lounge. "Of course, when I was a young man, I ran for Great Britain in the Commonwealth Games. People told me that I could have become a professional athlete, but I decided to concentrate on my first love."

"A different hobby?" a younger man replied as I stepped through the door into a cosy salon with a fire below an immense chimneypiece and its marble mantel.

"No, accountancy."

I would have recognised that voice on Mars, let alone in Wales. It will still ring in my ears when I'm a hundred years old. I must have been a little stunned to hear it again for the first time in a decade; I walked straight into a low table and yelped out in pain.

"Izzy?" my original stepfather Arthur declared. "Izzy Palmer? I'd know that poor posture anywhere."

"Ar-thur!" I moaned and, in a snap of the fingers, I was sixteen years old again.

"I mention it only for your sake, not mine, Isobel. I've always said you could make something of yourself if you only stood up a little straighter."

I slouched my shoulders, bowed my head and mumbled out a defence. "I have made something of myself, thank you very much."

He stood up from the leather Chesterfield sofa and waved one hand through the air as if he'd only just remembered something. "Oh, of course. Your little detective agency. Are you still pursuing that?"

He was far greyer than when he'd been married to my mother, and I already thought he was ancient back then. His prickly eyebrows climbed up his forehead, then dangled there in silent speculation.

"I'm not just pursuing it. I'm making a grand success of the business. We've solved over…" Bother! I couldn't remember how many murders I'd solved.

One hundred murders!

"…one hundred murders!"

Even out-of-touch Arthur knew this was a lie.

It could be worse. At least you didn't tell him what a great accordionist you are.

"Well done, young lady." His patronising voice was even more painful to hear than his boasting. "I'm sure that your mother is exceedingly proud of you. How is my dear Rosemarie? I hear she's done something or other in the theatre recently?"

He was the king of diminishing other people's achievements and bigging up his own. After a single minute in his presence, I felt like pushing him into the fire, and I am not normally a violent person.

This does raise the question of whether he drives a black Ford saloon.

I'd dismissed the idea that my old nemesis was my current nemesis, but with his appearance there at the house, I was willing to reconsider.

Arthur was a human black hole and could suck all thoughts, conversation and attention from a room with a snide comment or boastful claim. This meant that I'd completely ignored the third person there, even though he was standing eagerly to attention, waiting for me to talk to him.

"Hi Izzy."

"Hello, Edmund." I tried to sound composed. "It's nice to see you again."

"Oh, so you know each other, do you?" Arthur asked, but I ignored him as I examined my handsome friend.

Eager was just the word for Edmund Porter. It was a very different attitude to the smoother-than-ice persona he'd had when I first met him at his family's estate after his mega-rich father had been killed. His sister had told me that he had been through a lot when I saw her in prison, and he'd already been out of sorts at the party-cum-suspect-ID-parade that we'd thrown. Perhaps the stress of breaking up a relationship shortly before his no doubt grand society wedding had sent him loopy, and he'd brought me there to kill me. That still wouldn't explain the presence of my ex-stepdad, who was pulling on his elasticated braces like a clown as he waited for me to explain what was happening.

"Edmund and I go way back," I finally revealed. "I solved his father's murder on the very first try." I was probably trying too hard to impress the grumpy seventy-five-year-old with the crooked teeth and growing collection of facial warts.

"Yes, we're *good friends*." Edmund added a certain weight to these last two words.

To be honest, nothing had really happened between us when we'd first met. Though he'd flirted like rotten, I was distracted by my then-boyfriend's murder trial, and we never even went on a first date. Perhaps that was why he still liked me. I was his *one that got away!*

"What brought you here, Izzy?" Arthur enquired, and his eyebrows still hadn't returned to their normal homes.

"Well, Arthur, as it happens, I'm here on a—" I was about to show off about my detective skills when I heard footsteps in the corridor behind me and cut my explanation short.

I think we all flinched at that moment, nervous as to who might be creeping up on us when we weren't expecting it. I balled up my fists for some reason, as if I could fight myself out of anything more than a crisp packet. All three of us fell silent, so I wasn't the only idiot there. In fact, there was another one just arriving.

"Izzy!"

"Ramesh?"

We asked the obvious question at the exact same time. "What are you doing here?"

"More to the point," he continued, "why didn't you tell me you were coming? We could have shared the journey. I made a new road-trip playlist after we ruined the last one."

He already sounded put-out, and he didn't even know about the killer yet.

My three companions started talking among themselves, but I decided to count to sixty to see whether anyone else would arrive. It would have been a real pain to have to explain the whole thing again after someone else got there.

"If you'll all calm down a second, I'll tell you why I've come." They did just that and, though Ramesh was dressed in a blue velvet playsuit and would have slid right off the leather, Edmund and Arthur took their seats around the fire. "The letter I received to summon me here was written by a person who I believe must be responsible for—"

"Hello!" a new voice in the doorway cooed, and we all turned to look at the person who had arrived approximately forty seconds later than I would have liked. "I'm Noémi. Are you here for the—" My slightly wicked, though really very well-presented second cousin saw me, and the warmth in her drained away. "Oh, you're here too."

"Come in and sit down, Noémi. I was about to explain what I think is happening."

"I don't need to take orders from you, cousin," she said, then did exactly as I'd told her.

I cleared my throat and tried again. "Right, the thing is, I believe we've all been called here because—"

"Izzy Palmer?" a deep, pleasant voice called through the window and a minute later, a big hulking figure with wavy blonde hair and baby blue eyes had entered the building to get to me. "I can't believe you're here. It's such a surprise."

The man I'd once dated who thought he was Father Christmas was there in the room with me and he was no less of a hunk than he had been when I'd last seen him.

It looks like the word hunk really is making a comeback.

"It's nice to see you too, Nicholas. If you could sit down on the sofa with the others, I'll—"

"Santa!" Ramesh yelled and ran across the room to give him a hug. At least he didn't ask to sit on his lap. I should probably point out that my nice but delusional ex had forsaken his usual fur-trimmed coat for more seasonally appropriate attire. It was still red and white, but in the form of a sports jacket and jogging bottoms.

I stood there babbling like a very wordy baby. "Brilliant, great, fabulous." I waited for one more minute, then finally decided that the time had come to explain. "You see, from what I can tell, we've all been brought here for different reasons. Ramesh, I imagine you were expecting to meet someone famous?"

He nodded and looked a little proud. "Cher wrote to me personally!"

I might have got a little sidetracked by this. "And Patricia was alright with you leaving her with the baby and driving across the country to meet a singer?"

"Cher is not just 'a singer', Izzy. Her music changed the world. And don't get me started on what she did for that poor lonely elephant."

This was good advice, as I'd made that mistake in the past. "Fine, whatever." I turned to stepdad number one (chronologically at least). "What about you, Arthur?"

"As it happens, I was asked here to address the Welsh Society for the Preservation of Historically Significant Tax Returns (or WSPOHSTR for short). I'm going to give a presentation on effective filing techniques that will stand the test of time."

"Fascinating," I replied, more to wake myself up than anything else. "And what about you, Edmund?"

The handsome young CEO of Porter & Porter looked a little sly. "It doesn't really matter, but now that I think about it, it was something equally implausible."

His new friend Arthur looked put out by this, but I wouldn't let the stuffy old bore interrupt again.

"Well, in that case, I believe that I received the only truthful invitation."

"You didn't ask me," Santa with muscles spoke up.

There was a good reason for this, but I wasn't so rude that I could tell him it was bound to be something weird. "Oh, my apologies. What did your letter say?"

"I'm here for a magical helpers convention."

There it is!

To give you some context to just what an odd bod this fellow was, on our first date we had a lovely home-cooked dinner at his flat and then snuggled up on the sofa to watch 'Elf'… in February. I might not have found this too weird if he hadn't worn his Santa suit and referred to me throughout the evening as "little girl".

I'm not going to lie. I quite liked that part.

Don't be disgusting.

Hey, you're the one who went on a second date with him.

Yes, but—

And a third and fourth.

Maybe, but then I drew the line and ended things like a sensible adult… after we'd been out six times.

"I'm supposed to be meeting a lawyer who has uncovered something which will help me contest my mother's frankly unjust will," Noémi explained when I'd presumably been staring into the fire in silence for too long.

"There you go then," I said quite confidently. "Each of us has been summoned here for a different reason that we would love to be true. I believe that my invitation was the only one that's—"

"No, I don't accept that," Ramesh objected. "Perhaps mine is the real one and Cher will be here any moment to tell me that I'm her most important fan!?" I could tell that even he knew this wasn't true.

"I'm sorry, but I don't think that's it, Ra."

The poor chap was desolate and collapsed into an armchair, from which he went sliding straight off.

"Wait," Noémi demanded. "Why us? If someone is playing games with you, why would they have invited us along for the ride?"

"I can't say for certain." I walked closer to the fire then and looked around their faces for a moment to be sure of myself. I was aware that I hadn't told them about the killings yet, but I needed to build up to it. "All I know is that each of you has been involved in another of my cases. You were all suspects at different times, and I believe that someone has lied to get us here."

Chapter Fifteen

Before I could say anything else, yet another new arrival arrived newly. "Hello? Did we miss anything?"

"Oh, typical," I muttered under my breath as I turned to see my Uncle Bradley and former colleague Wendy in the doorway. "I knew that I should have waited."

The rest of the gang were comparing the cards and letters they'd received, and we were running out of chairs.

"Did you see anyone else outside?" I asked my uncle. "I swear, I am not going through this a third time."

Bradley didn't answer but came to give me a kiss on both cheeks. "Bonsoir, ma belle." I'd never heard French spoken in an East-Midlands accent before and it was… unrecognisable. "Let me have a look at you."

Of all the things that would happen during our stay at Bron-Yr-Aur – and let's be honest, things were going to get bad – this was still one of the worst.

"There's my little Ian!" He opened his throat and unleashed a laugh that sounded like a gannet having an argument with another gannet. It went, ak ak ak! "Oh, the old ones are the best." He was almost crying with laughter as he turned to the others to explain. "My not-so-little niece here has always reminded me of a boy I went to school with. That's why I call her Ian!"

This was pretty standard behaviour for my mother's dreadful brother. I had hoped that the time he got dumped by his much younger girlfriend shortly after I'd accused him of murder would have made a dent in his oversized yet fragile ego. Sadly, this was not the case, and I could do nothing but stand there feeling terrible about life as his laughter rang out once more.

"That was a nasty thing to do to someone you should have nurtured and protected," my hero put to him, and it was Bradley's turn to feel bad as he looked over his shoulder to see the final (for the moment at least) member of our party. "I mean it. If you think anyone here is impressed by such spiteful humour, you're wrong."

David came to stand next to me, and I felt superhuman. They were a bit late to come to my defence, but Edmund and Nicholas joined him, and Uncle Bradley suddenly looked the small man he'd always been. Twelve-year-old Izzy spent many a night dreaming of such a moment. I used to imagine myself directing lines from Jim Henson's 'Labyrinth' (my favourite film from the age of seven and up) at bullies from school and my horrid uncle. So perhaps it's no surprise that one popped from my mouth at that moment.

"You have no power over me!" I admit that I delivered it with a bit too much gusto, and half the people there looked at me like I was the wrong side of eccentric, but I felt invincible once more.

"Edmund," David said to shatter the silence without even a glance at me. "It's good to see you again."

I'd forgotten that they knew one another, and I was even more weirded out when Fake-Father Christmas joined them on the sofas for a chat. Seeing three men I'd held romantic feelings for all together was somewhere between my worst dream and my best nightmare. Admittedly, it also reminded me of the three-Spidermen-pointing-at-each-other meme that my mother keeps sending me when she presses the wrong buttons on her phone.

To be honest, it felt more like a coffee morning at a local church than a murder investigation. They were all getting along so well that I didn't feel it was fair to tell them that our lives were in danger. The unlikely guests formed little groups to get to know one another, and I went back to the mantelpiece to watch them. Wendy and my ex-stepdad were perfectly matched in their grumpiness, so they got along brilliantly. Arthur told Wendy about the joys of living in a retirement community on the Kent coast, and Wendy went into great detail on her love of stamp collecting.

Ramesh and Noémi hit it off, too. They were both largely impervious to other people's opinions and, as the case at my cousin's family home had been one of the few that Ramesh hadn't investigated with me, they had a lot to discuss.

I had plenty to think about myself and, with no one free to discuss the puzzle before us, I relied on my usual last resort.

Oi! I prefer the term "fallback monkey".

Shh! I need to think. First things first, we have to consider the possibility that one of the people before us is the killer. It implied on my card that the culprit would be here to meet me. The question is, was that the truth, or was it a ruse to confuse us from the beginning.

It might be.

But can we rule any of them out already?

It's possible.

I wondered if the presence of the black car meant that anyone else who drove here was innocent, but the killer could have come in the car that was seen around the time of Jack Campbell's murder, taken a taxi back to civilisation, then returned in a second car to throw me off the scent.

I suppose so.

They're certainly a collection of the nastier people we've crossed paths with… plus Ramesh, David and the poor deluded fellow who thinks he's a Christmas elf.

Don't be so close-minded, Izzy. Isn't it conceivable that he really is Saint Nick?

No, brain. No, it's not.

Aware that this was getting us nowhere, I was actually quite happy when Ramesh interrupted.

"My dear friend," he told me, "you are so good at bringing people together. Look at everyone getting along like old friends. There are those in life whose job it is to socialise and be fabulous, and others who must merely look on, knowing that they are the glue which holds the world together. Did I ever tell you you're my—"

I stopped him then, just in case he decided to sing 'The Wind Beneath my Wings'.

"I need your help, Ra," I explained. "While this lot are busy, we need to find out what we're dealing with."

"In terms of entertainment for the weekend?" he suggested incorrectly. "I was thinking the exact same thing. There are bound to be board games or something like that around here. But where?"

It was possibly the first time he'd ever looked like a serious detective. He put one finger to his lip and began to scout about the room for his prize. I did not allow this to continue for long before I grabbed him by the arm and pulled him to the hall.

"We're not looking for games, Ra. We need to work out what the killer is doing."

"Wait, you mean that the person who killed Jack, Marco and Eddie is here?" He looked suitably shocked.

"That's what my letter said, but I don't understand why anyone would invite all these people along."

He bit his lip as if he had something difficult to say. "That's what happens in all these silly stories, isn't it? A mysterious figure invites a bunch of apparently unconnected strangers together and then kills them off one by one."

"No, Ramesh, that's not what happens… Well, it sort of is, but the difference here is that these strangers aren't unconnected. They've all been suspects in one of my cases."

"Except your former stepdad," he was quick to realise.

He'd knocked me off track, but it was a good point. "Yeah, except for him. But what I'm trying to say is that it's impossible that there would be a connection between these people other than the one we already know."

"Is it?"

"Yes, it is."

"But really, Izzy. Is it truly impossible?"

"Yes, Ramesh. It is. I know our suspects too well for that. I'm the glue between you all, just like you said. For one thing, my uncle and cousin have never met you or David before."

"That's true." He had a bit of a think, then clapped his hands like a fairytale prince. "I've got it! Perhaps we're all Sagittarius!"

"You're not."

"Then you're right." He sighed in disappointment. "There's no possible connection."

Far from making progress, we appeared to have taken several steps backwards, and so I decided to get on with the task I'd planned.

"Let's explore."

He instantly perked up and followed me along the hall. "Are you sure you don't want to talk about the arrival of your lethal ex-boyfriend?"

"Definitely not."

"Fair enough."

Despite all this talk of murder mysteries, it felt like we'd entered a horror film. The long corridor before us was lined with skulls, mounted animals and the odd inexplicable bone. I was tempted to take Ramesh's hand as we tiptoed through the house, Scooby Doo style, but thankfully, I had the ability to tell myself that there was no such thing as ghosts, ghouls and monsters, which helped me to remain calm.

Forget about monsters. It's axe-wielding psychopaths we have to look out for.

We came to the first immense padded door off the passageway, and Ramesh and I silently debated between ourselves who should be the one to open it. I won by jumping behind him and acting terrified.

To our great relief, once he'd summoned the necessary courage to enter, there was another cosy space inside and not an axe or chainsaw in sight.

"Library!" I drooled, as I took in all the pretty volumes that lined the room. It made my own book sanctuary look a little sad and underwhelming.

"Come on, Izzy. There's nothing to learn in here," my companion insisted, once he'd checked under a table for the killer.

"Just give me a minute," I said, because I wanted to luxuriate in all that knowledge and the promise of fascinating tales. The room was divided up by subject which made finding the fiction section a doddle. It seemed that whoever owned the place had the complete works of Charles Dickens, which took my fancy at that moment, as I really hadn't read enough of his—

"Izzy, now!" Ramesh broke me from my book daydream, and I finally submitted.

"Fine, but I'm coming back here when we've caught the killer or everyone else has been murdered. This place is great."

After that brief, unnecessary interruption, we reached a few grander spaces. There was a sparkling dining room that appeared to have been laid out for our dinner, but just as I was about to explore, Ramesh called to me from the opposite side of the corridor.

"You have to see this, Iz!" He emitted a few yelps of joy, and when I went to find him, he was, perhaps inevitably, throwing an oversized balloon around a ballroom. "It's amazing!"

The room was half-filled with the inflated pearlised globes, and I wondered why so many of the places I visit these days look like weddings. The already glittery and glamourous room had been adorned with streamers and bunting, but best of all, by Ramesh's standards…

"There's a karaoke machine!" He was so excited that he got stuck at this moment and could do nothing more than repeat my name. "Izzy! Izzy! Izzy! I really think that you're wrong and Cher must be coming here. I must have written twenty-seven times to tell her that my greatest dream is to perform karaoke with her."

He kicked his balloon over in my direction and it travelled in a perfect arc across the room. "And the best part of it is that we wouldn't do a Cher song at all. We'd sing 'You're the One That I Want' from Grease." He did the internationally recognised gesture to suggest that he'd just *blown* my *mind*. He hadn't, but I appreciated his enthusiasm.

"Can we please keep looking for the reason we've been brought here?"

"Fine, but when everyone's dead and you're being boring in the library, I'm coming here to sing."

I considered pointing out that a massacre was the less desirable of the two options I'd previously outlined, but it would only have led to more inane chatter.

We kept on along the never-ending corridor. There were all sorts of rooms that probably had names that I didn't know. There was one that looked as though a posh lady might press flowers in it, and another where gentlemen would have gone to drink, smoke and escape from icky, yucky girls. There was also one with paintings of cats all over the wall, but I haven't a clue what that was used for.

Then, as we went further into the depths of the murky building, the spaces we found became less grand. There were broom cupboards and rooms filled with cleaning products. We turned off the main corridor to reach the kitchen and through there, we came to a larder and utility room. There was nothing to say that a killer had been hanging out at Bron-Yr-Aur, and not much sign of life in general, though I was surprised that the place was so well kept. Someone must have been spending a good bit of money to keep the place in such a condition. David said that the hotel had closed down three decades earlier, and a place like that would quickly go to ruin if left unattended.

"Izzy," Ramesh called after we'd split up to explore a clutch of small rooms in what I suspected would once have been the servants' quarters. "Iz, you've got to come here."

I was wondering what exciting find he'd made and couldn't decide between a signed photo of George Michael and a children's trampoline, but I left the office I'd been exploring to find him.

"It's not what we were expecting," he said rather seriously, and when I entered the near empty room, I realised just how right he was.

Sitting up perfectly straight on a rickety wooden dining chair was a man I'd never seen before. It looked as though he'd been dead for some time.

Chapter Sixteen

"Who is he?" Ramesh could only wonder as I moved around the body to get a better look.

The dead man has been tied to the chair, but I got the impression for some reason that it was not to keep him in one place so much as to display him for our benefit. There was a cable tie around his neck that kept him upright. It looped around the high back of the chair, though his arms and legs were free. He could easily have stood up… if he'd been alive, I mean.

"I've been wondering ever since I arrived who had been looking after the place. Someone had to get the house ready for us. So perhaps this guy was the caretaker."

"Or the owner?"

I looked at the man's clothes and couldn't rule out the possibility, but it didn't seem right somehow. "I don't think so. I think that whoever owns this place doesn't come here often. It's probably some rich old family who have ten houses around the country and only come here for a weekend every other Christmas. They'd leave this poor man in charge the rest of the time. Perhaps the killer was the one to light the fire, make up the bedrooms and prepare the party in the ballroom, but someone must have been looking after the building before that."

"How can you be sure that there are bedrooms for us?" Ramesh was just as un-squeamish as I was these days when it came to blood, guts and corpses, and he bent at the knees to get a better look at the dead man.

"Because the whole thing is very theatrical. This is the sort of killing that *you* would plan if you ever wanted to murder someone."

He smiled at me then and put one hand to his chest. "Thank you, Izzy. That's such a sweet thing to say."

"The fire in the lounge was lit so that we would all congregate there. The dining table has been laid for us to share a dinner together."

"And the ballroom is ready for me to crank out the tunes."

"Exactly." There was a question that deserved to be asked at that moment, but I was still studying our first victim… of the day at least. He looked as though he was in his sixties, though they do say that death can make people look older. He wore a patchy, checked shirt and paint-covered trousers, and his thin grey hair was messy on his head. "I think he was probably killed sometime yesterday. It was a good twelve hours ago at the very least, but I'd imagine longer." I took a step closer to look at the colour of his skin and open one eye. "I don't know enough about the topic, but judging by the lack of a wound, I'd say he was probably poisoned."

Ramesh stood back up and crossed his arms across his chest as if to hug himself. "Look at you, knowing things. You're so clever."

"I'm not sure that knowing how he died helps us much. It would be more useful to know why he was killed, and why his assailant would want us to find him."

"Perhaps whoever did it is proud of their work and wants to show it off. If I was a top-notch killer, I'd want everyone to know it."

"Thank you so much, Ramesh." I'd found over the years that it was better – i.e. quicker – to compliment my best friend whenever he said something irrelevant instead of correcting him.

"Can we go and see the others now? It's almost teatime, and I have a hankering for whatever tasty snacks our ever so welcoming killer has laid on."

"We should call the police first," I told him. As much as I'd like to have solved the case alone, I could see that the time had come to share the workload, even if it meant I might never find out what was behind the killer's scheme.

I looked at the dead man, whose name, I'd decided, was probably Leonard. He rather reminded me of my dear old dad… the real one, not the other two.

I took out my phone, and Ramesh shrugged and turned to leave. "You must admit, it would make a good title for a book. 'A Corpse Tied to a Chair."

"Nah, no one would read it." I dialled 999, but the call didn't connect. "There's no signal. Can I try your phone?"

Ramesh had special pockets sewn into all of his most elaborate outfits to hold the essentials, though you could never be sure where they were hidden. He was terrified that he might spoil the line of the ensemble, and so it did not surprise me in the slightest when he raised his right arm to show me where his phone was.

"How ingenious," I said, rather than pointing out that it would be a bad idea to keep it there during hot weather. I dialled the number again and got the same dead tone. "Perhaps it's the storm. Is that a thing? Do storms still affect phone signals?"

"Yes, it's quite common." I sometimes forget that Ramesh actually knows about computers and the like. "If a power line is down, or there are simply too many people using the service and the mast can't cope with the demand, then that would make the signal drop out. Being so far from civilisation as we are only makes it more likely."

I checked my phone again to see whether Janet Ellinson had got back to me, but there were no new notifications except a newsletter from a shop selling personalised cat accessories. I bought one pair of earrings from pet-à-porter.com for Ramesh about five years ago and they've never stopped mailing me. I really must get around to unsubscribing one day.

As we retraced our path through the house, I considered exactly how I would tell the rest of the group what had happened. I had to act on the principle that the killer was there amongst us. Every last person had a reason to be angry with me, except for Ramesh. I suppose it's possible that he was harbouring a well of undisclosed rage, but it would have been the first thing since we'd met that he'd failed to describe to me in far too much detail.

Among the ranks of potential killers were two ex-boyfriends and a guy I'd almost dated, who, according to his homicidal sister at least, was far more besotted with me than I'd ever known. Backing them up, we had my least favourite uncle, my least favourite cousin, my least favourite stepdad and – as Bob had overtaken Wendy by paying an assassin to kill me – my second-least favourite ex-co-worker. It's fair to say there were plenty of explanations for why one of them would have wanted to mess with my life before potentially ending it.

When we entered the grand old lounge, I started by counting the number of people to make sure that no one new had arrived, but there was no change on that score. Equally surprising was the fact that the other guests had gathered around a table in front of the fire to play Monopoly. So it seemed that one of Ramesh's predictions had finally proven correct.

"If you wanted to be the boot, you're too late," Uncle Bradley announced as I came over to make sense of the scene.

"Who would ever want to be the boot?" I had to ask. "Surely everyone wants to be the top hat."

Arthur became very snooty at this moment. "I'm the top hat. I'm always the top hat, as you well know, Isobel. I didn't think we'd have to go through all that again after *last time.*" He shuddered, as if the one occasion I'd chosen to be the top hat on my fifteenth birthday still haunted him.

Father Christmas smiled in our direction. "I'm the thimble, Izzy. I thought it was the most festive."

"There's only the battleship left," Edmund told me almost apologetically. "You can share with Ramesh… or… me?" His eyes were full of hope at this moment, and I hated to let him down.

"Nope, I'm not playing Monopoly."

"Don't be such a killjoy, Izzy," my nasty cousin Noémi told me in her pretty voice with her pretty hair and nice clothes.

Ooh, look at me, I'm Noémi and everyone thinks I'm so great.

Not that we hold a grudge.

Of course we don't!

She smiled her pretty smile and finished her point. "If you can't let your hair down when you've been tricked into coming to a scary house up in the mountains, when can you?"

"Practically any other time," I murmured. "I am busy right now trying to work out what's happening."

Arthur decided that this was the perfect moment for him to talk more. "What Izzy isn't telling you is that she swore never to play Monopoly again after she lost to me some years ago."

I tried not to react to the loathsome man. I promise I did, but people like him get under my skin. "It wasn't because I lost. It was because you cheated."

"Come along, Isobel. We've already talked about this." He pinched the end of his nose and looked disappointed in me. I knew that look well. "It's not cheating to be much better than one's competitors."

"No, but it is cheating to filch five-hundred-pound notes from the bank when you thought that no one was looking."

He shook his head in apparent amazement. "Oh, dear me. We do have very different memories of that day."

"It doesn't matter," Ramesh said to back me up, "Izzy isn't playing, and besides, we just found a dead—"

I was close enough to kick him to keep him quiet. "Pigeon. We found a dead pigeon, the poor little creature."

"At least he died in a comfy place," Bradley said whilst looking around the room as though considering moving house. "Who owns it anyway?"

We all turned to the only Welshman in the room.

"What, just because I'm Welsh, you expect me to know the history of an old house in the middle of nowhere?" David managed to pretend this was not the case for a good four seconds. "Fine, it belonged to an old opera singer at one point in the sixties. She used to have a classical music festival here. When she died, it went to her rich family. They rented it out to a hotel chain who gave up on the business in the nineties and it's been abandoned ever since. But that doesn't mean that all Welsh people know one another."

This caused a stir of laughter, and Bradley couldn't resist a dig at the Welsh – who were one of the many groups he blamed for the downfall of his central heating business. "Come off it, Dai, m'boy. There's only about twelve of you in total. Of course you all know each other."

David wouldn't take the bait and walked over to the window to peer out at the worsening storm. The others soon busied themselves with the boardgame, and so I went to see him.

"You came," I said, but he didn't look at me at first. "I didn't think you would."

When he still wouldn't say anything, I was about to give up, but then he leaned closer to the window, and I realised he was just distracted. "That's weird. I thought I saw something moving out there."

"You thought you did, or you really did?"

He wiped his hand across the glass where it had fogged up, but the rain was coming down so heavily that it made very little difference. "I really thought I did."

"Then you really must have." I smiled at his joke and sat down beside him on the padded window box. This did not make it any easier to talk to him, but I knew I should. "Whatever your reason, I appreciate you being here."

"I didn't want you to get killed," he said a little too loudly, but no one was paying attention.

It was strange to be with him again. I thought we'd said goodbye for the last time that afternoon.

I knew he would turn up! My brain insisted. *What point would there have been in him making such a short cameo otherwise?*

"Well, thank you." For a moment, I just wanted to stare and perhaps poke him a bit to prove that he was real. Ideally, I would have asked him to pinch me, but that might have sounded a fraction too kinky. "I thought you said I was an idiot for coming here."

He forgot about whatever was or wasn't outside and looked back at me. "I don't believe that was the word I used. But after you left, I decided that if you were going to be…" he paused to find a better expression. "… foolish, the least I could do was make sure you were okay."

I didn't know whether I wanted to pull him in for a kiss or shout at him for abandoning me. I also had the lingering memory that he was the one who was supposed to be angry.

"I'm fine," I perhaps lied. "Though I can't say the same thing for the caretaker of this place. Someone killed him before we arrived."

"That poor man." He didn't sound too surprised by this, but then death does tend to follow me around like a needy puppy. "Shouldn't you be running about the place, looking for clues? Why haven't you told everyone of the danger?"

"Because I know how my uncle will react. He'll panic and do something stupid. My cousin Noémi will blame me for all her woes, my former stepdad will find some sly way to criticise me, and the killer will quite literally get away with murder."

"Come off it, Izzy. That's no reason to keep them in the dark."

"I literally gave you three whole reasons, not just one!" My voice went all squeaky, but I managed to get it under control. "We were evidently all called here for a reason, and I want to know what it is."

"But more people could die."

I realised that he was making sense and took a breath before replying. "Not if we stay together. Just give me a couple of hours, and then you can all head out into the storm and be on your way."

He clearly wasn't convinced that this was the best idea and, when I turned to Ramesh for support, I realised that everyone had disappeared. The Monopoly board was still there – though the top hat was missing, which made me think that Arthur had pocketed his favourite piece to ensure that no one else could use it – but there wasn't a person in sight.

Chapter Seventeen

If stealing a small metal playing piece doesn't make someone a likely murderer, I don't know what does.

"What…?" David began when he noticed that we were now alone, and I responded with a similarly intoned, "How…?"

We'd evidently been too involved in our own conversation to notice what had been happening around us, and I couldn't imagine why they'd gone off until I heard Ramesh's voice carry down the corridor to our comfy lounge.

"Ready or not, here I come!"

"Brilliant." There was more than a hint of sarcasm in David's tone, and he parroted my previous refrain back to me. "It's like you said. If we stay together, we'll be fine."

"All the more reason to help Ramesh seek out the hiders." I assumed this was the game they'd opted for in place of Monopoly, though, knowing Ramesh, he might well have added his own unique spin on it. It wouldn't have been the first time he'd suggested "strip hide-and-seek", though I doubted there would have been much appetite for such an activity.

We caught up with him quickly enough, which meant that all we had to do now was locate every other person in a gigantic mansion that we'd never visited before.

"Please tell me no one is going to take their clothes off," I begged my friend in a whisper as I tapped him on the shoulder. He'd been tiptoeing along the corridor in an over-the-top manner and now turned around with a look of horror on his face.

"Ah!" He almost jumped out of his skin when he noticed us, but the fear subsided quickly enough. "Don't sneak up on me like that."

"We called your name three times," my ex replied in that lovely smooth voice of his, which made me want to give up my house in South London and move into his mouth.

Mmmmmm... David's mouth.

Is that all you're going to say?

Yep.

No lewd comment? Just, *Mmmmmm?*

That's right.

Fair enough.

"You have a filthy mind, Izzy," Ramesh informed me, and I thought for a moment that he had heard my thoughts. "We are not playing *strip* hide-and-seek, if that's what you're thinking." He was rarely coy, but nearly blushed as he mumbled the truth under his breath. "Though I may have suggested it if I'd thought that anyone would agree."

I tried to block out the associated mental images, and David attempted to affix our runaway mine car to the tracks for a second or two. "What happened to Monopoly?"

"Soon after we started playing, Uncle Bradley tried to sell Wendy a second-hand boiler. Noémi flirted with Father Christmas, and Edmund had a tragic, far-off look in his eyes the whole time. As soon as Arthur started complaining about everyone buying the properties he wanted, Noémi suggested that this house was the perfect place for a game of hide-and-seek. Before I knew it, they'd run off, leaving me to count."

David had always taken Ramesh too seriously and had to ask a question as we peered into rooms and peeked under furniture. "How exactly do you play strip hide-and-seek?"

I talked over him. "How long a head start did you give everyone?"

Ramesh answered us both in turn. "I don't know, as no one ever agrees to play with me. And thirty seconds."

"Let's have a look around the kitchen, shall we?" David suggested, which made me worried that one of the others had stumbled across the caretaker's body. After ten more minutes of searching, there was no sign of anyone, and we headed upstairs.

"This is impossible!" Ramesh lamented when our exploration of the common areas on the first floor brought us no luck – though he was briefly distracted by a collection of disco records and an old gramophone. "It's taking even longer than Strip Monopoly. And, no, David. Before you ask, I don't know the rules of Strip Monopoly, because no one ever wants to play it."

He wiped his tired eyes on his velvet sleeve, and I cursed my luck for not bringing snacks. He always gets like this when he hasn't eaten for a while, and I normally carry a little packet of nuts or a muesli bar to perk him up.

"Remove one piece of clothing every time you pass go!" David declared with a surprisingly breezy air for a convicted murderer who had recently been released from prison, only to find himself at the scene of a terrible crime.

"Hmmm…" Ramesh considered this option as he crawled on his hands and knees to check behind a shelf. "That could end up being a very chilly game. Perhaps it would be better to wait for community chest cards."

David once again treated Ramesh as if anything he said was in any way sensible. "That's an idea."

"No, no, no," I said, mainly to make them stop talking. "The only way to play Strip Monopoly would be to save up money for clothes removal instead of houses and hotels. You could choose which person removes an item of clothing in exchange for a thousand pounds into the middle of the board."

They stared at me as though I was the weird one.

"You make it sound so seedy, Iz," Ramesh complained with a grossed-out look. "You have sullied the good name of Strip Monopoly."

I can't say how happy this made me. It meant we could finally talk about something else.

"I don't mean to sound judgemental, Ramesh," David began, "but knowing what you did about the dead body and the killer who brought us here, why did you go along with the idea of hide-and-seek in the first place?"

He looked surprisingly guilty. "It wasn't my fault. I tried to stop them when Noémi suggested it, but everyone was so excited that they sped off in no time. I couldn't think up a reason for why they shouldn't leave the lounge without telling them about the dead body or the vengeful killer."

"I'm sure it will be fine," I lied to stop him feeling bad. "It's fairly unlikely that anyone will die. And besides, you're an excellent seeker."

"Yeah, I am." This gave him the confidence he needed to increase his speed. "And without people doing stupid things like dispersing around a spooky house at entirely the wrong moment, horror writers would be out of a job."

David had been looking through a wardrobe full of old fur coats, but there was no sign of anyone (or Narnia for that matter). "I don't suppose you heard where they went when you were counting?"

"I would never cheat like that in such a worthy and hallowed game." Ramesh pretended to be offended, and the hunt continued.

It was becoming increasingly apparent that – much like Monopoly – hide-and-seek is fun in short stretches. The second floor of the building was particularly boring as it contained countless largely identical bedrooms and nothing else. The one point of interest was at the far end of the corridor, where the fancier suites were located. There was no one under any of the four-poster beds, or hidden in the bathtubs for that matter, but we did find names on several of the doors.

"My goodness, Izzy!" My friend hadn't looked so amazed since Patricia agreed to their double Barbra Streisand couple's costume the previous Halloween. "You predicted the future! You knew that the killer would assign us rooms."

"I'm not a fortune teller. I've just read the same murder mysteries that the killer evidently has."

"Which I suppose could be a clue," David more helpfully pointed out. "We're looking for someone who can read."

"That rules out my uncle." My eyebrows did a quirky dance for some reason. I'm sure that I looked like a bad comedian waiting for a laugh.

The three of us fell silent, and I had a sensation that I'd experienced before on my cases. There was a tension rising in me. It was almost as if I really did possess some sixth sense, and I knew that a hugely important discovery was about to be made. As we got closer to the end of the very long corridor, the truth hit me. At the rate that people had been dying, I felt certain that the killer had struck again and, at any moment, we were about to find a dead—

"Izzy, you do understand how to play this game, don't you?" Arthur bellowed from the other end of the floor. "We have all hidden, and you have to find us. I've been waiting far too long for it to be entertaining anymore."

Why do I fall back into old patterns of behaviour so readily? I hadn't seen the man in over a decade. He'd divorced my mother twelve whole years ago, in fact. So why was it that I still whined and huffed like a teenager as soon as his grating voice attacked my ears?

"I know how to hide-and-seek. Thank you, Arthur!" It was not just the distance between us that made me shout. "But this is a very big house, and it has a lot of rooms. If you wanted the game to be over sooner, you shouldn't have hidden so well."

"And now she complains because I'm too good at playing." He shook his head as if to say, *I despair of you, Isobel. I really do.* "I believe that everyone is hidden on the fourth floor. Feel free to look for us when the moment strikes you."

He turned around and walked up the stairs, so we doubled-back on ourselves in order to go after him.

So much for your sixth sense that something important was going to happen.

I decided not to engage with this point, mainly because I was still fuming at Arthur. I wasn't even the one who was supposed to be seeking! That was Ramesh's job, but no one had criticised him.

Once we'd found the right floor, it was a doddle to locate our quarry. Father Christmas was such a big chap that his feet stuck out from the end of the bed that he was hiding under.

"You got me!" he said, full of his usual cheer. "Which is good because I have a question."

I half expected it to be, "What do you want for Christmas?" But don't worry, it was something equally mad.

"I was just wondering what time the other magical helpers are getting here. Do you know the itinerary?"

I left Ramesh to explain the whole we-were-tricked-into-coming-there situation as David and I searched out the others.

"Typical," Uncle Bradley said when we found him squeezed in beside an old water tank. "I never win anything."

Noémi had simply gone to sleep in a comfy bed. Wendy was smoking a fag out of a window and barely noticed when we caught her, and Edmund looked as haunted as ever.

"I knew it," Arthur announced triumphantly when we located him under a chair in a small reading room. "I knew I'd be the winner. You simply can't keep a good man down."

He talked to Wendy the whole way back downstairs about the clever strategy he'd employed, but she said nothing. In fact, she hadn't said much since she'd arrived, and it wasn't like her. My former colleague was prone to grand, dramatic denunciations. She hadn't even taken the time to insult me.

"That was anti-climactic," Ramesh announced as he flopped down on one of the sofas. He lay horizontally so as not to fall straight off again.

"Somebody has removed my drink," Arthur complained when he returned to his previous spot.

"You probably just drank it and forgot," I snapped, in the hope he would stop talking.

"No, no. I don't just mean the glass I poured for myself or the second one that I gave Edmund. I'm talking about the bottle of whisky that I brought with me. I always travel with a twelve-year-old single malt from the Isle of Mull." I'd forgotten that he was a whisky bore on top of everything else. "I left the bottle on the table nearest to the fire, and it's not there anymore."

I could see how nervous this made my Uncle Bradley. He still didn't know about the killer but, from what I heard from my mother, he wasn't great with stress since he'd been a suspect in his cousin's murder.

"Who's been messing about with things while we were supposed to be playing the game?" His gaze travelled around the room to interrogate each person there. "And for that matter, what happened to the central heating job I was promised? I was told there would be a bonus for me if I could get the work done quickly. So which of you hired me to come here in the first place?"

"More importantly than any of that," Arthur talked over him, "what does the theft of a bottle of whisky with a recommended retail price of forty-two pounds fifty say about the thief?"

"I think you had better tell us exactly what's going on here, Izzy," Noémi walked into the centre of the group to declare. She had the confidence that I longed to command.

Despite her great presence and immaculate style, everyone was looking at me. I should have told them everything from the start, but after so many interruptions I hadn't been able to get through the speech I'd begun.

"Here's is the thing." This was a nice bold opening statement. All I needed to do now was tell them about the programme of violence in which they'd become entangled. "You have all been suspects in previous murders that I have investigated."

"No, I haven't," Arthur had to interrupt.

"You might not have known it," Ramesh said to help me out. "But you very much have."

The old dullard looked put out about this, and so I chose not to explain that I'd considered his potential as a killer whenever my cases were personally linked to me in some way.

"Three other previous suspects have recently been murdered. Just as you received letters inviting you to come here, I was sent a card by the killer which stated that, if I didn't come alone, more people would die."

There were a few gasps at this point. Edmund had to lean against the wall for support. Noémi swooned, though I think that was mainly to make Father Christmas catch her, and Wendy lit another fag.

"I came here because I knew that people I cared about could be in danger. I came to catch the killer, and I can only think that he or she is in this house right now." This stirred up the atmosphere once more.

To my surprise, it was David who stepped forward to question this point. "You surely can't say that for certain. How do we know that the killer is even here? Maybe he killed those three people and sent us letters to distance himself from the crime."

"You're forgetting about the caretaker we found."

Uncle Bradley had been warming himself by the dying embers of the fire and grabbed a porcelain vase from the mantelpiece to smash it in the hearth. "Which caretaker? And how could we be forgetting anything when you clearly haven't told us what's going on?"

"I'm sorry, Bradley." Though I was no great admirer of my uncouth uncle, I didn't want to upset him unnecessarily. "I was only trying to protect you. I hoped to learn what was happening before I said anything, but Ramesh and I found a dead body near the kitchen. I've no proof, but I think it was probably the man who prepared the house for our arrival."

This revelation stunned Uncle Bradley. He froze where he was, his eyes fixed onto mine, and I don't believe he blinked for the ten seconds before he bolted for the door.

"Wait," I called. Though we ran after him, he had a good start on all of us and was almost at the front porch by the time I reached the corridor. "Seriously, Uncle Brad. Don't do anything silly."

Like staying in a house with a killer who has a hunger for violence and a personal vendetta against the man's niece?

He shot out into the rain, and I picked up the pace to talk him down. "It's not safe in this weather," I shouted as he unlocked his van and swung the door open.

Unlike a house with a killer who—

Yes, thank you. I get the message.

The wind was not just howling but screaming out like a dying man. The rain fell like hammers from a tower and the clouds overhead were so dark that it felt as though the day had given up and called it a night.

Bradley reversed out of the space he was in and shouted at me through the window as he drove past. "You should have warned me as soon as I got here, Izzy. You're as mad as the blasted killer!"

Even as he pulled along the drive and down the hill, I kept after him. Perhaps it was the sound of his tyres screeching on the tarmac that pushed me onwards, or the desperate speed with which he escaped from Bron-Yr-Aur. Outside the property, the road immediately got steeper and there was a hairpin turn through an avenue of trees. Something about the noises his van made told me there was a problem and, a moment later, there was an immense crash. The van had pummelled straight into a tree trunk, and his car alarm began to wail.

Chapter Eighteen

David, Edmund and Saint Nicholas (my triumvirate of exes) were with me, whereas the others had stayed behind and looked out from the dry porch.

"Bradley!" I called in some anguish.

We got to the site of the accident in thirty seconds, and there he was – his head resting on the steering wheel, with blood all over it. I turned away; I couldn't look. It was one thing to find strangers and vague acquaintances dead, but he'd been a part of my life ever since I was born. While it's true that I had a better relationship with my newsagent than my uncle, the sight of his lifeless body was too much to bear.

"This shouldn't have happened. Even if the killer didn't stick a knife in his back or poison the man, they're still to blame in my book," David said as I buried my head in the shoulder of Edmund's well-tailored jacket. I should probably say that I hadn't made a conscious decision to choose him over the other two. He was simply the closest handsome man at that moment.

I think we all jumped as Bradley straightened up and looked out of the window at us. Father Christmas definitely stifled a scream.

"I'm not dead," said the man in the blood-spattered van. It was an old vehicle, and he had to wind down the window manually before saying anything more. "The brakes failed. I know I was driving too fast, but I couldn't slow down and went straight into the tree."

David opened the door and inspected the damage. It didn't seem that the transit had airbags, so Bradley was lucky that the wound to his head wasn't more serious.

"How do you feel?" the competent former manager asked, much as if he was checking on the well-being of an employee who, for example, has recently discovered that her grandmother needs a hip replacement.

Bradley groaned and touched his shoulder to test the pain there. "I've felt better."

"Do you think you can walk back to the house?" Father Christmas offered him a large, muscular hand.

Gosh! Even his hands are muscular!?

Between the jolly giant and David, they managed to support Bradley's weight, as Edmund and I followed them back up the path to the house.

"Do you have any signal?" I asked, as my phone still wouldn't connect.

He took his out and tried as well. "It says I have five bars, but when I call, nothing happens."

"Same for me." I considered what the best thing to do was, and a vague memory struck me of a time when people didn't carry telecommunication devices in their pockets, but they were anchored inconveniently to one specific place. "When we get back inside, we'll have to look for a landline. We need the police, an ambulance and eventually a tow truck."

"Wait a second." We were back in the courtyard in front of the former hotel, and Edmund ran over to a sporty blue Porsche that had been there when I first arrived. The car seemed to glow as he approached it, and a moment later, he was inside.

He turned on the engine and then his voice came out to me. "Mine too." I struggled to interpret this, but he ducked back out of the car to explain. "The brakes are cut. I'm guessing the killer did it on every vehicle in order to keep us all here. You can ask the others to check if you like, but I doubt there's much point."

I tested my own car and tried to imagine how the killer had gone about this task. "How long would it have taken to do everyone's cars?"

He didn't answer but tugged me towards the house; having a conversation in freezing-cold rain isn't as much fun as a chat beside a fireplace. When we got back to the smoky, wood-panelled lounge, Arthur was explaining the best way to make a fire to whoever would listen. To give credit where it's due, she'd got the thing blazing.

Bradley was laid out on the sofa, clutching his head. David was looking after him as best he could, but Noémi – who if my understanding of genealogy is any good, was his first cousin once removed – had no interest in his plight and was praising sexy Santa for his heroic deeds.

"I found a phone, Izzy," Ramesh told me, coming in from wherever he'd just been with a rotary-dial, corded device in his hand. "I've tried it in different sockets around the ground floor, but they're all dead."

"Could you choose your words more carefully," Bradley complained, as he was enjoying playing the victim.

"Sorry," Ramesh murmured before turning back to me. "All the terrestrial phonelines seem to be… without life."

"Thanks, Ra," I told him and wanted to say more, but my head was reeling just as much as my uncle's.

"We have to get out of here." I believe this was the first thing Wendy had said to the group. "We can't just sit here and wait to be murdered."

"We can't go anywhere without cars," I told her in as kind a voice as I could muster. "Bradley's brakes were cut, and mine and Edmund's didn't respond when we tried them just now. I think the killer is clever enough to have found a way to keep us here."

"Then we'll have to go on foot," Arthur concluded in his usual, I-know-all-the-answers, why-does-everyone-have-to-make-everything-so-complicated voice. "It's as simple as that."

"In a storm?" Ramesh put to him. "The nearest town must be ten or fifteen miles and let me tell you this, sir, this is a knock-off Dior velvet pant suit I'm wearing; I will not expose it to the elements any more than I have to."

This was not my biggest concern in the situation, but he'd raised a good point… well, at least half a good point.

"We really don't have the clothes or supplies to trek through the storm." I had no desire to say the next sentence, but there was no other option. "We'll just have to stay here for the night. Hopefully, the storm will break, and we can leave at first light."

This brought a fragile calm to the room. I have no doubt that some of the more cantankerous members of our party – I'm talking about you, Arthur and Noémi! – would have liked to disagree, but there was no other option. We were stuck… in a big scary house… with a killer.

"Who suggested the game of hide-and-seek?" David asked once Bradley's wound was well staunched with tissues. "Who was the first to say that you should leave this room?"

Ramesh had already provided this information, but either David had forgotten the answer, or he wanted to make a point.

The suspects looked about at one another until several pairs of eyes came to a stop on Noémi. "Fine, it was me, but I didn't know what was going on at the time."

"That must have been when the brakes on the cars were cut," David continued.

"I barely know how to cut an apple, and I haven't the first idea about cars. I only suggested the game because everyone had lost interest in Monopoly."

It was odd to have to reconsider someone's potential as a killer. I'd ended up eliminating each of them on my previous cases, but that didn't mean they were innocent now. Noémi was particularly good at playing the innocent, and she batted her eyelids in Nicholas's direction.

"I believe you, young lady," he told her, and she hurried over to find solace in his arms.

"Fine, then tell me what happened when you went upstairs," I asked the group. "How did you all decide to go up to the top floor?"

"That was Arthur!" Edmund declared in a more animated tone than before. "He said we should get as far away from you as possible."

My (thankfully) former stepdad threw both hands in the air in indignation. "I only said that in order to find the best hiding places. It stands to reason that the further away from the seeker you go, the better the hiding place will be." He was evidently proud of this complex strategy.

Edmund wouldn't let him off so easily. "Or you knew that, if you could persuade everyone to go upstairs, you would have time to take one of the staircases back down here, avoiding Ramesh, Izzy and David. Then you tampered with the cars and ran back up to the fourth floor. I heard someone moving around in the corridor when I was hiding."

Arthur puffed out his cheeks. "I admit that I eventually got tired of waiting for anyone to find me and went down to tell them to hurry up, but I didn't go anywhere near the cars."

"A likely story!" Bradley sent a jibe across at his former brother-in-law. "I've never liked you, Arthur. My sweet sister could have done a thousand times better than marrying you, and thankfully she has since!"

"What about Edmund?" Arthur asked with wobbling jowls – as the best form of defence is generally to accuse someone else of murder. "He was here when I arrived. Who's to say that he isn't the killer?" When no one responded, he decided that another dose of his voice was what we needed. “That must be it. He killed the caretaker, set up this place for us, and then hung around until we all arrived. It would have made no sense to leave and come back.”

“Nice try,” the new top suspect replied, “but I only got here ten minutes before you. If you remember, you commented on my wet hair when you arrived.”

Arthur was stumped by this, and I must admit that I’d been enjoying them doing my job for me, but when no one had anything more to add, I realised that I’d have to get on with it.

“There are two things we need at this moment. The first is to find the killer, and the second is dinner.” I could practically hear their tummies rumbling as I said this. “I’ll deal with the former and Ramesh will be in charge of the latter.”

“But, Izzy…” He looked like a lost puppy at that moment. “I don’t have any internet signal. How am I going to watch cookery videos on my phone if I don’t have a signal!?”

Almost involuntarily, we all took our phones out to see whether anything had changed.

“I’ve got nothing,” Noémi said.

“Ditto,” Wendy added.

“I haven’t got a phone,” jolly saint Nick shocked Ramesh by declaring.

“Wait! I’ve got a text message!” I practically sang. “There’s a journalist in London who I called when I arrived here. She’s looking into who owns the house and who the black Ford out in the carpark is registered to.”

“And you didn’t think of telling her to call the police if you failed to get back in touch by a certain time?” Wendy finally showed a glimpse of her true grumpy self.

“I… Well, I didn’t… That actually would have been a good idea.”

David stepped in to ask something relevant. “What does her message say?”

I tapped the screen and there before me was a long description of the history of Bron-Yr-Aur. “It’s about the house,” I said as I scanned the message. “It was built in the nineteenth century, and there’s some stuff here about the opera singer who owned it.”

“How very useful,” Wendy grouched.

"It passed down through her family, but it doesn't say anything about the current owners."

"Is that it?" Arthur was severely unimpressed. "Our first contact with the outside world in hours, and it's of no use whatsoever?"

"Did she at least include a recipe that might help me make dinner?" Ramesh looked extremely hopeful, and I would have to disappoint him.

"I'm afraid not."

He looked as though he would throw his phone in the fire but managed to calm himself down in order to muse dolorously. "What did people do before the internet?"

"You'll just have to look for a cookbook." I turned around on the spot before deciding who should help him. "Nicholas, could you go to the kitchen and lend a hand?"

"Of course, Izzy!" he immediately scampered to the door, and I realised that Danny wasn't the only man I'd dated who possessed a puppy-doggish energy.

Hmm. I wonder why you chose him just as he and Noémi were cosying up to one another.

My cousin was furious at my power play/incidental interference, depending on how you wish to view my actions. "And what are you going to do, oh great leader?"

"I'm going to do what I do best," I answered a little smugly.

Bowling?

"I'm going to interview my first suspect." I already knew who I wanted and pointed across the room. "Edmund, come with me."

Chapter Nineteen

Just across the hall from the place where we'd set up camp was an equally large space that I hadn't entered until now. I imagine it had served as the bar when the house had been a hotel, and sure enough, there was a healthy supply of drinks in a cabinet in one corner. Sadly it was locked, and I hadn't a clue how to pick it, though perhaps that was a good thing. My suspects' spirits were agitated enough without adding spirits to the mix.

"It's not me, Izzy. I hope you know that," Edmund insisted as I dreamed of the Naughty Hot Chocolate cocktail I would not be drinking.

"Sorry? What's not you?"

"I didn't kill anyone. I didn't bring you here to die, and I don't know anything about the letters that you all received."

"You all? Don't you mean, we?" Ooh, I was pleased with this fast thinking. If he was the killer, it only made sense that he wouldn't have sent one to himself.

"Yes, of course, *we* all received."

I came to sit in front of him beside the rain-spattered window. That side of the house was more protected from the elements than where we'd previously been, but this also made it darker. The simple bronze chandelier above our heads was doing its best, but the selection of differently shaped forty-watt lightbulbs could do little to fight off the darkness of the heavily upholstered room.

"You didn't reveal what was in your letter."

"Because it's not important," he said with just a hint of anger. "If it was, I would tell you."

He'd been so arrogant when we'd first met. His zillionaire father was found dead in his family's sprawling home in the country, but he'd danced about the place as though he were on holiday. He'd shown no fear of being fingered for the murder, partly because he knew he hadn't done it, I suppose. But all that had changed.

The man sitting before me was in a bad state. He was like a method actor who'd gone too deep into a torturous role. He barely looked at me as he spoke and kept glancing down at his hands. His legs jerked every few seconds, as if he'd been connected to the electric supply and regular jolts of energy were keeping him alive.

"That's not how this works," I told him. "I'm not saying that you're to blame; in fact, you're somewhere near the bottom of my list, but I still need to know what brought you here."

He rolled his shoulders in an attempt to get more comfortable in the tightly sprung armchair. "Can't you just trust me? If you don't think I'm the killer, I mean. Can't you just take my word for it that you don't need to know?"

"I'm sorry, that's not possible."

Yeah, Edmund! Izzy's far too nosy for that.

Instead of answering me directly, he put his hand inside his still wet suit jacket and extracted a small white envelope. The handwriting on the address was different from the card I'd received. It was as if the sender had tried to make it look friendly rather than threatening.

Dear Edmund,

I feel like we missed our opportunity when we first met, but it's never too late. I know this must sound crazy, but I've got a friend who owns an incredible house in the mountains in Wales. I'll be there all alone this week. If you think we've still got a shot, you should come to meet me on Thursday afternoon. I'll be free from four.

If you believe in second chances, I can't wait to see you at Bron-Yr-Aur in the Brecon Beacons.

With lots of love,

Izzy Palmer

I couldn't help laughing at the final words. "Sorry, I don't mean to be unkind. I just think it's funny that such a personal letter was signed with my surname. Did the killer add it in case you couldn't remember who I was?"

He managed to see the funny side. "Perhaps there are lots of women called Izzy who are after me. Perhaps I get such invitations twice a week, and the killer knew this and didn't want me to be confused."

"That must be it." I found myself replying in the same comfortable, flirtatious way in which we had once spoken to each other. "If you'd thought that it was from Izzy Simpson or Izzy Montague, I guess you wouldn't have come."

"Exactly. I have no interest in those other Izzys."

I opened my mouth to tease him again, but I couldn't do it. The very fact that he was there proved that he held feelings for me, and it would have been cruel to point it out. The truth was that I'd previously assumed he flirted with every woman he met. I'd never imagined for a moment that I was anything special to him, but apparently I was wrong.

As I sat there formulating another question, the possibility of the life we could have built together played out in my mind. I saw us walking hand in hand on his estate of Vomeris Hall. I pictured us having dinner together with his two non-criminal siblings around a big table at Christmas. I imagined what our kids would look like, and then the bubble of a dream burst as I considered what his murderer sister would have thought of all this. I can't imagine that Audrey would have stood by and allowed her brother to fall in love with the woman who put her behind bars.

"You want me to believe that you couldn't be the killer, and yet you may have more of a reason than anyone else here," I eventually told him.

One of his eyebrows raised a little higher. "Oh really? Enlighten me."

"Your sister is still locked up for your father's murder. Your brother was put away for his swindling. You might even feel some loyalty to your old butler, who was caught up in their crimes. If you were the killer, this letter would help promote the idea that you bear no hard feelings for the part I played in ripping apart your family."

"You're clever," he replied, but not in the combative way that most of my suspects would. He really meant it as a compliment. "To be perfectly honest, I came in here thinking that I hadn't any possible motive, but you can always find the angles, can't you? You know just how to see the worst in people. It's quite a skill."

I tried not to be offended and focussed on the most important point. "You didn't answer me. Are you saying that you weren't upset by anything that happened?"

"That's exactly what I'm saying. My family needed to be torn down into its constituent parts. It was the best thing that could happen. We grew up in the shadow of a contemptible man. He tried to mould us in his image and failed, but it turned us into hybrid monsters: neither good nor bad."

"How poetic," was all I could think to say at first. "Do you know that I visited your sister in prison recently?"

He hesitated over his answer. "I did hear a rumour. I don't speak to Audrey directly, but our sister Daisy does. She's really the only good one among us. She believes in charity and redemption and all those pretty lies that we teach children." His eyes travelled up to the ornate wooden ceiling and back down, and then he stopped himself, as though aware that he was rambling. "My point is that she told me that Lady Audrey had received an august visitor."

I felt I owed him an explanation. "Thinking back through my cases in the hope I might identify who'd been doing all these terrible things, it occurred to me that she might blame me more than anyone else I've put in prison. It's not just that she was caught, but that she was so confident that her plan would work."

"If I remember correctly, she made the mistake of inviting you to the scene of the murder."

"She actually paid me to investigate," I replied. "I've built up a bit of a name for myself since, and so criminals tend to take me a little more seriously these days. Audrey made the mistake of thinking that I would trust the evidence she laid out for me instead of following my own instincts."

He smiled then. "Yes, you did a brilliant job, and Audrey deserved all she got. Arrogance is a common failing in my family."

"And yet you don't seem as cocksure as you once did."

My words clearly rattled him. "Surely killers have to be arrogant to believe they can get away with murder. If you're saying that I no longer possess such a characteristic, then we can end the interview there."

I bowed for a second to concede his point, then tried to speak more clearly. "What I'm trying to say is that it would be a lot easier to understand why you were summoned here if you told me what's happened over the last few years since we met."

He stayed perfectly still for the length of time it takes to sing

'Happy Birthday'. I sensed that the cogs in his brain were whirring and that, like a futuristic computer on an old TV show, the issue would take a few moments to process.

"I fell in love," he eventually revealed. "I fell in love, had my heart broken, and all the king's horses and all the king's men can't put poor Edmund together again." There was a resigned, perhaps even detached tone to his voice. "Has anyone ever hurt you, Izzy? Has anyone ever let you down so badly that you didn't think you could live anymore?"

I had to think about the answer. I thought I'd dated every kind of low-life and non-entity, but I hadn't been through what he had. "No, I can't say they have. I'm thirty-three and barely any of the relationships I've had in my life have given me happy times to look back on, but no one's ever tormented me the way that I hear your fiancée did. They either didn't like me in the first place, they reminded me of a brother, or they were totally insane."

Or they did like you but had recently murdered someone.

"Then congratulations are in order." He began to laugh, but that joyful, frightening sound was killed in a second. "You are lucky that no one has ever taken your heart, put it in a little box and dropped it in the middle of the ocean. That's how it felt when I realised what I was to Ella. I was just a toy for her to play with, and do you know the worst part of it?"

I'd hoped that he didn't expect an answer, as there was something about the emotion running through him that was difficult to comprehend. "No. I can't begin to imagine."

"The worst part of it is that she blamed me for everything. The person who had cut me off from my friends, made me think that I was worthless, humiliated and degraded me at every chance she got, told me that I was being unreasonable. When I broke off the engagement, Ella said that the only reason she'd treated me badly was because I'd never had enough room in my heart for another person. But I was the one who had planned out my whole life with her. I knew where we would live and what I wanted to call our kids. I can still see us together, old and grey and in love, but that wasn't enough for her. The only way that woman knew how to love was by destroying my confidence so greatly that I couldn't imagine another person loving me."

I watched him for a moment, and I could see the pain that ran through him. He wasn't the same person I'd briefly known; he was a raw nerve.

"I can't comprehend what she put you through. But perhaps it's best to forget the ending and think only of the happy times you had. You must have loved her if losing her hurt you so much." I was worried that this just made me sound insensitive, so I decided to make a fool of myself instead. "I've had any number of disasters in love. There's the boy who thought I was a boy, the time I accidentally punched my boyfriend's mother, and I'm not going to go into all the men I dated who had unhealthy obsessions with particular body parts, but I bet you didn't know that nostril fetishes were a thing!"

I'd hoped this might make him laugh, but he just looked scared. That didn't stop me, though. In fact, I ploughed right on! "There's one story that even Ramesh doesn't know. It was when I was at university. I'd been with a bloke for most of my time there and really thought that he would be the one. Our final term came, and neither of us had the courage to discuss what we were going to do next. We would occasionally mention the idea that we might end up living in London, but we never fixed on any details and so, in the very last week before graduating, I decided to take the bull by the horns."

"Oh, Izzy, what did you do?" At least he was sucked into my cringeworthy story.

"I booked the best hotel room in Southorpe-on-Sea – in the three-star Seychelle Guest House – and I got there early to cover the bed with rose petals… well, carnation petals, as they were cheaper. I lit candles and put on soft music. I had the whole thing planned out."

"Tell me you didn't sing him a love song."

Cringing is a powerful tool. I really had made him forget his problems for a moment.

"I didn't just want to sing my love to him. I was going to perform a version of 'We've Only Just Begun' by the Carpenters and accompany myself on the accordion. My mother's always told me I have a beautiful voice."

He hid behind his hands at this point.

Your plan is working perfectly!

"He was called Mick, and I planned to drop his name into the song every time it was supposed to say 'luck'."

He was breathing more heavily now, practically wheezing in fact, but it soon turned into a painful laugh. “Make it stop, Izzy. I can’t take anymore.” He peeked out at me, then changed his mind. “Actually, no. So many bad thoughts are going through my head right now, you’ll have to finish.”

“We went out for a fancy dinner to La Catapecchia della Pizza[2].” This really set him off. His jags of laughter were so loud and squealy that I’m sure, had anyone happened to pass the room at that moment, they would have assumed I was murdering him. “And then I surprised my beloved Mick by breaking off our romantic walk along the seafront to enter the hotel.”

“Just so you know, I’m imagining that the candles you lit had caught the curtains when you were out, and your hotel room was in flames.”

“I wish! We got up there, and I was about to whip out my accordion when I thought, *No. If I’m going to do this, I’m going to do it right.* So I cut straight to the proposal.”

“You asked him to marry you?” He was clutching his sides, but the reality must finally have come home to him as he stopped laughing. “That’s actually very sweet of you.”

“I got down on one knee, said those magic words, and do you know what Mick did?”

He couldn’t produce the requisite sound and so, his mouth hanging open, he shook his head.

“He laughed. He saw the petals and the candles and the accordion there at the ready and he laughed at me for being a sap. My first proper boyfriend uttered two sentences that night which I will never forget. He said, ‘That’s what I like about you, Izzy. You’re always good for a laugh.’”

Edmund was laughing then, too, but at least he apologised. “Oh my goodness, that is heartbreaking. I am so sorry.” The immense sound that ripped out of him shook the candelabra on the table between us. “It’s not just funny, it’s tragic.”

He looked in his pockets for a handkerchief but, finding nothing, he had to dry his eyes on the sleeve of his fancy jacket.

“I aim to please,” I said, and despite the painful memories that my

2 According to my Italian friend, this sophisticated sounding restaurant is a mistranslation of Pizza Hut, that is closer in meaning to Pizza Slum. And, yes, the best jokes are the ones you have to explain.

aborted proposal brought back, I managed a giggle of my own.

"What happened afterwards? Did you move to London together? Did you at least get lucky?"

"No, and no. We cuddled until the sun came up. Or rather, I fell asleep on his shoulder as he talked about the role-playing novel he planned to write and, at the end of that week, we went our separate ways quite acrimoniously."

He said you had a face like a plate!

"He kindly confided in me that he could never have married me because I had a face like a plate." Remembering just how seriously I had taken this at the time, I burst out in hysterics. "What a horrible person! Thank goodness we didn't end up together."

We both needed some time to calm down after that, but once our sobs of laughter had subsided, he seemed a lot more cheerful than when we'd gone in there. "Thank you, Miss Palmer. You always seem to know just what to say."

This may have been the least accurate statement in history, but I didn't correct him. "Well, I'm certainly always good for a laugh."

I pulled him to his feet and, as we walked back through the room, he asked me two final questions. "I have to ask; do you know what happened to him? Did you dodge a bullet?"

"Yes, and sadly, no." Of all the breakups in my life, the one with Mick was the most painful, and it knocked my confidence for years to come. This may well have been the first time I had looked back on it and not feel those old wounds stinging. "He wrote his role-playing novel and became a millionaire. He's a guru to many hairy, tattooed men who spend their evenings rolling dice and playing with metal figurines. I saw him once years later in London. He was getting out of a black Mercedes and, for some unfathomable reason, I went up to say hello."

Edmund put his hand to his mouth then but managed to speak. "Tell me you didn't ask him to marry you again."

"Even worse. He thought I was asking for an autograph and grabbed my train ticket from my hand. He didn't even recognise me."

More laughter ensued.

Chapter Twenty

It occurred to me that I'd gone into that room to interview a suspect but ended up providing a free therapy session. There must be a name for a type of treatment which exposes a patient to mortifyingly embarrassing tales in order to help them forget their troubles.

How about Cringe-o-therapy?

It'll do.

We found that the main lounge was now deserted, so we went to search for the others in the kitchen.

"There's still one question I didn't get to ask," I told Edmund as we wandered. "You accepted that your sister Audrey isn't an Izzy-ite."

"I thought your fans preferred to be called Palmerettes?"

"Not important. Back to what I was saying. My question is, do you think she could hate me so much that she would orchestrate this whole thing from prison like some mafia kingpin?"

His brow furrowed then, and I could tell this wasn't a topic he had taken the time to consider. "How did she seem when you went to see her?"

"Terrifying."

"I can imagine that." He wasn't quite as cheerful as he'd been when I'd sacrificed myself on the pyre of my own embarrassment, but he managed a smile. "I doubt she would have agreed to your visit if she really hated you, though. It's not your fault that you saw through her scheme. I'm sure she's cursed you any number of times as she falls asleep at night, but she must know deep down that she's only got herself to blame. For all she complains about our terrible father, she could have left home and got a job somewhere else rather than hacking him to death."

"Oh, that's a pity." I bit my lip and probably shouldn't have shown just how much this disappointed me. "I mean, it would have been nice and easy if she was responsible. Though I don't know how she would have convinced someone to go to so much trouble." We were walking past the entrance to the ballroom at this moment, and I spotted another flaw in my theory. "Hitmen might accept payment to whack someone, but I bet they'd draw the line at inflating all those balloons in there."

When we got to the kitchen, there was an unexpected sight to behold. Everyone was having a wonderful time.

"Pancakes!" Ramesh sang with joy when he saw me. "We found all the ingredients in the fridge. Who in this blessed world doesn't love pancakes?"

Noémi surprised me by getting her hands dirty cracking eggs. David was grating cheese for the savoury fillings. Nicholas was mixing drinks. Arthur was charged with preparing the batter, and Wendy would have the most important job of all.

"Izzy, I'm flipping mental!" she said as she mimed her forthcoming task. She laughed, and it was honestly the first time I could remember her producing anything less than a caw.

"Of course, the secret to a good crêpe," Arthur deigned to explain, "is the mixing. It's all in the wrist." Everyone was so smiley that it was hard to be angry with him.

Even Uncle Bradley, who was propped up on a bench by the wall, was watching events with a grin. "Hey, Izzy, Izzy, have you heard the joke about the bishop, the call girl and the public house?"

It seemed that not everything had changed after all. "First answer me this, Bradley; do you think that I want to hear the joke about the bishop, the call girl and the public house?"

"You should listen, Izzy," David of all people told me. "It's actually quite funny."

I sighed and gave in. "Fine, go ahead and offend me. I'm ready."

Bradley smirked and looked about at the others, who were apparently just as excited as he was.

"Right, so this bishop had to call into a pub to see a parishioner who needed guidance. He did what he had to and, as he was leaving, he spotted a girl dressed very tartily—" He must have noticed my disapproval as he reconsidered his choice of vocabulary. "She was dressed in an inappropriate manner for a family establishment, and so the bishop went up to her and said, 'Young miss, would you happen to be a woman of the night?' and the woman replied, 'Yes, your grace,' and so the bishop said, "Well in that case, if you ever need help or spiritual guidance, you should call in to your local church, and the staff there will do all they can to help you.' He was a fair-minded individual and a very holy man."

There was silence for a moment before everyone burst out laughing.

"Do you get it, Iz?" Bradley's head injury clearly wasn't too serious, and he proceeded to bang the bench with his fist in amusement. "Everyone expects that type of joke to be naughty! The bishop didn't sleep with the girl or cast damnation down upon her; he tried to help her in a non-judgemental fashion." For once, the joke was funnier for its explanation, and I had to laugh at the cautious way my uncouth uncle spoke.

"I'll give you that one, Bradley. It's pretty funny... by your standards."

"You cheeky girl, if I wasn't injured, I'd take you over my knee."

"Now who's being naughty?" Ramesh piped up and, by this point, anyone saying anything would have made them laugh. It didn't take me long to realise that they'd been knocking back cocktails ever since they'd left the lounge.

"Where did all this stuff come from?" I had to ask when the joking had gone on too long.

"There are boxes of food and drink under the counter," Saint Nicholas explained.

"And it didn't concern anyone that the killer bought it and left it here for us? No one thought to wonder whether it had been poisoned?"

They looked guiltily at one another, each of them searching for the person who should have been responsible for such things. Perhaps inevitably, it fell to our manager-director to answer.

"I checked the seals," David explained. "I think it would have been difficult to slip poison into any of the containers."

"And we can't just starve to death," Noémi added.

I considered responding that we could always eat the rich, though since she'd been disinherited, there was a good chance I was better off than her.

They waited in suspended animation for my response, and I eventually put them out of their misery. "Fine, if you're sure that every bottle was tamperproof, and every packet sealed, I suppose we can keep going."

A cheer went up and the pancake making continued. It was perhaps the most jubilant scene I could remember on one of my cases, but then this was no normal group of suspects. For one thing, they'd all lived through such suspicion before. It made me wonder whether our previous encounter had made the killer believe that they would be successful where other culprits had slipped up. It was either that, or they didn't care about getting caught. Perhaps they were driven by such hatred that all they wanted to do was break my spirit and destroy my confidence. But if that was the case, who had I hurt so badly that they would feel that way?

Ramesh had another pocket on his pant suit for a small Bluetooth speaker and he had put on his legendary disco playlist, so that everyone was shimmying and grooving as they worked. Everyone but Edmund, who not only lacked a role in the factory line but had taken a bottle of bourbon from the box under the wooden breakfast bar and was knocking it back neat.

Though I'd been charmed by him in our interview, he was certainly the least stable of the people before me. He kept ping-ponging from happy to sad with brief stops at manic and *woe is me*. He hadn't denied the fact that he had strong feelings for me, and I was torn between great sympathy and pointing him out as the killer.

Why would he want to hurt you, though?

Perhaps… perhaps he blames me for the dissolution of his relationship. Perhaps his fiancée knew that Edmund still liked me, and that was the real reason they broke up.

In reply, my brain started laughing. *Sure, Iz. That must be it. After all, men constantly lose their minds over you.*

I had to wonder why my internal monologue so often sounded like my cynical mother and what that said about me.

"Izzy?" a voice broke through my silent rambling, and I looked up to see Wendy flipping a pancake in the pan. "What do you think about that, eh?"

There were cheers and applause from everyone watching, though I had a more helpful response. "That looks great, Wendy. But you're supposed to leave the batter to stand first."

That certainly killed the good mood, but it did give everyone an extra half an hour to drink Nicholas's fruity creation – and Edmund had more time to sit in the corner staring morosely into his Jim Beam. I didn't exactly join in the festivities, though Wendy and Ramesh's Travolta impersonations were suitably entertaining. I was taking my time to consider every last person there.

Clearly the killer had provided nice food and alcohol to set us off guard, and I could only assume there were darker times were to come. The culprit's first goal was achieved; we were trapped at Bron-Yr-Aur, and the next step could only be more violence.

David was just as circumspect as I was. He sipped his drink rather than tipping it down his throat and regarded the odd bunch around him as the curiosities that we were. I wondered if he was having the same thoughts that I was.

Wendy was the first to catch my attention. She'd been a cruel, belligerent bully during my time at Porter & Porter, but she was a different person to the new generation who worked there now. The kinder side to her personality was apparent there in Wales, but what if she was the architect of our meeting and her conversion to this fun and friendly person was just an act?

There was a certain logic to her being the culprit. She'd had an affair with my murdered boss and was furious with me when I'd uncovered just what a monster he was. Add that to the fact that she knew Jack Campbell, who was the first to die this time around, and she seemed like an obvious choice.

On the other hand, she really was good at flipping those pancakes, and can we really say that is a likely characteristic of a serial killer? Surely such demented individuals would never do anything so jolly. Psychopaths probably use a spatula.

Cool. So that's Wendy ruled out. Next!

It would be wrong to dismiss the possibility that Ramesh himself was the instigator. For one thing, he loves organising parties, and could easily have whipped up this little bash. It should also not be forgotten that he was once one of my suspects. There was a brief period – approximately twelve hours, if I remember correctly – when I considered him to be Bob's most likely killer. He had been bullied and abused by the man for years and I thought that he'd finally snapped.

He hadn't, of course. In fact, he was the sweetest, most loveably insane person I'd ever met. But what a twist that would make! Can you imagine? A few more people die, and I bounce from suspect to suspect before finally realising that – after twenty or so non-pet-related criminal investigations together – my best friend is the real killer! That would be a clever ending, though I've spoilt it now, so that's no good either.

I longed for the worst of all my fathers to be to blame, but Arthur spent so much of his time explaining boring facts to people that I doubt he had time for revenge. I couldn't dismiss the importance of the antagonistic Monopoly game on my fifteenth birthday, of course. Nor our family trip to the seaside when he refused to talk to me because I wouldn't accept that classical was the only real kind of music. Oh, and he was particularly unhappy when I bought him an Andy McNab book for Christmas, when he preferred Chris Ryan. Now that I come to think of it, he could be a precious little snowflake. Of course, as a teenager, I hadn't lived enough to realise just what a whiner he was.

Noémi and David were the only members of the group who I knew to have committed a crime – unless you count some of Ramesh's more garish outfits. My second cousin had been responsible for a particularly long con – in which she got her boyfriend to sleep with her mother to obtain money for the care of his supposedly ill father. It was despicable by anyone's standards, but I wasn't the one who uncovered it. Her mother was too clever and spotted their plan. When it came to the question of whether Noémi's swindling was proof that she had a killer instinct, the answer was no. Of course, the fact that she ended up stabbing her brother in the shoulder might just tip the balance.

Uncle Bradley was another fun choice. I think that even my mother – his own sister – would be unsurprised if the man she'd spent decades apologising for on a weekly basis had made such a hash of his life that he'd turned to… whatever was going on up on that mountain. He'd always been a desperate figure, but since his fiancée left him, his rich cousin who'd propped up his business had died, and he was dethroned as the central heating king of the East Midlands, his life had become a mess. Which explains why he was a pain, but not why he'd blame me for it.

So that just leaves Nicholas… I'd never learnt his surname. The only way I'd been able to track him down after we first met was because I knew he attended a pacifist society in London – which worked in his favour on the first case that had involved him and wouldn't hurt this time. When we were dating, he didn't appear to possess a phone or use the internet, and his small Balham apartment was mainly filled with toy-making equipment. The idea that he could be a killer was both enticing and appalling. Overall, I'd say he was mainly there to make up the numbers, but I suppose there are just as many movies about killer Santas as nice ones, so I couldn't say for certain that he was innocent.

Which left me where, exactly? All of them and none of them could be the killer. All of them and none of them could have tempted us there. What I couldn't say for certain was whether the extensive information that our puppet master clearly possessed on me was known to the wider public. Almost all of my cases had received a good write-up in the papers.

Hmmm... I'm not sure most people would use the term "a good write-up" to describe murder investigations.

The case involving Marco Romanelli had caught the attention of the European press, and my first one was such a novelty that a few British newspapers depicted me as a young Miss Marple. But perhaps there was something that the killer had mentioned in the letters which would help to narrow down the suspects.

For the moment, all I could do was go along with the others. Enough pancakes had been produced for three each, which led to the eternal debate of whether we should have two savoury and one sweet or vice versa. There was cheese and ham, tomato, pesto and chicken breast as fillings for the main course, and Wendy wisely put the combinations we made back in the pan for a minute to melt the cheese.

I'm going to go out on a limb here and say that she is just as nice as she now seems.

Who would have thought that the preparation of pancakes could teach us so many moral lessons?

In a long line, like the animals in the Hundred Acre Wood, we paraded to the dining room with our tasty treats, and then Ramesh returned to the kitchen with a trolley he found to transport the drinks. Everyone was in high spirits, and it really didn't feel as though we'd recently found a body or believed that Bradley had been killed in his van.

The wonder of pancakes!

I think it was more likely the wonder of alcohol that set the mood, but either way, we wolfed down our dinner.

"You know," Bradley said, glancing about at the expensive

furnishings, "I could get used to living in a place like this. Right swanky it is."

It was true that, though there was a sense of neglect to most rooms in Bron-Yr-Aur, the dining room was still in good condition. The tablecloth was in rich red damask, and it matched the backs of the upholstered chairs. There were ten of them spaced out around the table that spanned the length of the room, but only nine were occupied. I'm sure that Noémi would have liked to make that eight… not because she wanted to kill anyone (necessarily), but because she moved her chair as close as possible to Nicholas and would undoubtedly have sat in his lap if he'd let her.

She must have been a naughty girl if Father Christmas won't even allow that.

Although this was not the guest list I would ever have chosen for a dinner party, it was a nice feeling to know that people could get on even in the most adverse situations.

"I think we should play a game," Ramesh announced and, with a wink for me, he ran off to get supplies. "It's called, 'Who's Hates Izzy Most?' And it's a lot of fun."

He'd started to hand out slips of paper and pens, but I felt I should stop him. "Ra, I'm not sure about this."

"You don't know the rules yet."

"I can guess them!"

He winked once more, presumably to say, *This is the perfect way to gather evidence on our suspects,* and then he proceeded to ignore me. "All you have to do is write down why you and my dear friend Izzy have crossed swords over the years, and the person who comes up with the best story is the winner. Everyone has to argue their case, and then we'll vote on who is the most deserving entry. Don't you think that's a clever game?"

"Genius!" my own blood uncle exclaimed and set to work scribbling. "How do you spell *conceited?"*

"Very well," I said to exact a modicum of revenge. "And when that's done, we'll play, 'What's the Most Annoying Thing That Ramesh Has Ever Done?'"

I don't think that David said a word the whole time we were in there, and he frowned at this dubious pastime. As helpful as the game might have proved for the investigation, I wasn't looking forward to eight other people tearing me to shreds, so it was lucky that, just as things got going, there was a heavy bang on the ceiling above us, and we all fell silent.

"There's someone up there," Wendy announced in a frightened whisper. "We're not alone."

Chapter Twenty-One

David was the first on his feet. He's always been a strong man, but whatever exercise he'd done in prison had only made him fitter. He launched himself across the room and was through the door before I could catch up. I didn't look back to see who was following us but sprinted to the nearest set of stairs and then up to the first floor.

David paused on the landing to listen and, sure enough, we could hear a door slamming shut somewhere. At that, we both shot along the corridor to a point that was approximately above the dining room. Only one door was open and so he stopped and poked his head carefully around it.

"It looks empty."

I followed him and found myself in a large room with two ping-pong tables and a door leading off on either side.

"I'll take this one," I told him, but he grabbed me by the arm to disagree.

"No, Izzy. We should stay together. I don't want you getting hurt."

This was far from the most romantic thing he'd ever said to me, but it set my heart beating faster, despite myself. Ever since I'd seen him that afternoon, I'd been holding on to the fact that I was angry with him for forcing me from his life, but every time he spoke, every glance he bestowed upon me, made it hard to think of anything but long walks and Valentine's Day cards, moonlit dinners and horse-drawn carriages. He was a murderer, and I couldn't trust him one bit, but there was no question in my mind that I'd ever stopped—

"Izzy, come on!" He threw the nearest door open as I stood gawping.

Get it together, Izzy! This is zero hour. Go time. The final countdown!

I was all pumped up by now, but that room was empty too, and it appeared to have once been a small hairdressing salon. Or rather, there were pictures of people from the eighties with lots of different hairstyles, at least. And so, instead of coming face to face with the killer, I considered what I would look like with a perm.

David showed no such hesitation but shot back through the table tennis room to the far door. This time there was at least something to find behind it.

"Arthur's whisky," he murmured as we took in the sight of the half-empty bottle that was lying on its side on the top of a small round table.

There was a bright green military-style jacket on the chair next to it, and I was fairly certain from the smell that someone had recently been eating in there. I caught the definite scent of pickled onion crisps.

My goodness, Izzy! If this detective gig doesn't work out, perhaps you can enrol as a police dog.

"That must be what fell over." I pointed to a suit of armour on the floor not far away. It was holding an axe that was now buried in the floorboards of the small sitting room.

"Whoever tipped it over must still be hiding nearby," David concluded, and before I could answer, we heard the sound of someone dashing along the hall away from us.

Try though we certainly did, we were too slow to catch a glimpse of the fleeing figure. By the time we'd gone back through the neighbouring room and made it to the corridor, the mysterious armour-tipper had disappeared.

"There were ten chairs at the dining table," I said, thinking out loud. "Ten chairs but only nine of us."

David wasn't listening. As soon as he had a sense of which way our fugitive had gone, he started to move, but I had another idea. I followed him at a good pace, but when he took the stairs down, I went up a level. In the space of a minute, I'd navigated the long passageway to reach the run of bedrooms we'd been assigned. I saw Ramesh's name first, with Wendy's opposite. I found David's, Nicholas's, Noémi's, Edmund's and Arthur's before coming to the very end of the corridor, which we hadn't explored until then. There were three more rooms I hadn't seen before. My Uncle Bradley's was on my left. Mine was straight ahead and, to my right, on a printed paper sign, was the name of an old nemesis who hadn't shown her face yet.

Eilish Hart

I read the words, and something stirred deep within me. Obviously, if you haven't paid obsessive attention to my cases over the last few years, my big dramatic moment doesn't add up to much. If the truth be told, Eilish had only been involved in two of my less substantial, really comparatively short investigations, but suddenly the world I'd entered that day made sense.

Eilish was my flatmate at university. She was also one of the worst people I'd ever met. She'd taken a prime cut of steak from my freezer compartment and now that I say it, I do realise that's not as bad as any of the murders I've investigated. But a little over a decade later, when we'd crossed paths a second time, she was no less pleasant to be around. Though, to be fair, I did offend her by accusing her of murder on the basis that she'd once nicked some meat.

So perhaps she was no Genghis Khan, but she had said some very hurtful things about me when I'd first arrived at university and yes, that once again makes me sound as if I've held on to a grudge far beyond its shelf life. But if you'd seen Eilish's stupid hair, you'd— Nope, it's happening again. Nothing I'm saying is evidence of her evil nature in any way.

However, the fact that she'd been hiding in that house from us, had stolen Arthur's whisky and proceeded to run away when we'd gone to see what had happened suggested something more sinister was at play. And we mustn't forget, though I don't blame you if you have, that Marco Romanelli was murdered directly in front of the waterlogged donkey stall where Eilish worked. I'd seen her standing in the shadows when we went to inspect the scene of the crime. I'd even waved, and she ignored me entirely, presumably because she didn't want too much attention before exacting her diabolical plan in Wales.

The only thing I could think was that my conviction that she was a killer had turned her into the very thing she had denied being. I'd driven her to murder… which didn't reflect too brilliantly on me.

"There's no sign of anyone," David told me when I got downstairs.

"Did Ramesh and the others hear anything?" I asked, but as they hadn't even followed us to see what had made the noise, I didn't hold out much hope.

"We'll find out soon enough." This was the kind of thing that people on cop shows say that you never really hear in real life. It would have been cheesy coming out of most people's mouths, but in David's soft Welsh accent, it sounded just perfect.

"Of course I didn't hear anything," Ramesh replied a minute later when we rejoined the group. "Wendy took over my Bluetooth speaker and played Burt Reynolds' only album very loudly. There's a reason that he didn't record a follow-up. It was painful."

I must have made a face then, and it wasn't just because I knew of his love for David Hasselhoff's 1985 *masterpiece* 'Night Rocker', which, he liked to remind me, was a number one hit in Austria. No, the reason I looked at him like that was because I'd foolishly been expecting him to be at least a tad curious over whether we'd tracked down the killer.

"Don't look at me with your judgy face, Izzy." He stamped his foot then and reminded me of Pacino when he was in a bad mood. "We tried to remain nervous. We all tried very hard to consider the danger you'd placed yourselves in, but you took too long, and then someone suggested a dance party, so that's what we did."

"You had a dance party to the music of Burt Reynolds?" David felt the need to ask.

"For goodness' sake, David, try to pay attention. It was not through choice."

Just behind him, Wendy and the others were boogying about to the sound of a bluegrass guitar with Reynolds telling a story over the top in a folksy voice. She was really getting into it, and Arthur was do-si-doing around her. Despite his objections to the music, Ramesh couldn't resist tapping his toes and side stepping in time with the beat.

"Ra, I need to tell you something," I pulled him aside to whisper as David went in search of a drink. "I think that Eilish is here. There's a good chance I've driven her to kill."

"Ah, that's a shame. Who's Eilish?"

"My teenage nemesis who we met again in my university town when we investigated a series of terrible murders."

"Nope, doesn't ring a bell."

I huffed and kept going. "She once stole a steak from me, and I never forgave her?"

"That does sound like you, but I'm afraid I can't place anyone called Eilish." He tapped his lips and had a good think.

"She wouldn't let you ride a donkey even after you threw a tantrum?"

He immediately stopped dancing. "That psychopath! I knew from the very first moment that she had evil in her. What should we do? Place a piece of meat under a box with a long stick that will trip when she goes to eat it? Leave a trail of breadcrumbs down to the cellar and then lock her in? Tie her to a windmill propeller?"

"Where would we find— Actually, never mind." It's impossible not to get sucked into his madness at times. "I just want you to keep an eye out for her. I don't know for certain that she's the one who brought us here, but there's a weird kind of logic to it. For all the terrible people we've met over the years, few have taken such a personal dislike to me as Eilish Hart… Well, few who aren't in prison, at least."

"Leave it with me," he nodded knowingly, then continued dancing to the music he claimed not to like. He moseyed towards Noémi, who was already draped over poor Papa Noël. My uncle was still too weak from the run-in with the steering wheel of his van to get up for a jig, but he was doing all the arm dancing that he could manage.

The only person who refrained from the festivities was Edmund. I really hadn't done a good enough job of picking up his spirits, and I wished there was some way to bring him into the fold.

If a man isn't happy at a murder-scene hoe-down, when will he be?

I considered telling the others about Eilish, but I didn't see what good it would do, and so I went to talk to him instead.

"Is there anything I can do to turn your frown upside down?" I asked and immediately regretted sounding like a school guidance counsellor.

He clapped his hand and smiled in that hazy, imprecise way that only severely drunk people do. "You can grab a glass and help me finish this bottle before I pass out."

"Ooh, tempting, but perhaps rather than me joining you in a frankly worrying state, you could stop drinking and save us both a lot of trouble?"

I doubt he heard me as, instead of answering, he started rambling about his ex. "The worst thing about it is that I loved her. I truly loved her. She was sweet and evil and despicable and lovely, and I just wish the first month we spent together could have lasted forever."

He did a comedy drunken hiccup then, like a cat in a cartoon who accidentally swallows a bottle of beer when trying to catch a mouse. It slightly undermined his profession of love.

"It could be worse." I looked across at David, who was being manhandled by Wendy. I think she was trying to dance with him, but he must have turned down the offer, as she was moving his arms around like he was her puppet. "You could be in love with a murderer."

I suppose it took a few seconds for this to sink in, as those cloudy eyes of his travelled about the raucous scene in front of us before he responded. "David? You're talking about David, aren't you? You do still love him then?"

I nodded, though I can't say for certain that he saw. "I doubt I ever stopped."

"I wouldn't worry. As far as murderers go, he's one of the good ones." Another hiccup, and he looked as though he might fall face forward out of the chair. "Is that why you never called me?"

I wanted to answer, but I couldn't think of a response that was anything but insensitive.

"No, it's alright, Izzy. You don't have to say anything. You're a nice person. Nice people don't end up with rotters like me. I only ever meet gold diggers and nutters and the occasional backstabber. You're better off with David." He rose to standing then and took a moment to steady himself. "I think it's time I went to bed, Miss Palmer. But may I say one thing before I do?"

"Of course." I stood up to tower over him. I was long past the point of slouching to try to look shorter than the men I was with, and to be honest, I don't think he had much of a problem with my above average height in the first place.

"I want you to know that you're a good person, and I appreciate everything you've done for me this evening."

There wasn't much I could say to that, and so I went with, "You're very welcome."

He waved this away impatiently. "No, no. Listen, cos I won't have the courage to say it in the morning. I think you're great, Detective Palmer. I think you are one of the top four women I have met in my life. And I'm even including family members in that."

I couldn't help laughing at him. "You are very kind," I said, though I could have substituted that last word for *drunk*.

"I mean it, Izzy. You're a sweet, lovable person and you don't think highly enough of yourself."

"Yeah, okay." I glanced at the others and, when I turned back, Edmund was suddenly much closer. I don't know if it was the drink or his clumsy attempt at making a pass, but his lips brushed against me and he sort of leaned there for a moment, supporting his weight on my cheek. There was an awkward five seconds or so before he could right himself and, when he did, instead of addressing what had just happened, I said, "Are you sure you're alright? Do you want me to see you to your room or something?"

"Now there's a proposition, you saucy madam." He was already stumbling away. "But I'll be fine."

"I'll take him up there," David said in a tone that was as serious as a novel about… urmmm… poverty, maybe? And I realised that he'd seen the whole thing. "We wouldn't want anything bad to happen."

I stood right where I was and couldn't speak. I should have made light of the whole thing, but my tongue wouldn't do as it was told. They disappeared from the room, and I stood there hating myself.

So we solved one mystery that night. Who hated Izzy the most? It was Izzy.

Wait, this isn't going to turn into one of those weird psycho-whodunits where it turns out that the detective is suffering from a split-personality and is actually the killer?

Me? Suffering from a split personality? Whatever gave you such an idea?

Ha ha ha ha ha! I really don't know!

Oh, how we laughed!

The silent laughing came to a stop, and I was suddenly glad of Burt Reynolds's brief attempt at a music career. No one had noticed my bout of gormlessness, or perhaps they were just so used to it that they didn't say anything. When I came back to the land of the living, I was vaguely aware that there was something I'd forgotten.

I racked my brain trying to remember what it was and, when it finally came to me, I knew in an instant that I was already too late. Cue yet another scene of me running upstairs. Good old Father Christmas saw my panic and gave chase, which led to Noémi coming screaming after us. Ramesh never likes to be left out, so he was a little way behind. This just left Arthur, Wendy and Bradley jiving away obliviously. My last glimpse of the room reminded me of the final minutes of a wedding disco before they turn the lights up, and everyone realises that they don't look as cool as they'd imagined.

"David!" I yelled, as I thought he was more likely to hear me. "Edmund!" I added as, why not?

No one called back, but I was still only on the first floor, and they would easily have made it to the second by then. I'd had plenty of things to curse myself for that day, but this was the biggest. I knew why all that alcohol had been left for us, so how could I have fallen into the killer's trap so blindly?

"David, where is he?" I shouted down the corridor when I saw him coming towards me. "Where did you put Edmund?"

"I made sure he got into his room and left it at that. I'm not his babysitter." He clearly couldn't understand what the trouble was, but turned around when I ran straight past him to the door which bore Edmund's name.

There was a terrible sound as I reached the larger suites that the killer had assigned us. It was like a ton of bricks falling to earth, and potential explanations listed in my brain. The reality was somehow even worse.

"We fell for it," I said to myself as much as anyone who happened to have followed me.

I stood in the doorway to Edmund's room and took in the scene. There was a four-poster bed against the far wall. Its thick wooden posts were ornately carved with birds, leaves and woodland animals, and it looked old and expensive, but the bed itself was a mess. It was hard to make out what had happened at first, but there was a net hanging down on one side of it and, in the centre of the bed, a large collection of heavy iron weights were dotted across the bedcovers. I was praying that Edmund would slope from the bathroom and ask what all the noise was, but I knew it wasn't going to happen. As my eyes made sense of the carnage, I could make out a pair of arms and legs beneath the shrapnel and a splash of blood soaking into the bedsheets.

Chapter Twenty-Two

I wanted to cry but I couldn't. I wanted to run from that house and never have anything to do with murders and murderers again, but I couldn't. David and Nicholas moved past me to see whether there was anything they could do for poor Edmund, while Ramesh and Noémi stayed behind to comfort me.

My cousin had never been a touchy-feely sort of person, and she'd rarely said a kind word to me, so I wasn't expecting to feel her arm around my waist and her head on my shoulder as Ramesh did the same on the other side.

"It was all set up for us," David whispered, before changing to a furious shout. "Make sure that no one goes into any of the other bedrooms."

He'd evidently realised the same thing that I had. The booze, the food, the warm welcome: we'd been lulled into a false sense of security before the killing began. I should have realised why there were names on the doors. Our tormentor wanted to divide us up so that we were easy to pick off. I wondered when the attack on me would come, which is a very selfish thing to consider when standing over the body of a friend.

"There was a net suspended from the top of the four posts." Father Christmas pointed up to the section that was concealed by a navy velvet curtain. "When Edmund lay down on the bed, the net was loosened and the weights fell on top of him. That poor, poor man."

It felt wrong for that symbol of childhood innocence – or at least an eccentric man who believed he was Santa – to appear in such a violent scene. He looked down at Edmund and saw the same tangled mess that I'd witnessed when I first arrived. The only silver lining I could find to any of this was the fact that the victim had been about twenty-four sheets to the wind when he collapsed on his bed and a ton of metal crushed him. I had to hope that he didn't suffer for long.

If there were doubts over whether his sister didn't like you before this, you can be sure that she's no fan now.

"I don't know what to do, Izzy," Ramesh mumbled into my shoulder, and I assumed that the sight of yet another dead body had sobered him up. I appreciated his affection but knew that I could no longer wander about the place, hoping that no one else would get hurt. They were all there because of me, and I was the one who had to catch the killer. So I stopped being such a baby and found my voice.

"No one touch the body or the metal or even the bed. We should leave right now to preserve the crime scene."

David and Ramesh stepped back outside, as if the room itself could hurt them.

"I'll see if I can get a signal anywhere," Noémi announced and escorted her red and white admirer from the room. They swayed off down the hall ahead of us as David shut the door to Edmund's bedroom.

"I'm sorry," he told me, his voice softer and more considerate than ever. "I know you liked him and… Well, I'm sorry."

I wanted to interrupt. I wanted to tell him that, until that day, I'd thought of Edmund as a rich playboy who saw me as a curiosity. I'd never imagined that he wanted a relationship. Of course, I couldn't say any of that because the man was now dead, and it would have sounded insensitive. So, all I could utter was a brief, cold, "Thank you," as we returned to the ground floor.

The dancing in the dining room had wound down, and Burt Reynolds's album had presumably come to an end. Wendy and Arthur were lying on the floor together, and Bradley had fallen asleep in his chair. All that was missing was the definitive sound of a needle jumping past the end of the last track to tell us that the party was truly dead.

I didn't see what good it would do to disturb them, so I turned instead to the younger members of the group.

"I still have to interview everyone." I admit this sounded like a futile gesture. What sense was there in treating a haunted house like Bron-Yr-Aur as a normal crime scene? Well, it gave me something to cling onto, so that's what I would do. "Noémi, I need you to come with me."

I imagine this was the last thing she wanted. She would probably have preferred to make the most of the sadness of Edmund's death to get closer to sexy Sinterklaas. I didn't care about that, so I told David to make sure that no one else left and took Noémi to the ballroom.

"I need to ask you something above all else," I told her as soon as we were alone. "Do you hate me?" I probably sounded like an overemotional child, but I had to get a sense of the girl before me.

I'd been eleven years old when we first met, and her cruelty and rejection had scarred me for years. On our second meeting, she'd at least pretended to tolerate me before showing her true colours. So who was she now?

"That's a very strange question to ask, dear cousin," she said in an offended tone. "I don't think that I hate anybody."

I hadn't expected any more from her, but I was determined to get it. Standing in the middle of the pine-floored room, I pushed on. "You have every reason not to like me. I was there to witness the greatest shame in your life. From the sound of things, you were lucky to avoid prison for what you did to extract money from your mother. No one would have known about your crime if I hadn't been there."

There were no chairs for her to lounge upon, and so she tried to look sultry and confident standing up. "Yes, but it would never have come to that if I hadn't chosen to do such a thing." Her smile grew, and the weight upon her shoulders seemed to lighten. "I'm a different person. I've learnt my lesson."

I wasn't buying it. "Your mother was so horrified by your behaviour that she killed herself and made it look as though you were to blame. I'm sorry if it makes me a cynic, but I struggle to believe that you've seen the light."

"I'm not saying I'm a saint. I'm telling you that I'm not the person I was. People can change, Izzy. Or do you believe that your lovely David is nothing more than a murderer?"

It irked me that she even knew who David was, let alone what he had done. Happy with her retort, she wandered away to kick the balloons on the other side of the room. They were larger than the type you get at children's parties and looked like giant pearls.

"There's a difference between him and you," I told her. "He did a bad thing for a good reason and served his time. You did a bad thing for yourself and got away with it." I wanted to find a way to scratch the surface of her well-buffed exterior. "What happened to your boyfriend?"

"Which one?"

"The one who helped you swindle your mother?"

She considered the question for a moment. "I'm afraid you'll have to be a little more specific."

"The French one!"

"Keep going."

I let out a groan. "His name was Frederic or Ferdinand or something like that. The only boyfriend I've ever met."

It finally clicked. "Oh, Fabian! No, no. As soon as the excitement of our underhand scheme had gone, and it was clear that Mother had left me next to nothing in the will, I realised that little Fabi wasn't for me."

"I take it all back. You truly are an innocent flower."

She kicked the closest balloon so that it went ricocheting into the others. "You're missing the point entirely. After Mother died, I was left with practically nothing. I had a flat and about £50,000 in savings."

"That's not nothing by most people's standards, you—"

It was probably a good thing she interrupted before I said something rude. "But I had no career or friends. Even my brother didn't want to see me."

"Maybe because you stabbed him?"

Nothing I said had any effect on her. She was determined to finish her explanation. "Fine, forget all that. The worst thing that happened was that I drove my own mother to suicide. I have to live with the knowledge that she didn't just want to escape from this world but punish me so greatly that I would end up in prison for murdering her." She had to take a deep breath then and, for perhaps the first time in my life, I caught a fragmentary glimpse of the person beneath the expensive makeup. "I treated her like dirt, but if you'd ever asked me who I loved most in the world, it was her without a doubt. I realised after she died that it is possible to be a terrible person without realising it."

She truly sounded sorry for her behaviour, which only made me more suspicious.

"You didn't just fish a few quid from her purse, you swindled hundreds of thousands of pounds from her. It wasn't an accident. You plotted to defraud her so that your already comfortable existence would be even more luxurious."

I wanted her to disagree. I wanted to hold on to the idea that she hated me for the part I'd played in her downfall. I wanted a nice simple solution to everything that had happened that month, but she wouldn't be the one to provide it.

She moved deeper into the sea of balloons, like a sinner wading out into a river to be baptised. And when she was surrounded, she stopped and turned back to me. "You're right. Everything you've said is true, and that's why I can't blame you for what happened. I blame myself. If anything, you saved me. I was an awful, awful person, and you showed me the error of my ways." She smiled then. Perhaps it was the cliché she'd just spouted that caused it, or perhaps it was a sign of her gratitude. "And there's another, more concrete reason I could never hate you."

"Oh, really." I should have dialled back the cynicism, but it came so naturally.

"If it weren't for you, I would have been found guilty of my mother's murder. And you can be sure that they wouldn't have let me out for good behaviour or whatever stroke of luck befell your boyfriend. I would have spent decades in there. And that was what enabled me to pick myself back up again. When I was all alone without a friend in the world. When I really felt that there was no point in living, I realised how lucky I was to have a second chance. And that was all thanks to you."

I suppose it was the emotion of everything that had happened that night, but I felt tears forming in my eyes and really wanted to believe her. More than that, I wanted her to be an actual cousin, and not just some nasty girl I saw once a decade. Perhaps she sensed all this, as she moved towards me, and the balloons bounced against one another a little more violently than before. One knocked into another, and the chain reaction led to the whole flock of them bristling and bumping and, in a moment, there was an ear-splitting crash.

I saw Noémi's shock as a line of large china plates that were sitting on a high shelf came smashing to the ground, one after another like dominos. The first was already in pieces right where she'd been standing moments before, and the look on her face was one of pure horror. It took me a moment to work out what was happening, but it was clear that the china was all linked together and, when one fell, it brought the next one down with it.

The room was immense, and the shelf spanned all four walls, so that it took the best part of thirty seconds for this seemingly spontaneous reaction to finish. By the time it had, I'd reached Noémi and put my arms around her as she stood there shaking. The sound of silence rung in our ears as the crack, crack, crack of plate after plate – like an undiminishing echo – finally subsided.

"It's another trap," I said to explain the strange spectacle, though not why anyone would have done such a thing. "One of the balloons must have had a cord tied to it which sent the crockery falling."

"This one was…" She pulled me closer, and I could hear her sobs just that little bit too loudly. "This one was for me. I should be dead like Edmund."

Chapter Twenty-Three

Whatever I might have thought of Nicholas's sanity, he was a genuinely kind and caring person. He was the perfect choice to look after the shaken victim of the most recent attack. Of course, I have no doubt that people have questioned the real Father Christmas's sanity from time to time. A bloke who dresses up in red and flies about the place doling out gifts for free? He must be some kind of crazy socialist!

David had taken the time while I was away to make coffee for everyone. This meant that a few of our companions who had enjoyed the drink a little too much looked rather embarrassed as they sat in the lounge once more. At least Bradley was walking about again, and the wound on his head had stopped bleeding, but he wouldn't make eye contact with anyone. I noticed that Wendy and Arthur were no longer buddying up, either, but had placed themselves on opposite sides of the fireplace and seemed deeply interested in the carpet beneath their feet.

As the room we'd spent the most time in without anyone suffering an injury, the lounge seemed like the safest place to be. I was trying to remain objective about the identity of the killer, even as everyone there showed me their best faces. It felt as though each suspect was interviewing for a job. I was well aware that none of them were going to give too much away for fear of incriminating themselves, and so it was down to me to see through their careful phrasing to what lay beneath.

Noémi was a perfect example of this. There were few people I'd known in my life who I thought so poorly of. Several of the murderers I'd sent to prison were more sympathetic characters than my second cousin. She was the definition of a spoilt brat. So of course she was going to tell me that she'd changed and it was all thanks to me.

The biggest problem was that I'd believed every word of it. Was this a sign of softness or stupidity on my part? Should I have raked her over the coals until she confessed to her crimes? It did not go unnoticed that, at the key moment of her emotional speech, she caused – whether unwittingly or not – a literal chain reaction which created any amount of noise and spectacle but left her entirely unscathed. If I'd had to pick one person from the group based on their attitude alone, then it would be Noémi Castleton.

Except, that wasn't quite true. If I was making that decision based on personal experience, there was someone who would have tied for first place in the nasty stakes.

"We have to find Eilish," I announced to break the silence, and it made me wonder what everyone else had been thinking about all this time. "I don't know why anyone would bring us here or why they felt the need to kill off my past suspects if I'm the one they want, but this is something I can control."

"Sorry," Wendy said in a cautious voice, "but who's Eilish?"

"It's a long story," Ramesh replied wearily. "But basically, she's Izzy's nemesis."

"I thought I was your nemesis." Wendy's ill-timed joke was delivered in an apologetic tone.

"Her university nemesis," her ex-colleague clarified. Wait, I mean her ridiculously dressed cat-loving, new-father, former colleague, not me or David. Gosh, what a lot of Porter & Porter employees were there. It was a bit like a reunion.

Oh, please no. Not another reunion.

David helped get the conversation back on track. It was one of his many talents. "Her name is on one of the bedroom doors, and we think she was the one who took the bottle of whisky and made all that noise upstairs before Edmund was killed."

Arthur put his hands to his head at this moment as if the most distressing thing that had happened that night was the theft of some scotch.

"How are we going to find her?" Ramesh's frivolity had long since drained from him and he contemplated the task before us with uncharacteristic solemnity.

"I haven't a clue." I peered about the room as though this would provide the answer. "We already know how difficult hide-and-seek is in this house. She could be anywhere."

"Come along, Izzy," Arthur demanded in his public-school-teacher-from-the-fifties voice. "You can do better than this. Pull yourself together and find the solution."

"What help have you been?" David stepped into the circle of sofas to ask him. "All you've done since I got here is criticise."

"I beg your pardon," Arthur replied as he rose to his feet, ready for an argument.

"Fine, you're forgiven." David stared the man down.

"That's not what I meant. I meant…" Suddenly rather nervous, Arthur looked around him for support and even Wendy wouldn't return his gaze. "I was just trying to encourage my stepdaughter."

"Former stepdaughter," Ramesh said, so that I didn't have to.

"Yes… former…"

Nooooo! Don't make us feel sorry for you, Arthur. You are a swine and you do not deserve our sympathy.

Exactly!

But look at him, Izzy: that poor guy. Make it better!

To stop my brain from getting too emotional, I decided to defuse the situation… whilst hopefully showing the old bully the error of his ways. "Don't worry, everyone. Arthur doesn't mean any harm. He just speaks without thinking."

My mother's second husband nodded slowly in my direction. "Thank you, Izzy. That's very…" He couldn't find the right word so left the sentence unfinished.

"We could split up into groups and search the house simultaneously," Nicholas suggested, as Santa doesn't like it when children argue.

"It's too dangerous," David replied with a huff of breath. It was past eleven o'clock by now and we were all tired, so I could understand why he would be so frustrated. "For one thing, we don't know what other death traps the killer has set. I think we should stay here all together, wait out the storm, and hope for the best."

Before anyone could disagree, I felt the most unexpected sensation. No, it wasn't some revelation that came to me at just the right moment. It was a buzzing in my pocket.

"I've got a signal!" I practically screamed with joy and pulled out my phone to see what it was. A few of the others gathered round as I saw that there were about thirty missed calls from Janet Ellison, a few from my mother, and a text message from my stepdad – I mean, my nice stepdad back in London. It just said…

Good evening, Izzy,

I hope you are very well.

In case it isn't automatically clear, Greg was formal in all his written correspondence.

A journalist called by to talk to us. She tells us that you've gone to Wales for some reason, and she can't contact you.

Please let us know that everything is alright.

Best Wishes,

Gregory

"Write back!" Ramesh yelped. "Quick, Izzy. Write back while there's still enough of a signal. Tell him to send the police."

Noémi had already taken out her far fancier phone and was trying 999 herself. "I can't connect. I just keep getting the same dropped call sound."

"Me neither," Wendy confirmed. "You must be blessed, Izzy." She still had the same grouchy voice as when we'd worked together, and it was hard to conceive that the things she was saying to me were now… nice.

Noémi was walking back and forth around the room to search for a signal and, by the time I pressed send on my message, it was already too late.

"Nothing," I told the others. "I get that little clock symbol, so it's not even leaving my phone."

"We can't just stay here." Ramesh was definitely more serious than he'd been all afternoon. He likes nothing better than a costume change, so I was surprised he hadn't swapped outfits to signify the switch. "A group of us should go looking for Eilish and the rest of us can walk around the grounds in the hope we can contact the police."

David had slipped into his role as not just the manager, but the wise head and conscience of the group. "Very well. But if you're going outside, use the torches on your phones to check you don't stand on anything nasty."

I could see a few of them thinking, *Does he mean dog's mess?* And so I put them out of their misery in the most polite way I could think of.

"Thank you, David, for making the very good point that the killer could have set traps outside as well as in."

Uncle Bradley was a man of very simple humour and had to clutch his tummy. because he was laughing so hard. "Here, Iz. I thought he was talking about—"

I decided to change the topic. "So everyone's clear on what we have to do?"

There was no discussion of who would go where, as pretty much everyone believed that they would be the person whose phone would achieve the miraculous feat of contacting the authorities. The others all left the room. David and I looked at one another but stood right where we were, either side of the tall window where we'd sat to talk hours earlier.

"Of course, I don't know for certain that Eilish is to blame," I muttered.

He seemed happy to have something to talk about. "I've been thinking about that, and we know that the car brakes were cut when we went to look for the others. Do you remember that I thought I saw something through the window?"

"Do we really know anything?" I felt I had to ask. "The killer could have been hiding outside and doing each car as people turned up."

"Which would suggest even more that it's Eilish we're after. I assume you were in here with the others before I arrived?"

It was hard to keep the events of that never-ending night straight in my head, and so I tried to think back through what had happened. "I got here sometime after four o'clock. People arrived in ones and twos, and I guess you were here by five. Is that right?"

I don't think he invested the gesture with any particular meaning, but he wandered closer, and it made me feel both more nervous and somehow safer. "That sounds about right."

"Okay, well, between those times, Ramesh and I went off to look about the house and that was when we found the already dead man."

"Who you think must be the caretaker?"

"That's the one." It really says something about my life when there are so many corpses that it gets hard to distinguish between them.

"So you're saying that one of the group could have slipped out while you were exploring. They saw to the cars and then joined in with hide-and-seek so that they'd have a chance to do mine."

"That's assuming they cut your brakes along with everyone else's, but yes." I sat down on the window seat and felt as though I'd been on my feet for days. "Noémi was the one who suggested they play it, though I doubt that would be enough to convict her of murder. And it was Arthur who told everyone to go to the top floor of the house. That would have given him time to mess with the brakes if he was to blame."

He didn't answer immediately but dropped to sitting and, just for a moment before he pulled away, I could feel the warmth of his arm against mine.

Stop being a silly little romantic, Izzy. First stop the killer from murdering us, then you can be all lovey-dovey with Hannibal Lecter.

I would have pointed out that David was not, to my knowledge, a cannibal, but I didn't like where that conversation would have taken me, and we really had been talking about 'The Silence of the Lambs' too much already.

"The question I keep coming back to is why?" I couldn't imagine what he was questioning, so I waited for him to explain. "Why set the traps?"

"That's obvious," I told him, as I was a far more experienced detective than he was. "The killer couldn't guarantee that there would be enough time to murder people without anyone noticing. Imagine that Arthur had gone off with Ramesh and come back with Ramesh dead. It would be obvious that Arthur was to blame."

"You think that Arthur is the killer?"

Yes.

"No, that was just an example. By getting here before us and leaving tricks and snares about the place, the killer could ensure that they could complete the plan without detection. What they can't do, however, is guarantee that the nasty surprises they've designed will actually work. To be quite honest, the falling plate routine in the ballroom just now was dramatic but ineffective. The chances that Noémi would be killed by one of them were pretty low."

Something must have occurred to him then, as I could see just how excited he became. "Have you considered the fact that Noémi herself may have known what would happen when she kicked the balloons? Perhaps she was the one who set the plates to fall in order to suggest that she's suffered an attack and isn't the killer."

I tapped his hand patronisingly, and not just because I wanted to feel his fingers under mine. "Have I ever asked you whether you know how to do your job? When you were my boss, did I pop into your office to check that you were using a spreadsheet correctly?"

"Sorry, Izzy." He flipped his hand around to squeeze mine and my throat got blocked for a second. I swear that I couldn't breathe because my heart had leapt from my ribcage in an escape attempt.

Rather than melt in front of him or show just how much electricity he had sent through my body with this simple and – let's be honest – fraternal gesture, I kept talking. "I have every possible twist known to detectives and murder mystery readers up here." I pointed at my skull in case he didn't understand. "Killer fakes an attack to prove her own innocence? Tick. The narrator is secretly the culprit? Hopefully that doesn't apply in this instance, but also tick. Every suspect is to blame? Double, triple, quadruple tick."

He had a habit of waiting for a beat or two before responding, and his eyes seemed to draw a circle around me as he did so. "I should never have doubted you."

"No, please do. If no one ever doubted Poirot or Miss Marple, the killers would be far warier and probably not commit any crimes around them. People underestimate me because I'm a youngish woman with weird friends and no formal qualifications to be a detective. It certainly helps me worm out the culprits."

He smiled, not just with his lips, but his eyes too. There was a dancing light behind them, and I had to look over to check that the fire had burnt down, as it was so much like a flame that I felt it must be a reflection.

I thought he would offer another light-hearted reply to continue our easy banter, but he stopped himself and had something more important to say. "I didn't just come here to make sure you were okay, Izzy. The truth is that I couldn't stand to leave things as they were when you left my house. Not only because I hate the idea of you seeing me as a pathetic man with no job, living at home with my parents, but because you were right."

"I was right?" I echoed, as I wasn't used to anyone saying such a thing. "I mean, of course I was right, but it happens so often you really must be more specific."

"When you said that I should have trusted you. You were right."

I was happy to go along with this but knew that I hadn't said anything of any great value. I'd gone to Swansea to tell him off but lost my voice and fainted instead.

"And before you say it, I know you didn't utter the words, 'you should have trusted me'. I read them on your unhealthily pale face as soon as you arrived. And so, you were right."

I wanted to respond, but I couldn't. My throat was oddly numb and even my movements were sluggish. I think I took my hand from his, but no words emerged from my mouth as I had intended. Instead, I just studied him again to see if I could detect any other differences that had emerged in the years we'd spent apart.

I must have taken too long, as he soon went back to what he was saying.

"I should never have pushed you away from me, not just when I was arrested and before the trial but ever since. I should have written really very dull and repetitive letters to you every day and not made you feel miserable because I decided that the only way you could be happy was if you lived your life without me. You should have been the first person I saw when I came out of prison."

I wanted to cry or laugh or touch him then, but nothing came. It felt like one of those dreams where good things start to happen and some nagging self-awareness tells you, *Don't get too excited, Izzy. This is very unlikely to be real.*

That's me! I do that for you, and you are welcome!

I wanted to tell him that, if this was how he felt, there were no more obstacles left and we could finally be together, but instead I sat with my head slumped, looking down at my hands. I wanted to go back to how things had been on our first date. I wanted him to reminisce about charcuterie boards and make fun of me for sitting on avocados and my spontaneous Welsh accent.

When I finally looked up again, it wasn't at him, but at the far corner of the room where the wood-panels on the wall met the plaster moulding. It took me a moment to work out why this was noteworthy, but then it suddenly clicked.

"Look at that." I pointed across at a beige box with a metal grill on the front. "It's a speaker."

He must have thought I was changing the topic for the sake of it, but he maintained his gentle tone of voice. “Izzy, I don’t think you understand what I’m trying to say.”

I let out a really inappropriate laugh and was only thankful I didn’t say anything rude. “No, David, I don’t think you understand what I’m trying to say. That speaker must be part of a P.A. system. I’ve seen more of them in other rooms around the house. I reckon it was installed for announcements when this place was run as a hotel. You know the kind of thing.” I put on a funny voice as… well, it couldn’t get much worse than it already was. “‘Hello there, beloved guests. In five minutes in the tea lounge, Del Smalls and his very big band will be performing the hits of Gershwin. Meanwhile, if you’re in the mood for a dance, our tango teacher, Señora Mickelson, will be running her thrice-weekly beginner’s class in the ballroom. There’s something for everyone here at the Bron-Yr-Aur Hotel.’”

This impromptu skit had gone on far too long and so I was incredibly grateful when he interrupted.

“Izzy, why are you saying any of this?”

“Because we can send a message to Eilish. If she’s here in the building, we can tell her to come out and talk.”

Chapter Twenty-Four

Weirdo.

My brain wasn't happy, and it/he/she wasn't the only one.

Incompetent weirdo.

I'm sorry. I really am.

Incompetent, never-knows-how-to-read-the-room, boyfriendless weirdo!

David didn't look too pleased either as we searched the house for the control panel for the speaker system that I imagined must exist and, perhaps less likely, still be in working order.

"I at least have an idea where we should look this time," I told him with all the false confidence of a person who has interrupted a tender moment with the love of her life to say, "Look at that!"

At least you didn't run off when he was facing the other way.

"That's good," he murmured, but no more would be said until we found our prize. I'd noticed when I first arrived that there was a small room near the front door which would presumably once have functioned as a reception. There was a door that I figured must lead to the back of it in the bar where I'd talked to Edmund, so that's where I took us.

"See," I exclaimed, as though this was an argument I just had to win. "There's the microphone and control panel. I had a feeling they would still be in place."

We'd entered a very drab office with a few dusty desks and stacks of chairs that hadn't been used for decades. At one end of it, there was a corner table which held the P.A. system. Though the hotel may have closed down in the 90s, as David had previously said, this machine must have been installed thirty years before that. It had dials! Dials! What machines do people make today that still have dials?

Toasters?

Touché.

"I'll give it a go," David had rediscovered some of his usual smoothness and sat down at the desk.

For a moment, he looked like a Second World War radio operator, and I half expected him to pick up the headset and listen in for mayday calls. He flicked a few switches, but there was no sign of life, and so he brought his fist down in front of him in a gesture of slightly exaggerated disappointment.

"You might want to plug it in first," I suggested, and bent down to do just that. "It's amazing how much better things work when they have electricity buzzing through them."

"You, Izzy Palmer…" He held extended one finger to show exactly who he was referring to. "…are hilarious." This might have been true, but my comment hadn't even raised a smile.

This time, when he flicked the power switch, the little meters flashed a cosy orange colour, and the needles started moving on the gauges in front of us. He pressed a button and tapped the head of the microphone so that an audible thud could be heard coming from the room next door.

"Your turn." He got out of my way, and I took his place at the mic.

As tempting as it was to shout, *Good morning, Vietnam!* it was almost midnight, and we were up a mountain somewhere on the border between Powys and Carmarthenshire.

"Hi, Eilish," I said instead, and my own voice leaked back through the door to me a split second later. "I imagine that was you that we heard upstairs earlier. Your name's on one of the bedroom doors, too, so I suppose you received a letter to come here. It was probably offering you something nice or the chance to meet someone interesting. That seems to be the pattern that the killer used to get everyone to come."

I looked up at David and he urged me to say more.

"I know it must have been scary when you got here and saw me with the others. We obviously haven't had the best relationship over the years, and I imagine that you were worried that I would accuse you of a crime again. I have a bit of previous as far as that's concerned, which is why I thought I should talk to you like this. You see, I don't think you're to blame for what's been happening here. If you even know what that is in the first place."

I was starting to ramble, so I took a deep breath and tried to concentrate. "All I really want to tell you is that I think you'd be safer if you come out from wherever you're hiding and tell me your story. We've already found some dangerous traps in this house, and I think you'd be better off if—"

"Izzy?" a voice whispered from over in the doorway and so I yelled, "Quick, David, get her!" There was a blur of movement and I called out again just in time. "No, stop, I didn't mean it."

Eilish and David looked at me like I'd been born with half a pound of cheese in place of a brain.

"I don't know what came over me." I held my hands to my mouth in shame. "The most inappropriate thing possible popped from my mouth, but I didn't actually mean to say it. Doesn't that ever happen to you?"

"No," Eilish grunted. "And it wasn't funny."

"It wasn't supposed to be!"

Of the three of us, I believe that David looked the most uncomfortable. His eyebrows hadn't descended twenty seconds after I'd made my boo boo. My brain, meanwhile, found the whole thing hilarious.

Ahhhhhhhhhhhhhhhhhhhh! Ha ha ha! Ahhhhhh!

Stop it! You are always getting me into trouble, and I've had enough. Be normal!

"I really am sorry," I promised Eilish, in the hope I might win her trust again. "I just need to have a conversation. I swear that I'm not trying to pin anything on you."

She eventually shrugged and turned around to head back into the neighbouring room. I wasn't sure at first what this meant for our potential interview.

"Well, are you coming?" she stuck her head back inside to enquire in her usual gruff tone, and I hurried forward to follow her.

She sat down in the very same chair that Edmund had been in a couple of hours earlier and looked quite pleased with herself. "I was asleep behind the drinks cabinet. Your chattering woke me up."

"Why didn't you hide somewhere further away?" David asked with a note of concern in his voice.

Eilish curled her lip like he was stupid. She may not be the deranged delinquent I'd made her out to be, but she was certainly the least charming person in England (and perhaps beyond). "I tried that before, and a bloody suit of armour went and tried to bloody kill me."

"We saw the aftereffects," I said. "What triggered it?"

Eilish clearly wouldn't trust me for some time but rolled her shoulders like a boxer and answered all the same. "I didn't do nothing. I just walked up to him, and he fell on me. I thought I was gonna die."

To be quite honest, in her green army vest and black jogging bottoms, she looked as though she could have beaten a suit of armour in a fight. This, combined with her closely shaven head, made her look like a boxer in training.

"And then you ran?" I took the chair opposite hers and David stood behind me, ever the dedicated overseer.

"That's right. I couldn't make out what was going on here. As far as I know, you lot could be one of them sex cults you hear so much about."

I was about to ask her what this meant, but I really didn't want to know.

"That doesn't explain why you hid from us in the first place," David said before my brain could force me to talk about sex cults. "You could have come through the front door and introduced yourself like everyone else."

She snorted at this. Her porcine features had only become more pronounced since our university days. "Doubt it mate, not after what I saw."

"What did you see?" he and I both asked at the same moment, and I, for one, was thinking that we'd finally found the key to the whole case.

"I saw you arriving just after me, dit'n't I, Izzy?"

"Oh."

"That's right. I drive five thousand miles across Britain..." I have to interrupt for just one moment to point out that Southorpe to the Brecon Beacons is about a five-hour drive in normal conditions. "...and whose car do I see pulling into the car park but Izzy bleeping Palmer's." She didn't say bleeping, of course, but this is a family friendly TV programme. "I was tempted to turn around and head home, I can tell you. But after you didn't get out of the car for a few minutes, I crept inside the house and saw a couple of blokes chatting away in the lounge. I decided to explore the place before I spoke to anyone."

"That must have been Edmund and Arthur," I explained to David. "They got here before me."

Eilish continued her tale. "I walked about the house trying to understand why the British Society of Donkey Handlers would hold their annual AGM here."

David looked seriously confused by this, and I was torn between explaining the mention of donkeys and correcting Eilish's redundant use of the first word in the phrase annual *Annual* General Meeting. I figured we were already on shaky ground and went for the former.

"Eilish runs the donkey stand in Southorpe-on-Sea."

The previous snort was replaced with a sniff. "I don't just run it," she said most proudly. "I own the place. I bought it outright last year. That must be why the BSDH asked me to be their chairperson. If the rain in Britain ever stops falling this season, I'm hoping to make a killing." Her smile curled up at this moment, before she noticed her poor choice of words and issued a correction. "Wait, I don't mean a real killing. I've never so much as broken no one's arm before, no matter what Skunk from The Shank and Garotte might tell you."

There was a definite wince on her face as she recalled whatever terrible memory this brought back to her.

"So you had a look around the house…?" David prompted her ever so politely in his sweet and musical voice.

"That's right, I had a poke about, and do you know what I found?"

"A bottle of whisky?" I dared ask.

"Nahhh, that was later when you were all storming about the place. I found a dead man tied to a chair. And that was when I really freaked out." There was a hint of fear in her usual undeservedly arrogant tone. "Seriously, I lost my head and just ran. There were voices coming from the front exit, so I bombed it upstairs and hid in the first room I came to. It was basically a cupboard, but there was a box in it I could hide behind and, about ten minutes later, you lot opened the door and were talking about all sorts of weird stuff. I waited until you were gone from that floor and then legged it outside as fast as I could."

She needed a moment to calm down, and I waited for her to continue. That didn't happen, so I rudely prodded her along. "And then what did you do?"

"I got to my car alright, but when I had to reverse out of the space, I could tell that something was wrong. The brakes weren't working."

"So you weren't the one who cut them?" David asked, as he'd apparently been forming some conclusions of his own. My sleuthing was already rubbing off on him.

Miaow! I wouldn't mind rubbing off on—

Stop it!

She gave him some serious side-eye. "Why would I cut the brakes on my own car? You reckon I'm a total idiot or something? Mate, do you reckon I'm an idiot? I've got a degree!"

It was nice to see that Eilish hadn't lost her ability to fly off the handle over nothing. She normally got like that when she'd been drinking.

"No, I didn't cut my own brakes, nor anyone else's, if that's what happened."

David looked at me then and I knew what he meant. He meant, *This feels significant. Either there's someone else running about here cutting people's brakes and setting traps, or one of our existing suspects used the hide-and-seek game as an opportunity to divert attention.*

I looked back to say, *Or Eilish is lying, and we can't trust a word she's just said.* And, to my surprise, he nodded as though he'd understood. For a moment, I felt as though our minds had melded, which immediately made me worried that he knew all that my brain has been thinking.

Hellooooo there, David. How you doin'?

I don't know whether Eilish noticed this silent back-and-forth, but she continued her explanation without calling us names. "I wasn't going to hang around outside in the rain, and I didn't want to get killed in my car if a murderer spotted me, so I came back into the house, nicked the first alcohol I could find – which, by the way, tastes as though it cost too much money. What's wrong with supermarket-brand white rum? Eh? What's wrong with not taking out a mortgage to buy a bleedin' drink?"

There really was no answer to such a question. I felt as though I were interviewing an angry goldfish who needed regular reminders of the task at hand. "I will pass your thoughts on to the person who bought the whisky. What happened after that?"

She became sullen. Nope, that doesn't make sense. She became even *more* sullen. "I drank the whisky, dun I? I went up to one of the rooms I'd already heard you looking in and got drunk to make the time pass."

She wiped her nose on the back of her tattooed hand. In case anyone was wondering, the tattoo was of a cartoon Margaret Thatcher with an axe in her hand, sitting on the back of a large pig who was chasing a farmer who bore a striking resemblance to Freddie Mercury. Yes, it was surprisingly detailed and, no, I have no idea what any of it was supposed to mean.

David leaned against the back of my chair as he asked another sensible question. "Right, so that was when you upset the suit of armour. We understand that part now, but—"

"No, mate." She paused for the count of five, as if to show just how much she disagreed with his understanding of events. "I didn't upset him. He went for me. A great big metal soldier with an axe lunged straight for me, and I knew that you people downstairs would have heard, so I hid in the room next door and, when I knew you were occupied, I legged it again. Only this time, I didn't go outside. I came in here." She tapped her head to show how clever she was. "I knew you'd all think that I'd done a runner, but I was close by the whole time."

Her laughter sounded like someone nailing their hand to the wall over and over again. It was a muffled yelp of repeated agony and surprise.

"But Eilish…" David said to return to his previous point, "why were you scared of Izzy in the first place? You must have known that she wasn't the killer. She solves murders wherever she goes."

I'd rarely met a person whose smile instantly made her look more intimidating, but that was just one of the unique wonders of Eilish Hart.

"Hey, you're right. People are always getting murdered around her. I've never thought of it like that before. If I was of a suspicious nature, I would question why the police have never considered her a suspect."

"People don't get murdered wherever I go," I had to contradict them. "I go to the supermarket all the time – to buy avocados for my mother, or because I'm out of pre-mixed cocktails – and no one has ever been murdered." I realised that there was one small caveat to add. "A man did once have a fatal heart attack as his trolley passed mine and, yes, I was the last person that he ever saw, but he was not murdered (to my knowledge)."

Eilish flicked her fingers through the air so that they made a clicking sound. "Ahhh! Izzy's like a honeypot for murderers. You can't deny it, mate. You attract killers the way rich elderly widowers attract morally dubious young women."

David couldn't hold in a laugh at this comparison, whereas I was surprised that Eilish knew such long words.

"Can we please get back to more important topics?" I begged. "Two men are dead in this very house. My uncle came close to losing his life, and my cousin very nearly suffered a graze or two. I really shouldn't be the focus of this conversation." I believe that my sanctimonious tone did the trick, as they fell noticeably quieter.

Yes! One-nil to Izzy. Well, more like one-three, as Eilish scored a procession of screamers just before. But you're back in the game at least.

"Eilish, as my colleague was asking," I continued and immediately felt weird for describing my ex-con ex as my colleague. "Why was it that you were scared of me when you saw me arrive?"

"Because I know that you're out to get me." She scrunched her lips together and, for a moment, I was worried she wouldn't explain this bizarro statement. "It can't be a coincidence that some fella gets whacked in my town and you show up. Yeah, I saw you with that overly excitable friend of yours. I saw you poking your nose in, and I was already worried that you'd pin the blame on me. So you can imagine how I felt when I drove twenty-seven thousand miles across Britain…" Again, I'd like to stress that it really is only a two-hundred-mile drive. "…and what should I see when I'm sitting in my car putting on my donkey ears for the meeting, but the woman who's been out to get me since we were kids."

I looked at David again, as I couldn't think how to respond. He clearly wasn't faring much better but did what he could.

"I don't believe that Izzy would ever stitch someone up," he tried. "She's so honest that, when a man who loved her committed a foolish crime, she accepted his decision to confess to murder. A less scrupulous person would have stood in his way, but not Izzy." I couldn't look at him. I kept my eyes straight ahead, as it was almost too painful to hear. "In fact, one of the things I have always admired most about her is the integrity with which she lives her life. I've tried very hard to be as good a person as she is, and I know I'll never come close."

There was such kindness in his voice that I was tempted to stand up and put my arms around him. I'd spent the years we'd been apart trying to convince myself that David Hughes was nowhere near as good a person as I remembered. I had to repeat over and over that he'd killed a man, when plenty of other options had remained to him. The truth is though, I was wrong. He was a murderer, but the nicest one in the world. He'd killed a monster to prevent others from suffering, and that didn't stop him from being the well-meaning soul that I'd fallen in love with.

And so, with Eilish watching us in her usual disgruntled manner, I turned to look at him. Our eyes met, my heart throbbed, and Eilish Hart started laughing.

"Ahhhhh, you soft idiots. Why don't you get a room and stop making me want to vomit?"

Chapter Twenty-Five

"That wasn't as helpful as I'd been hoping," I confessed as we left Eilish to return to her bed on the floor.

"No, and I feel a bit queasy after talking to her." David certainly looked it. "She's quite… unpleasant, isn't she?"

"The last time we met, she told me that she had plans for a Damascene conversion to become a better person, but presumably she got distracted and forgot."

Speaking of the easily distracted, Ramesh re-entered the house as we reached the hall. "No luck with the phone signal. Though I did find a twenty-pence coin, so it wasn't an entirely wasted trip." From the look of his drenched and windswept companions, I very much doubted they would agree with this sentiment.

The conversation ground to a halt as David took his phone out and everyone stood peering into their devices. It would have been annoying enough if they'd had any signal, but they all looked so desperate without one that I felt I had to say something.

"Seriously? Are we so ruled by technology that we can't spend one night without the internet? None of us are so young that we've forgotten a time when we didn't have a miniature computer in our pockets."

Ramesh released a groan as if to say, *Please, Izzy! Don't remind me.*

I continued in my stern, Mother-knows-best voice. "I genuinely think the world would be a better place if these things had never been invented. I wish we still lived in a time when we actually had to talk to one another. We've lost so much— Hang on a second, I think I've got a message."

They huddled around to bask in the glow of the screen on my cheapo phone that Mum got free by ringing up the company to make a fuss after I dropped the old, equally bad one in the toilet.

"What does it say, Izzy?" Noémi demanded to know. "Tell us what it says!"

"It's from the journalist I asked for help. The black car outside was seen at a couple of the other murders." The phone was slow to load because… well, it's temperamental like that. "She says it was sold for scrap a couple of years back and there's no record of it since then."

My heart sank, and there were a few moans around the group as this dead end was revealed.

At least Ramesh still held out hope. "What about the message you sent to your family? Did it get there?"

I closed the SMS that Janet had sent me and opened the other app. The phone was slow again, and people began to groan.

"How is it that your phone is the only one that gets a signal?" Arthur complained. "It must be running on stone-age technology that is unaffected by meteorological conditions." This was probably the only thing he said that day which triggered a laugh.

I was unmoved by his complaint. "I'll have you know that the ExtraMobile 32X Very Good Phone is the number one handset in certain areas of the Russian countryside. You can take your iPhones and your other brands that I can't think of right now. I'm happy with this one." I'd never been so proud of the brick in my hand, though I don't think I'd convinced anyone else of its value.

"It still hasn't loaded!" Nicholas practically cried before going to bang his head against the wall.

You know things are bad when Father Christmas stops believing.

"Here it is!" As if by magic (very slow magic), the message appeared on the screen before me, and all eyes fell on the little beauty once more. "Nope, it hasn't sent."

This even made me feel like running out into the storm. All the hope I'd invested in finding Eilish and hearing back from my family had brought us nothing. We were alone there. Trapped in a building that might just kill us, with a group of people I couldn't trust and no way to contact anyone who might be able to save us.

I doubt there's any hot chocolate either.

This might have been the moment when it all got too much.

"It can't be helped," David told the others. "We'll stick to our original plan. We can fetch blankets and coats or what have you from the cars, and then we'll find cushions to make beds in the lounge. I'll kindle the fire and we'll all stay together tonight, safe and sound."

There was some murmuring of acceptance at this moment, but one person still wasn't happy. "Safe and sound so long as the killer doesn't put a silent alarm on his phone and slit our throats in the night." Wendy had clearly given this scenario some thought.

"It's simple." Ramesh put an arm around his old enemy to explain. "We'll make a pact that no one is to kill anyone else until we leave. How does that sound?" He glanced from person to person, but most of the suspects continued staring at their useless devices.

Arthur was the exception. "I still haven't heard an explanation for why any of us would want to hurt Izzy in the first place."

Ramesh immediately sized him up. "Perhaps you're related to one of the people she locked away and we don't know anything about it." A new possibility exploded into his brain just then. "Perhaps one of you of is out for revenge on Bob's behalf!" He once more turned to address the group. "Come on, everyone. Tell the truth. Are any of you here connected to the man that David slew?"

Is slew the past tense of slay? I think I'd have gone for slaw.

As in coleslaw?

Now that you say it, it doesn't sound right.

As there were no takers for Ramesh's not-quite-as-absurd-as-it-might-sound suggestion, he gave up and let me speak. "I don't think you're on the right track, Ra. And even if you were, I doubt the killer would confess just like that."

I heard Uncle Bradley whisper to Wendy, "I'm related to the guy who does the voice of the speaking clock," which I happen to know is a lie, but Bradley has never been very good at boasting.

It would take David to get the unruly bunch under control. "We're not going to achieve anything by standing out here. I'm going to make everyone some tea. Noémi and Nicholas, can help me, and the rest of you can get settled in the lounge."

He didn't wait for their agreement but marched down the hall away from us so that his nominated helpers soon followed. I felt less safe as soon as he was gone, and I almost shouted out the most feeble request I could imagine, *Try not to get killed!* The words stuck in my throat, and I stood staring after him until he was just a blob in the distance.

"Okay then," I said in a hollow voice, and I clapped my hands in the hope I might sound more confident. "Let's do as the man said."

I didn't have anything in the bag in my car except some entirely inappropriate sparkly dresses that my mother had bought me and some equally awful hippyish clothes I had worn as a teenager (which my mother was also responsible for buying). I went out with the others nonetheless and did what I could to help by shining the incredibly weak torch of my incredibly weak phone into the boots of their cars.

I was most amazed by Wendy, who looked as though she had come for an outdoor expedition. She had ropes, bolt cutters, a net of some description and what looked like infrared night goggles in her car. I figured she would be the person to stick with if we had to trek down the hill in the morning.

Ramesh, on the other hand, had brought a rhinestone sleeping mask, Celine Dion pyjamas and life-size pillows of his wife and child. "Don't look at me like that, Izzy. You know this is the only way I can get to sleep." I suppose I must have continued looking at him like that, as he broke down and said, "I miss my little family so much. Please tell me we'll get out of here alive!"

"You'll be fine, Ra," I promised. "It would take a true psychopath to want to hurt someone like you."

What I didn't tell him was that I'd been scared ever since I found the graffiti in Southorpe that this would be my last case. Even though there were only a few hours to get through before we could leave, the weight of a thousand different forces was pushing down on me. It wasn't just the pressure to find the killer and save lives; it was the building itself, looming over us in the darkness. It was almost as if the place had been built to taunt me. Add that to the manifestation of so many demons from my past, and the reappearance in my life of a man who, until very recently, I believed had five more years to serve in prison, I think it's fair to say that I had a lot on my plate.

I didn't dare look in Arthur's boot for fear of what he might keep in there, and Uncle Bradley's van was too far away and too crumpled for a quick stop off, so it was time to head back inside.

Wendy surprised me when we got to the lounge by collecting cushions for everyone and offering me a spot closest to the fire. It was a thoughtful gesture, but I knew that Arthur would complain he was cold all night if I didn't give it to him, so Wendy and I made camp on the other side of the sofas.

"I'm glad we've got a moment alone together, Izzy," said the woman I had once described as a cross between a school dinner lady and an evil leprechaun from a horror film – mainly because she was wearing a lot of green at the time. "I wanted to talk to you when you visited the office, but…"

She came to an unexpected halt, and I didn't know what to say to her as I lay down on my meagre cushions and shuddered beneath my lightweight jacket. I really should have stayed by the fire.

"You see," she eventually continued, "I realised some time ago that I wasn't very nice to you when we were working together." She really was struggling to get her words out, and her groggy voice was even groggier than normal. "I don't know why it happened, but I got swept up in the world of office rivalries. I've been at Porter & Porter so long that I can't say when it happened. I used to be a kind person; I'm sure that's true. But somehow I transformed into the office bully. I thought it was my job to act as a moral arbiter and cast aspersions on anyone who didn't live up to my standards."

She didn't look at me as she spoke, but gazed at the fire which Ramesh was trying to reignite. I had expected him to just blow on it very hard, but it turned out he was quite the boy scout and soon had it roaring.

"A year or so after you'd gone, and most of my friends had retired, I suddenly realised that no one cared what I thought any longer. Perhaps I'd always been oblivious to it, but I became aware of the whispers and rolling eyes whenever I entered the room. The young people working there weren't scared of me, and they didn't care that I was a manager. I finally came to see that the only way I could fit in was if I acted like a decent person."

Her voice broke then. The woman I'd always thought of as being impervious to the opinions of those around her was crying before me.

Say something nice, Izzy. Do the right thing.

But I couldn't force myself to speak. I just lay there, like a kid on a school camping trip, watching her drunken teacher discuss her deepest secrets. The fact is that what Wendy needed more than anything – much like my old technology teacher, Mrs Pearson, had that night in the tent in the New Forest – was someone to listen. So that's what I did.

"At first, it was pitiful." She laughed at herself then, but the sound was filled with sadness. "I was trying to be their friends, and it just wasn't working. Nothing I did or said made anyone think I was any nicer. And then…" She finally turned to look at me. "And then I heard them talking about you one day, and I began to tell stories."

I didn't say anything, but I put my hand in hers. I felt it was the least I could do.

"I told them how you and Ramesh would hide in your private den in the server room – though I didn't tell them it was me you were normally hiding from. I talked about your love of books as if I had nurtured it. I laughed my head off remembering the staff talent show when Ramesh came in dressed half as Kelly Clarkson and half as Kylie Minogue and sang a mash-up called 'Since U Been Gone, I Can't Get You Out of My Head'. Of course, you'll remember that, at the time, I told everyone that he was a despicable pervert who shouldn't be allowed to get away with such things. But as I repeated these tales as if they were my own, I came to realise just how much I liked you both."

She took a deep breath and seemed human in a way that I'd never imagined before. "I insulted and tormented people because it gave me power, and yet it never made me happy. When you first came to work at the office, you were so different from everyone else, and you helped bring Ramesh out of his shell. I don't think that even I knew it at the time, but you did the same to me. I started wearing more interesting clothing so that the two of you would notice. I embroidered my boring old skirts with cats and pineapples and unicorns, but it wasn't enough. I was still the same nasty person, and you called me out for it, when what I really wanted…"

She looked up at the ceiling and blinked over and over again to fight the emotion. "What I really wanted, though I would never have admitted it, was to have friends like you. No matter what I said or did, you always looked after one another. You were true friends, and I've never been so jealous of anything in my life."

Her words faded out entirely then as the tea arrived, and she turned to look into the darkness on the other side of the room.

Don't be so mean, Izzy! Give her a hug.

It must have been a surprise for Wendy to find herself enclosed within my massive wingspan. I gave her the biggest cuddle I could manage and said, "Then I guess we'll have to be friends, too. And you can tell everyone in the office all about our adventures."

She really was sobbing by now, but she was the kind of person who always had a handkerchief tucked into one sleeve. She produced it with nimble sleight of hand, then dabbed at her eyes.

"Thank you, Izzy. I really mean it. Whatever else happens here, I'm glad I finally got the chance to tell you how I feel."

I gave her a proper hug this time, rather than a surprise attack from behind, and then David appeared, and a herd of rhinos rushed to grab mugs of tea.

"There's plenty for everyone," he assured the others. "There's no need to push."

Ramesh was disappointed that there was no sugar, and so he went to the kitchen to look for some with Nicholas whilst the rest of us sipped at the pleasantly burning beverage.

"Tea goes straight through me," Bradley confessed. "I'll need someone to take me to the lav' after this." Even my awful uncle had a sweet side to him, and he sounded like a little boy asking his teacher for permission.

"That's a good point," Arthur agreed. Sadly, I've yet to find much to redeem my former stepfather. I'll let you know if anything comes to mind. "We'll all have to go to the WC before long."

As they were talking, I noticed a scrap of paper on the floor beside my makeshift bed. It was left over from the game Ramesh had begun earlier in the evening. I picked it up to keep the place tidy and didn't question what it would say until I was staring straight at it.

As I read the four words written in angry block capitals, all the comfort that my chat with Wendy had offered was ripped away. I felt more exposed than I had at any moment since I'd crossed the border into Wales.

"Who wrote this?" I said, getting to my feet to hold up the piece of paper. "Who hates me so much that they would think this?"

"I don't have my glasses," Arthur replied, squinting in the light of a few weak standard lamps and the glow from the fire. "What does it say?"

Noémi had to step closer to see. "It says, 'Izzy destroyed my life.'"

No one moved for ten seconds as I considered who was to blame. In a moment, life returned to the room, and the suspects spoke over one another.

"I only complained about your poor gamesmanship," Arthur got his own defence in before anyone else could. "Do you really think I would say such a thing?"

Noémi was next. "I told you; you saved me from prison."

Wendy jerked her head back to our neighbouring cushion pile, presumably to reference everything she'd just told me. David stayed exactly where he was, looking stern, and Uncle Bradley whined out a defence of his own.

"Come on, Izzy. You know I love you really. You're my niece, and I'd never say nothing so nasty…" He must have realised that he'd said such things before and amended the statement. "Well, not seriously, at least."

I walked over to the fireplace and threw the paper into the grate so that the edges turned red, then black as the flame caught hold of it. In a matter of seconds, it was gone forever.

Chapter Twenty-Six

Yes, I know. I shouldn't have destroyed evidence but imagine being trapped in a house with all the worst people you'd clashed with in your life and, after coming to believe that they weren't as bad as they first seemed, finding out that someone there really did blame you for everything that had gone wrong in their life. It was enough to drive a girl to burn a little piece of paper.

And I must say that, when that scrap of white had carbonised and disintegrated into a billion particles, I felt a great deal better.

"I've had another thought that might explain the reason for the traps," I told David as we escorted the group along the corridor. "I said earlier that they helped the killer carry out the plan without fear of being identified, but there's another benefit too. It distances our existing suspects from the crimes. It makes it seem as though there's someone else here with us."

"Isn't that possible?" he asked in a whisper so that the others wouldn't hear.

"Of course it is, but we've seen no sign of anyone but Eilish since we got here. We know the brakes on our cars were cut, but that was during the longest period of the evening when we were almost all apart."

He responded with a brief humming sound, as if he agreed in principle but had his doubts.

"You were the last to arrive, weren't you?" I asked. "And you didn't see anyone out in the car park with a pair of pliers or a knife lying beneath one of the cars."

"No, but it would have been easy to hide there. We know that Eilish managed to dart about the place without anyone noticing."

"That's the thing. I reckon she was the person you saw through the window. It makes me wonder whether the killer overheard what you'd seen and, when Noémi suggested they play hide-and-seek – presumably so that she could be alone with Nicholas – the killer saw the opportunity to trap us here and went back outside as soon as we were occupied."

We'd arrived at the toilets that gave off a decidedly public-school vibe. They were split into ladies' and gents' facilities, and the rest of the group walked gingerly through the neighbouring doors as we stood talking. Ramesh had a lengthy skincare and toiletry regime to get through, so I knew we would be there for a while.

"Give me your phone," David requested with his hand out.

I unlocked it. "Why? What are you going to do?"

He took it from me and started to type something. "I realised that two of the three texts you received were old-style SMS, as opposed to internet-based messages. I figure this gives us more chance of getting through to someone."

I watched as he spent a minute writing to each of my parents and Janet Ellison before handing the phone back.

"There's still the possibility that Eilish is to blame," he suggested, once the task was complete. "She certainly had the most freedom to set the traps and cut our brakes. Perhaps the suit of armour upstairs fell because she triggered it when she was setting it up."

I considered the possibility. "That could be it, but I really believed what she told us in the bar earlier. I can totally imagine her hiding because she thought I was persecuting her. You know the Spanish have the same word for *chase* as *persecute.*" Judging by his expression, he did not get the significance of my random comment, so I moved us on. "She knew about the recent murders, and suddenly saw me wherever she went. I think I'd be a bit frightened if that happened to me."

"Someone must be capable of all this." His voice became more nervous, and it was quite alarming to glimpse his less confident side. "You can't just believe everything that everyone says."

I bit my lip for a second before answering. "You're right. Noémi convinced me that, far from being angry with me for exposing the con she played on her mother, she was grateful I'd identified the real killer and saved her from a life in jail. And Wendy, of all people, just told me that she regretted the way she treated us at Porter & Porter."

"Wendy?" David responded. "Wendy Wendy? Our Wendy?"

"Yeah, she feels terrible about it."

Ramesh kept walking in and out of the gents brushing his teeth, as he doesn't like standing still for too long. "Does Wendy have a surname?" he asked.

"Yes, it's Robinson." David narrowed his eyes, clearly feeling that we should have known this after working with the woman for years.

Ramesh curled his lip as if he didn't care either way. "I always imagined that she was mononymous like the singer Prince or Tony the Tiger. Continue."

"The thing is," I said, ignoring the interruption, "I have to believe the people who've explained themselves to me because the killer – the real killer, who set this whole sick plan in motion – is clearly motivated by hatred. I don't think someone like that could stand before me and say such nice things. What's scared me from the very beginning is just how personal this is. I wondered as I left home yesterday whether this was my 'Curtains'."

David took a step closer and looked down at me. I doubt he got the reference, but the general meaning was clear enough. "I won't let anything happen to you, Izzy." He put both hands on my arms as if he wanted to pick me up off the floor. I could immediately feel his warmth on my skin, and it travelled through my body. "I promise I won't."

I closed my eyes and waited. I'd been waiting for three years and nine months, but instead of the touch of his lips on mine, there was a sound of falling masonry, as if someone had just knocked down a wall. We ran towards the men's toilets and, from the sight of the figures who peered out of the open cubicles, I realised that something had happened to my uncle… again.

"Bradley? Are you okay, Uncle Bradley?"

His only reply was a scream of agony. I felt quite helpless as there was a heavy door separating us from him but, luckily, Nicholas came to the rescue.

It's about time he did something. Otherwise what was the point of him coming here in the first place?

He stood back against the wall and aimed a sturdy boot at the position where it was safe to assume the lock would be. "Stand back, Bradley. I'm coming in."

The force he could summon was almost as impressive as the effect it had on the door as it splintered and then tipped forwards off its top hinge. With another kick, the door was freed entirely, and Nicholas passed it to David as if it was made of balsa wood. Ever the gentleman, Nicholas moved aside for me to do what I could for my uncle. At first, it was hard to imagine what that was. He was covered over and surrounded by large red bricks and appeared to be knocked out cold. I looked at the top of the cistern above the toilet and was fairly sure what had happened.

"Bradley, are you conscious? Can you hear me?"

I bent to look at him and removed the bricks that I could from his lap. There was even one still nestling on his shoulder and blood was pouring from his head. Someone passed me a wad of wet paper towels, and I pressed them to his forehead to stem the streams of thick red liquid.

For a tense twenty seconds, he just sat there, slumped over with his trousers around his ankles and his eyes closed. He looked far worse than he had in his van, and I really was worried that I would have to ring my mother – when the phones were working again, obviously – to tell her that her brother had been murdered by a rigged toilet chain.

"Why does this keep happening to me?" he finally moaned, and I could breathe again. "Seriously, Izzy. I mean, I know I'm not the best bloke alive, and I should never have broken up with my Julie or called your cousin Axel a plonker all the time, but my head is killing me. Do I really deserve this?"

He held his hand to the wound as drops of blood made it through the paper and dripped from his eyebrows to the floor.

"Do you think you can stand?" I asked as I replaced the towel with a fresh one that Nicholas provided.

David was on hand to help and, once my poor battered uncle had raised his trousers, he was helped back to the lounge by the two strongest men.

"What a way to go," Ramesh said, shaking his head as he took in the carnage before us. "He was this close to death by dunny. How did it happen?"

I moved towards the toilet again and grabbed hold of the old-fashioned metal chain that led up through a hole in the cistern. Instead of making the toilet flush as it was supposed to, it tipped a white board that had been placed on top.

"The bricks must have been on there when he came in. He did his business and then flushed, which sent the load down on top of him."

"But why wouldn't he have seen them up there?" Ramesh leaned backwards to get a better view of the mechanism.

"Do you look up as you enter a toilet? Most people stare straight at the bowl to see what state the previous occupant has left it in. When he pulled the chain, he would have been right beneath it."

"It would have taken some strength to pull the bricks down. He must have thought it was sticking and really yanked it. It's lucky that he didn't do himself more harm."

I looked at the splashes of blood all over one wall of the cubicle and the fragments of bricks that had smashed on the floor. "Lucky is definitely the word for it."

Chapter Twenty-Seven

Bradley was spoilt for care and attention after that, so he couldn't have been happier. If my uncle could have anything in life, I'm fairly certain it would be a full-time butler. He was certainly all smiles as Arthur and Wendy dressed his wounds and fetched him drinks.

It was another point of confusion in my already messy brain. I felt as though I were swimming in an endless sea of potential evidence with nothing solid to point the way. Unable to rely on what I saw before me, I tried searching through a mental database of solutions from beloved whodunits to see whether I could make the case I was investigating bend to fit an existing solution. It got me nowhere whatsoever.

As much as I hated to admit it, I could finally see that not everything in life was like a golden age mystery. I was looking for a twist, but perhaps there wasn't one. Perhaps the killer was just a madman roving about the grounds of an old house. He'd seen me on television or read about me in the paper and become fixated. All it had taken was a few killings of my old suspects to draw me to a house in the mountains. And from there, he'd given me a puzzle that wasn't really a puzzle because the solution went against the rules of every mystery I'd ever read.

What a rubbish ending. Is that all we've got to look forward to?

Perhaps the story will finish with me squashed to death beneath a bookshelf. That would be a most fitting end for a girl who had spent her life thinking that the only thing that mattered was how soon she could consume her next detective novel.

As miserable as this was, it wasn't nearly so bad as the mood in the group. We should all have gone to sleep, but instead everyone started bickering in the hope of proving that they weren't guilty.

"I'm saying that it can't be me because I'm simply not that sort of person," Arthur insisted with his perfectly superior attitude. "There are those who have it in them to indulge such base, violent instincts, and those who can rise above them. It's normally clear from just looking at someone and… well, that's not me."

He turned to Noémi and David as he said this, and my cousin was the first to respond. "What are you suggesting, Arthur?"

He looked even more stuffy than normal. "I'm suggesting that you have a history of violence. Am I wrong in thinking that you tried to kill your brother?"

She was sitting on the sofa and had to pull back in surprise. "You certainly are. I merely stabbed him in the shoulder. I had no intention of ending his life."

"I think we should all calm down." David must have known this would do no good.

"You would say that," Bradley declared in a harsh tone. "We all know what you did."

I thought that my lovely ex might lose his temper and lash out, but he stayed perfectly calm. "I imagine you do, but can you tell me what I would hope to achieve by all this?" He held his hands out to motion to the house. "Can you name one thing I would gain from this ridiculous charade?"

My (regrettably still) uncle glanced at my (thankfully no longer) stepdad, but they didn't have an original thought between them.

"Well," Arthur tried, "isn't it possible that…"

"Exactly!" Bradley responded, before realising that Arthur hadn't got very far and shutting back up again.

"Perhaps you blame Izzy for your time in prison," Nicholas cautiously put forward. Father Christmas isn't the type to offend anyone.

"Fair enough." David got up from the chair in the corner where he'd been trying to sleep and walked over to the others in front of the fire. "That does make sense, but then why wouldn't I just kill her? Why mess about with you lot?"

The whole bunch of them looked guilty then, as though they realised they had accused an innocent man unnecessarily.

It was Wendy who eventually responded. "Perhaps you wanted to hide that you were the one behind it. Perhaps you wanted to put Izzy through all this pain without anyone knowing it was you." She came to stand next to me in solidarity as she spoke. "Perhaps that's the reason for all these horrid traps. If Izzy walks into one accidentally, then no one will know for certain that it was your intention."

It was a smart idea, though this would have made putting the bricks in the men's toilet a bit odd. And before I could point out that the same held true for anyone else there, David had an answer of his own.

"I blame Izzy for nothing." He let the words marinate for a few moments. Actually, that's a horrible description; he didn't soak them in tomato sauce. He simply paused to make sure that we'd given what he'd said its due consideration. "I was at my wits' end with a cruel man, so I took a knife and killed him. I regret my actions, but not Bob's death. It may well have meant that Izzy survived the assassination attempt that he ordered."

He was so clear, concise and confident that the devil's advocates in the audience gave up in an instant.

"Then what about you, Wendy?" Uncle Bradley asked, to switch focus. "We all know that you hated Izzy when you worked together. From what I remember, you were besties with Bob, too. Are you seeking revenge on his behalf?"

There was something that had been puzzling me for some time. "Sorry, but how are you all so well-informed on my cases? Bradley, how do you know that Wendy and I weren't friends at Porter & Porter? And how does Arthur know that Noémi stabbed her brother?"

I waited for an answer, but they all looked guilty again, so it fell to David to explain. "I suppose they've been reading Ramesh's blog."

Ramesh had evidently worked out what was coming, as he'd retreated to the other side of the fire and was pretending that the small stuffed version of baby Pacino was a real child.

"Ramesh?" I snapped. "What's this about?"

He was quick to come to his own defence. "It was a blog, Izzy – just a blog. I didn't think anyone would read it. I mean, it's 2024, not 2017! I thought it would disappear into the ether of the infinite internet, and I could use it as a place to store my thoughts. I never expected it to blow up the way it did."

"And when you say 'blow up', you mean…?"

"I mean that the Huffington Post promoted it, and it was featured on the BBC News."

I sank down into my bed then. To be honest, I thought there was a chair just behind me, and didn't expect to fall that far. "So everyone knows everything about our cases and anyone in Britain could be the killer?"

"Well… more like anyone in the world who could afford the airfare over here, but yes, your general summary was accurate."

I didn't bother standing back up again. I'd been boggled by the possibilities before, and now I was… even more boggled.

Luckily (or otherwise), the others were still squabbling and barely noticed that I was no longer part of the discussion. Arthur was clutching a towel to Bradley's bloody head, but that was not enough to join the two men in solidarity.

"Of course, there is one person who isn't mentioned in the blog," my uncle began, before pausing dramatically. "Arthur, old pal, you've never been caught up in one of Izzy's cases, have you?"

"And what's that meant to mean?" There was nothing that Arthur liked quite so much as feeling outraged.

"I mean that if the killer was selecting past suspects, you don't fit the mould. And that suggests to me that no one wrote you a letter. It suggests to me that you were a sender, not a receiver."

"You're just saying that because of the time I invited you to my time-share apartment in St Ives but had to cancel at the last moment as Rosemarie had booked the wrong dates. That's it, isn't it? I knew you'd never forgiven me for that. Your sister insisted I was being paranoid, but I knew."

"That was fifteen years ago," Bradley replied with a scowl.

"Oh, you've been counting, have you?"

"I don't know what you mean."

The chance to deflect the blame encouraged Arthur. He smiled as he pulled the towel away and pointed menacingly at his former brother-in-law. "What about you, matey? I'm sure I'm not the only one who's noticed that the two traps you triggered barely scratched you."

My uncle's jaw dropped, and he showed his displeasure. "Barely scratched me? I'm lucky to be alive."

A few other people took sides at this moment. Wendy came to Arthur's aid. Ramesh chose the underdog and Noémi egged them both on. But somehow, Nicholas's voice drowned them all out.

I suppose he gets a lot of practice with all that ho-ho-hoing.

"I just want to say that, in case you're all thinking it, I had nothing to do with the murders."

Arthur and Bradley instantly looked put out that the spotlight had been stolen from them, and so they turned their ire on the man in red.

"Literally no one is thinking that, Nicholas," Arthur informed him with a nice, slow eyeroll.

"That's easy to say, but I know what you must all think of me. Nicholas the lunatic who believes he's Santa Claus. Well, I'm not totally insane, you know?" Shouting this at the top of his lungs probably wasn't the best way to prove it. "I'm aware that, to most people, my life is pure fantasy. I know that's why Izzy only went on seven dates with me before she'd had enough. But I believe in giving a bit of magic back to the world. So I'm not sorry, and I'm not a killer."

Oh my goodness, we've finally broken Father Christmas.

"Well, mate," Bradley piped up, "I hadn't considered your guilt before, but after that little outburst, I'm rather inclined to do so."

"Careful, Bradley," Noémi stepped forward to tell him, and I really felt like going to sleep. "Nicholas is a good, kind man and I think he's wonderful." She walked over to the big festive beefcake, put her hands on his chest and looked up into his dreamy eyes. "I've never met a Santa like you before."

"Do you really mean it?" He melted at the sight of her, so at least I didn't have to feel guilty about breaking up with him. Though I swear it was only six dates we went on, not seven.

Perhaps he's counting that time his supervisor at the department store got murdered.

While I was chewing this over, and Old Saint Nick and my previously fratricidal cousin were cuddling one another, the place exploded one last time with voices from every direction. It got so bad that Eilish had to come in and tell everyone to keep it down.

"Seriously, I'm trying to sleep!" she complained and, as most people hadn't seen her before, there were some very scared faces. Happily for them, she was soon drawn into the mass argument. Even normally placid David and generally oblivious Ramesh looked like they wanted to tear someone's head off, and it was all too much after a totally too-much sort of day.

"Will you please shut up?" I climbed to my feet again to shout, and magically, they all did just that. I took a moment to breathe before I said another word. The silence was exquisite. "Thank you. Now, I could go on about how I'm the one the killer is targeting this weekend, or complain of the pressure there is on me to solve what feels like sixteen murders with no reliable clues, but I'm not going to."

Though you kind of already have.

"Yes, thank you, brain." Oops, I didn't mean to say this out loud, but they probably all thought I was weird already, so it didn't really change much. "The best thing we can do right now is stop talking and get some sleep."

Inevitably, Arthur had something to say about this. "But I don't think it's very fair that—"

Eilish too. "Hey, I was minding my own business in the bar until this all kicked off. I don't believe for one—"

"I'm the one who needs the most sleep around here," Ramesh added, because he doesn't like it when people have been ignoring him for too long. "You know what I'm like when I haven't had my full nine—"

"That's enough!" I called to silence the room. "Children, to bed!"

Chapter Twenty-Eight

This was wishful thinking on my part. Though the court jesters the killer had sent to torment me did calm down, I wouldn't get much sleep. There were no more arguments, at least, and I must admit that it was nice to sleep in the glow of the fire. It reminded me of the Christmas Eve when I was eight when Danny and I had camped out in the living room to wait for Father Christmas before inevitably nodding off soon after.

I woke a few hours later to one miniature bang after another. It sounded like silenced gunfire on a TV show, and I counted eight impressively loud thuds before I realised that it was the sound of car doors slamming shut.

I can only assume that spending any length of time in prison would turn the dormouse from Alice in Wonderland into a light sleeper, as David was up on his feet before I'd opened my eyes.

"It's the police," he yelled in jubilation. "The police are outside. They're coming to save us."

I'd read too many books where the police turn out to be the bad guys to get quite so excited as he was, but everyone who managed to rouse themselves seemed pleased. After a minute or two of rubbing my eyes and blinking, I did come to accept that this was a good result.

"Morning folks," D.I. Irons said as she followed a group of armed officers through the doorway. She was dressed in tactical gear and held a very large gun. "Is everyone alright in here? We had a call from your parents, Miss Palmer."

Well, it wasn't actually Irons, but it sounded a bit like her. I'd presumably rubbed my eyes a bit too hard, as everything was now blurry.

"Before your officers explore the house," David began, "you should know that there are potentially boobie traps all over the place. There's a dead body in a room near the larder, another in one of the suites upstairs, and the man in the armchair by the fire will need medical assistance."

"And my bottle of whisky was stolen," Arthur stated, presumably so as not to feel left out.

"I'll take you to see the bodies if it helps." David should have been a police officer – though I think it's fair to assume such a career path is now closed to him. He knew just how to take charge of the scene and told the inspector or what have you exactly what he wanted to know. Yep, it turned out that the guy in the bulletproof vest was a man, and Welsh, and thus bore really very little resemblance to D.I. Irons after all.

The inspector took off his helmet to reveal a fine head of curly blonde hair. He looked similar to a cherub I'd once seen on a Victorian Christmas card. "It sounds like you've been through quite the ordeal."

"You're telling me," the same old bore as before replied. "That bottle had a recommended retail price of over forty-two pounds."

The armed officers secured the house floor by floor as an ambulance arrived to tend to Bradley's laundry lists of injuries and Ramesh's suspected paper cut. David and I sat beside the window and watched the storm rolling away over the mountains. The sun finally appeared, and it was a peaceful moment after a night of perfect lunacy, but this didn't change the fact that everything was still a mess.

I was glad that we'd earned an exit from the house of horrors, but the problem remained that I hadn't caught the killer. I hadn't completed the job that I'd spent the most important part of my life training to do, and so my one hundred-per-cent record of success (not including stolen hamsters, who I suspect were accidentally sat upon) had finally come to an end.

"What happens now?" David asked, and I looked him in the eyes as a mix of exhilaration, fear and relief coursed through me.

"I haven't the faintest idea. All I know for sure is that I miss my bed and my shower and my oversized library. Which, now that I think of it…"

I got up to speak to the officer in charge. I hadn't had to say much to Inspector Narberth yet, but I'd watched him at work, and he was an impressive chap. Although he only looked about sixteen, his subordinates clearly respected him, and they immediately followed the orders he issued.

"How can I help you, Miss Palmer?" he asked once he'd finished reassuring Arthur that our cars would be dealt with as soon as possible and that fresh milk for tea was already on its way. "I don't suppose you can point us in the direction of the killer?"

"I'm afraid not," I told him, a little shamefaced. "I've never fixed on a clear theory for what was going on here. At least the black Ford is still parked outside. I believe it was used when Jack Campbell was murdered in Croydon. Perhaps it will contain forensic evidence that will lead you to the killer."

"That's a very good tip. Thank you. But I imagine there was something else you wished to know."

"How did you guess?" This was a rhetorical question as my whole demeanour at this moment screamed, *I was hoping for a favour.*

"We in the police are known for our skills of deduction." He tapped his head three times in comic fashion. "Though if you wish to know about milk or, for some reason I couldn't quite fathom, a copy of last week's Radio Times, then you can be assured that everything is under control in that department."

"Actually, I was hoping I might have an escort to inspect the library. If you've already checked it over, I mean."

He looked around for a moment and, perhaps realising that he was the senior officer, shrugged and agreed. "I don't see why not. You've already marched all over the house with the rest of this motley crew. So long as you're not planning to pocket anything, I think you can take a peek." He held his hand out. "After you, Miss Palmer."

There was no small talk as we descended that gloomy corridor one final time, and this gave me a chance to rack my brains for a solution. Although Uncle Bradley and Arthur's confrontation before bedtime had been unpleasant to hear, it had summarised certain possibilities. Arthur really didn't have much reason for being there. He'd never been a formal suspect in any of my cases and, while I considered him a major antagonist in my life story, it was unlikely that Ramesh would have mentioned him on his apparently world-famous blog.

Bradley himself had performed the classic trick – which so many good villains have tried over the years – of suffering through a failed attack not once but twice in the space of an evening to suggest his innocence. Of course, Noémi might have been going for a similar effect with the falling plates, and she was far more likely to have the organisational skills to pull off this grand scheme than my perpetually hard-done-by uncle. As for Santa, the very fact that he'd never entered into our thinking made him the dark horse challenger. If our really very undramatic breakup had led his already fragile personality to split, then it was just about conceivable that the peace-loving gift-giver had become a violent maniac.

I suppose it would be wrong of me to leave Ramesh out. He hates that. But with the time he devotes to answering my fan mail (ten minutes a week) looking after his son (40-50 hours) and maintaining his various online diva-devoted fan clubs (the rest of the time) he really would have been hard pressed to turn serial killer.

Before I could work my way through the rest of the list, we reached the library and went inside. It was majestic in the morning light, and the spines of the books seemed to glitter – to me, at least. I doubt that the inspector would have felt the same way.

"Was there something in particular you wished to see?" he asked as I stared at one shelf after another.

"Yes and no," I told him. "It's not as if I'm expecting to find a hidden room with the killer in it, or a signed confession. It's simply that this is where I feel the most calm. If I could live surrounded by books, I would be happy."

"How nicely put. I feel just the same about model railways." I glanced at him then and he must have felt this needed an explanation. "My father had a collection in our cellar. There was a huge platform there with miniature towns and a complex circuit of tracks running between them. One of my earliest memories was clambering around under the platform and popping my little head up through a hole in the middle to watch my dad working on it. Describing it now takes me straight back there."

It was a nice memory, and I smiled at him before recalling my own Proustian Madeleine. "I have a library like this that my mum's cousin left me. Sometimes, when I can't make up my mind on a case, I'll sit on the floor in front of it and allow myself half an hour to scan the book titles. After a minute or two, I find I'm not reading them consciously anymore, but exploring avenues of thought." I did this in silence for some short time, and then the truth hit me. "It doesn't seem to be working today."

"Oh, well, Miss Palmer. I appreciate you giving it a go. You can't be expected to solve every case. We police officers have to share the burden, though I must say I'm always impressed when I read about your cases in the paper."

You saucy minx, you. Tell us more.

I took one last turn of the room. "There were no traps in here, were there?"

"Not that we've discovered."

This triggered a possibility, and I knew that I would have to ask for another favour. "If you don't mind, I did have one more idea. Could we go up to the bedrooms?"

Very smooth, Izzy. He's a chunk of cherubic police love, and I approve.

He nodded and stood aside for me to leave. "I'll have to make sure that they've been checked over. There should be some constables up there now."

He wasn't as familiar with the place as I was, though I imagine that would change over the coming days of the investigation. I led the way up to the second floor, where the killer had chosen our rooms for us. There were police checking for traps in the first we came to, and others were milling around at the end of the hall in front of Edmund's suite, but it was my room I needed.

The door was open, and everything inside had been moved about and turned around, but sitting on the desk beside the window was an envelope with my name on it. Inspector Narberth saw it first and went for a look. He donned the necessary latex gloves and, checking that it wasn't sealed, slid the contents free onto the table. A piece of paper the size of an index card fell flat on the table for us both to read.

Dear Izzy,

I've been waiting for this opportunity for such a long time and now we're finally here together. The fact is that people are going to die before anyone can leave this house, and it will all be your fault.

Good luck making it out alive.

"He's sick," the hardened – though angelic – officer beside me declared as I read through the note a second time.

I didn't know what to think of this small find. It certainly didn't make the case any easier to solve. Giving up on the note, I walked over to my bed, which had been torn apart by the officers tasked with securing the room.

"There was no trap set here, either," I said, thinking out loud. "This wasn't how the killer planned to get me."

"What I don't understand," Narberth didn't respond directly, but introduced a point of his own, "is how this madman hoped to achieve anything. If it hadn't been for the storm, you could have called us immediately and escaped without any trouble."

"I thought that too," I replied. "Though my phone has been just as bad this morning as it was last night. I think the signal up here is poor at the best of times."

I was still puzzling over what looked to be an entirely safe room when one of Narberth's constables entered to see his boss. "May I speak freely, sir? Or perhaps we should talk outside."

He sat down on the bed and looked up at his officer. "I think you can say what you have to in front of Miss Palmer."

"It's the last room we've been checking, sir. It's the only one of the suites we've inspected in which the bed has been slept in."

"It might not have been last night," I pointed out. "The killer could have stayed the night before we arrived to get everything ready."

"Well, Constable?" Narberth tipped back his head to await his subordinate's thoughts.

"That wasn't all we found. You see, the wardrobe in there has a space behind its bottom drawer. We discovered a box with various items we believe the killer must have used. There are cable ties like the one around the caretaker Mr Powell's neck, and a box of rat poison which fits with the evidence we've seen on the corpse. There's a bunch of screwdrivers and other tools in there, too. I figure that they were used for setting the traps about the place."

"Whose room was it?" the inspector asked, and his colleague had a nervous glance in my direction before answering.

"David Hughes's. He's downstairs with the others."

There was some more discussion, but I didn't hear a word of it. I left the room and floated down two flights of stairs like a ghost no one has taken the time to be scared of. The evidence rejigged in my head so that I could fit everything back together a little bit differently. I saw David arriving – the last to come, with plenty of time to cut the brakes in the car park. I saw him coming down the hall after he'd made sure that Edmund got to his bedroom. I thought about the one scenario that I'd refused to believe and my whole body shook as I realised that it could be true after all.

By the time I got to the ground floor, several of my friends, loved ones and former suspects were making for the car park. I followed them out there and stood in front of the porch, no longer a ghost but a zombie tethered to the spot, unable to decide which way to turn.

"Ahh, Izzy. I was hoping to talk to you." Arthur was holding a box of bottles. I assume he considered them reparations for the whisky he'd lost. "I just wanted to say that I'm sorry we had to meet again under such strange circumstances."

I couldn't find the words to respond, and so I stared at him with all the tenderness of a lethargic scarecrow.

"And…" He was clearly trying to communicate something important, but I was in no state to help him. "And, well, though your mother and I may have divorced, I have always considered you a part of my family. I know I'm a prickly old hedgehog at the best of times, but I think very highly of you, and I'm only at the end of a phoneline if you should need anything."

He adjusted the box to free one hand and then squeezed my shoulder affectionately. If I hadn't already been in a daze, this would surely have done it. I had to hope he thought that I was simply overcome with emotion, which, in a way, I suppose I was. Smiling at the bridges he'd nimbly mended, he walked over to his white Audi, plonked the box in the boot with a jangle of glass, and then waved goodbye to his fellow suspects as a tow truck pulled his car away. Over on the other side of the porch, Eilish had a yellow hatchback that was alarmingly similar to mine. Wendy's car had about thirty comedy bumper stickers, and poor Edmund's snazzy blue Porsche would remain just where it was.

I turned in circles, watching the relieved faces of my fellow tormentees as David emerged from the house. He was all smiles.

Chapter Twenty-Nine

Once I'd provided a statement to the police and my car had been fixed at a local garage, I drove back to Croydon on my own. Four and a half hours in light traffic is a long time to dwell on a problem, but by the time I got home, I was fairly confident of the facts.

I called the police from my house to tell them what else had occurred to me, and there was still plenty to investigate before the killer could be arrested. None of that was down to me, though. I was just a witness this time around. As Narberth had told me, the police would have to do the rest.

The day after I got home was the press night for my mother's new tour. She was warming up in regional theatres before a three-month residency in the West End. With the money she made, she was hoping to move somewhere swankier than our little town on the outskirts of London, and I was pleased to hear that she planned to build an annex for when Dad and I wanted to visit. Knowing the friendship that existed between my biological father, his ex-wife and her third husband, I predicted this would be a regular event.

I went to see her in her dressing room at the Fairfield Halls just before the event was about to start.

"I don't think I've ever felt so nervous in my life. I know it might sound stupid, but it's the pressure that gets to you, isn't it?"

"Izzy," she looked a bit worried about me, "this really isn't helping. I have to go on in twenty minutes, and I'd prefer to be sitting here meditating rather than listening to you blather."

Danny, Dean and their two respective beauties at least pretended to listen to me.

"I'm sorry. I'm sorry. I just thought this was a really good idea for a million different reasons, but now I'm beginning to wonder whether I should even—"

Mother held her hand out from the chair where Fernando was doing her makeup. "This is nothing new, Izzy. You've been here before, and you'll be fine. I know the whole thing must have been a shock, but I have every faith in you."

"That's right, Izzy," Danny told me. "You'll be amazing, and we'll all be there for you."

Ramesh might have echoed this sentiment, but as my mother's official dresser, he was running in and out of the room, pushing rails of brightly coloured outfits and panicking.

I took a deep breath and continued. "I appreciate it. I really do. I doubt I would have made it through this week if I hadn't known you were all at home wishing me well. I'm aware just how lucky I am to have you."

Dean of all people – that's right, the computer geek who I'd assumed still lived with his mother: Dean Shipman from Bromley – came forward for a hug. His fiancée Fiona joined him and, before I knew it, they were all at it. They huddled around me, and I felt like a hot dog in a bun.

"Five minutes till lights out," my father came in to announce, as if it was almost bedtime. "Oh, a hug! Yes, please. Greg, you're missing out!"

So then there were two more people squashing me, which made Ramesh stop what he was doing to join in. Patricia and Pacino were next door, so he couldn't let them miss out, and I ended up with almost every person I loved in the world wrapped around me. For a moment, I felt like a superhuman Amazonian queen with my cloak of power… or something like that. I felt invincible and, when they peeled off one by one, the sensation stayed with me.

"You'll be great, darling," my mother told me with a tear in her eye. "You always are."

"Two minutes, Izzy," a stagehand peeked inside to inform me, and I smiled and stood up from my seat in front of the showbiz mirror.

"Okay. It's time." I didn't want to leave them, but I knew I had to, if only to free up a bit of space in that cramped dressing room. "I'll see you on the other side."

"I'm sure you'll be a natural," the middle-aged man with the clipboard told me. "There's no need to be nervous."

"Funnily enough, I'm not." I followed him through a corridor with black walls and various doors leading off it, and then we came to another identical one. He held a door open and handed me off to a colleague, who led me to the centre of the stage, where a seat and microphone were waiting for me.

"Have you got what you need?" the stage manager asked.

I sat down on the stool to get comfortable. "I think so."

"Great. Everything has been arranged just as you asked. You can start in about thirty seconds."

I nodded and took a deep breath as he dashed away. Thirty seconds felt like an hour, but then I saw a chink of light at floor level and the curtain rose up to show the audience an awkward young woman in a shimmering black dress, sitting on a stool before a painted backdrop of over-sized diamonds, giant strawberries and flying reindeers – which I could only assume had been made to Ramesh and my mother's ever eccentric specifications.

I looked to the front row where the press, various dignitaries and the people I'd invited were sitting, and I noticed one empty space. There was a polite round of applause as the people of Croydon realised that they weren't getting the superstar mother but would have to put up with her upstart daughter for a while.

I gave one last glance into the wings where my friends and family had now congregated and then leaned towards the microphone to speak.

Author's Unnecessary Interruption

Don't worry, **the book isn't over**. This is just a brief intermission. You see, as I was writing that last chapter, I debated with myself whether the best ending I could give our beloved Izzy was to leave it right here.

She is no longer the insecure, underachiever she was when I published her first novel at the end of 2019. She is still secretly as mad as any of us, of course, but she has finally come to believe in herself, which is what these books are really about. If you compare the first stories with this one, you will see that she no longer questions her ability at every turn, even if she struggles to solve the most difficult puzzle she has faced.

And so I love the idea of finishing the story here, with the ending left to your imagination. But I'm not going to do that, as I think it would be too cruel to you, my wonderful readers, who have read every nonsensical word I've written about this bizarre band of characters.

If you happen to be the kind of person who likes authors who experiment with the form of the detective novel and have just had your mind blown by a whodunit with a vague and indefinite ending, then great! You can consider the book complete and put it down, amazed by my at least comparative originality.

And if you're not? Then turn the page to read Chapter Thirty, and please excuse this interruption.

Chapter Thirty

According to Wikipedia, the main concert hall at the Fairfield can seat eighteen hundred and one people – eighteen hundred and two including me. Almost every great rock act of the twentieth century has played there from The Beatles to Bowie, Genesis to Queen, and a scene from The Da Vinci Code was even filmed inside the main room.

In other words, Lennon, Mercury, Phil Collins and Tom Hanks had all ceded the stage to make way for Izzy Palmer, and with everyone's eyes on me, I started to laugh.

"I'm sorry. I know you're here to see Bu-Bu La Mer." There were a number of excited yells at this point, and the people on the balcony stamped their feet impatiently. "If you can see it in your hearts to give me fifteen minutes of your time, I have a little story to tell."

I was concentrating too hard on what I had to say to stand up or walk around the stage like Steve Jobs. Instead, I sat rigid in the chair and, before I could think about beginning the tale, I had one more announcement to make.

I actually got a couple of cheers of my own then, and the balcony went crazy, so I could only think that my mother had filled it with our extended family. I was less appreciative of the man in the middle of the auditorium who stood up to shout, "Where's the squirrel?"

I ignored him and got on with what I had to say. "I'm sitting on this stage for two reasons. The first is because I want to clear my name. An article was published about me in the paper recently, and I think that even its author would accept that not everything it said was true."

I looked to the area where the press were sitting. The lights were so bright now that I couldn't make out any faces, so I just smiled in that general direction.

"I'm not going to refute all the things it said about me, as this isn't about my bruised ego. The best thing I can do to show you what a good detective I am is to tell you about the most recent case I solved."

I shifted in my seat to get comfortable and began in earnest. "You'll know some of the details by now, but not all of them. You see, over the last month, four different people who had been suspects on my previous cases were murdered. The third happened last week. My mother's manager, Eddie Vanguard, was slain in a secluded spot beside the Thames and, when the police went to his office to go through his files, they found a threatening letter from the killer addressed to me.

"This was hardly a major revelation, as I knew that I had to be connected in some way to the killings, but it suggested that the motive was an extremely personal one. I searched back through my memories to find the culprit, but no one person stood out. It was almost as if no one hated me, which was a difficult concept for me to entertain. You see, I was bullied at school and treated differently for my height, clothes and delightfully quirky personality. The same thing happened at university and again in my first job. In fact, I've spent the whole of my life thinking that I'm an eminently hateable person, so it was something of a surprise that I found this task so difficult.

"Another letter soon arrived, telling me to drive to the middle of nowhere in the middle of Wales to avoid anyone else being murdered. It was hardly my ideal getaway, especially as the last man I truly loved had recently been released from prison and I foolishly decided to call in to see him en route. David Hughes was the culprit in my first murder investigation, and the tragic thing is that, despite his crime, I never stopped loving him. It took me a long time to accept that, but I try to be honest with myself these days. I arrived at his house, aware deep down of how I felt, and presumably hoping that he would come running after me to the spooky house in the mountains.

"What I couldn't have predicted was that he had also received an invitation to my rendezvous with the killer. Of course, rather than just asking him to come with me, I acted like a total weirdo. We argued, and then I drove off into the countryside without him. My destination in the Brecon Beacons was a gothic affair that looked as if it had been transplanted from a horror film, but at least I would not be alone. In the car park when I arrived, I noticed four other cars, including the black Ford that had been spotted at the scene of one of the murders.

"Inside the house was Edmund Porter, a suspect from my second case when his millionaire father was killed. He was sitting in a cosy lounge with my former stepdad. Arthur and I had never seen eye-to-eye, and it somehow didn't surprise me that, even though I hadn't seen him for over a decade, he would be there in my nightmare castle.

"Sure enough, we were soon joined by other nemeses from my

cases. My Uncle Bradley has always been one of my most enthusiastic critics, and HR Manager Wendy Robinson rarely kept such barbs to herself when we worked together. My cousin Noémi and I have had a number of run-ins, though I had to hope that she'd forgiven me over time. It certainly didn't hurt that, shortly after she arrived, an incredibly handsome single man who likes dressing up as Father Christmas came to take her mind off things."

I knew they were in the audience to hear this. It was not just the faint smushy noises that told me. I'd invited all the suspects that night myself.

"David came to my aid after all, and even my sidekick and best friend Ramesh was there – who some of you may know from his award-winning blog 'The Confessions of a Fabulous Doctor Watson' and also for the work he does on my mother's costumes." There was a whoop or two, and I encouraged the audience to join in. "That's right! A big hand for Ramesh. He is, sincerely, the strangest person I've ever met, and I love him dearly."

I'd lost my place a bit by now…

You've gone through the suspects, and now it's time to say what happened.

Right! Yes, that's it. "So there we all were. Scary house. Murderer amongst us, and what should happen? Someone cut the brakes on our cars, and we were left stranded! Mayhem!" *Nope, wrong tone. You sound like a bad comedian again.* "Even worse was to come, though. We'd been lucky that no one had triggered one of the many traps that the killer had left for us around the house, even during a poorly timed game of hide-and-seek. One of them was eventually tripped on the floor above us. No one was hurt, but the falling suit of armour alerted me to our final suspect.

"Eilish Hart was an old enemy from my university days. She'd hidden in the house because she'd seen me arrive and thought that I was there to frame her for the murders. This might sound like an unusual reaction, but one of them had occurred right in front of her place of work."

I was trying to boil the story down to just the facts, but it was difficult to be concise. "So all in all, there were plenty of old antagonists who might have brought me there to exact revenge. But if

I think through the collection of people that congregated at that house, there was one person who was unfairly maligned… Well, I suppose there were two people… or even three, including me." I paused and started again. "There were several people at Bron-Yr-Aur who were unfairly maligned, and Edmund Porter was one of them. He'd been something of a playboy when I'd first met him, but the life he'd lived since then had not been a joyful one. Not only did he have to deal with the murder of his father, the imprisonment of his siblings—"

"And the family butler," an anonymous voice pointed out.

"Oh, right, you probably know most of this from Ramesh's blog. Well, I'm sorry, but I can't just expect everyone in the audience to understand what I'm banging on about."

"Get to the point!" the heckler heckled.

"I am trying!" I huffed an indignant huff and looked for a friendly face beyond the glaring lights. D.I. Irons was standing at the side of the auditorium, and I was fairly sure she would have slung out anyone who got too rowdy. "As I was saying, not only had Edmund had to deal with half his family being murdered or locked up, his last relationship had sapped the strength and confidence from him, and he seemed a shadow of his former self when I interviewed him. A short time later, he went up to his room, lay down on his bed and was crushed to death by the ton of metal that fell on top of him."

I allowed this revelation to settle. There were whispers, gasps and the odd sickly gagging noise, so I figured I should give it a minute. "A kind and gentle man was murdered, and I could only blame myself for not working out the killer's puzzle sooner. All the most likely suspects in my life were there, and I felt that the answer had to be staring me in the face. When I interviewed the suspects, several impressed upon me just how much they had learnt from their involvement in my earlier murder investigations. These were people who I had identified as likely killers, but in the end, it became clear that they'd grown and changed just as I have."

My legs had been locked in place on the little ledge beneath my seat and were beginning to fall asleep, so I shifted them around. "My suspects' apparent remorse only made it more difficult to imagine who the killer could be. I'd had this feeling from the beginning that the culprit was desperate to impress me. I could tell that they'd read the same books that I had and knew the structures I would expect from a murder mystery. It seemed logical that, whatever the solution, it would be informed by the novels of Agatha Christie, G. K. Chesterton and Margery Allingham, and so I kept searching for the twist that would make it a true whodunit."

"Perhaps you done it!" some wag called out, and I ignored him.

Now that would have been a surprise.

Shhh!

"I considered whether my own best friend could be the killer. The guilty party being the man who had accompanied me on the vast majority of my cases would have certainly come as a shock. It wouldn't have made much sense, but it would have been a great ending, nonetheless. I wondered if my estranged stepfather..." *Is that a thing?* "... had spent the last eighteen years desperate for vengeance after the time I refused to accept him as the winner of a game of Monopoly – which, now that I think of it, would have been fairly original. Petty, but original."

Arthur was there and, as pretty much everyone else in the audience had something to say, he decided to shout a quick, "No one likes a sore loser, Izzy!" which I made sure to ignore.

"But those solutions didn't fit. They were just thoughts circling my mind, whereas the simple conclusion, the one that I should have come to early on, still evaded me." I was speaking faster now, gradually building towards a crescendo. "You see, there was one twist that was almost too perfect. Imagine me staying in love with a man who was found guilty of murder and, only after he'd been released years later, discovering that he was so incensed by the part I played in his conviction that he despised me. Imagine the boyfriend I've held up as a genuinely nice guy transforming into a maniac."

The atmosphere had changed in that vast cavern of a room. I could feel the tension, and my voice, as it boomed through the speakers, had taken on a reedy quality. "It was a perfect solution, because it was the one I chose to ignore. David could have got me there to the lonely mansion just an hour from where he lives."

"Depending on traffic!" a Welsh voice in the audience shouted, but by this point, I'd learnt to talk over such comments.

"He could have tortured me with the ghosts of all those old foes before bringing about my death. The evidence was all there. Not just the location, but the fact that he knew the place and could tell me about its history. I'd been sucked in by the idea that he wasn't even going to go until he knew my plan, but what if he was the one who'd arranged the whole thing?"

Rhetorical questions? Never a good idea.

"Then he deserves locking up!" an angry fellow declared, and I was tempted to enquire whether he'd ever been to a theatre before, as not every performance requires audience participation.

"Yesterday morning, after our night of suffering was finally through, and my Uncle Bradley had endured multiple head injuries, a possibility occurred to me. I began to notice evidence that had meant nothing before, and I reconsidered how the killer had cut our brakes. It had happened when we were all in different rooms in the house, so any of the suspects could have cut them, but I never questioned whether the last person to arrive had already done so. David Hughes could have gone to the house in advance to set up the traps and kill poor Mr Powell, then cut the brakes of each car as we arrived."

There was a murmur of what I took to be excitement at this moment, but then I realised that I hadn't actually mentioned the caretaker before.

"Ahhh… bother. I'm so sorry. I forgot to tell you about Mr Powell. You see, when we got to Bron-Yr-Aur, the man who looked after the house while the rich owners were away had already been poisoned, and we found his corpse in a room near the kitchen. I should have mentioned him before, but it doesn't change the story too much, so I'll go back to what I was saying."

I fell silent then and tried not to show that I'd forgotten what I'd been—

The evidence against David.

Right. Yes. Got it!

"As David lived so close to the scene of the crime, he could have murdered the caretaker and set everything in motion, then driven home in case I should call to see him." I've no idea how politicians chatter away in parliament without needing a sit-down. I was sitting down, and I was still exhausted. "When the possibility entered my mind, I knew just what a fool I'd been to ignore it. I mean, he'd been with Edmund just before he died. He'd taken him up to his bedroom so that the inebriated victim didn't have to go on his own. But what if, instead of keeping the poor man safe, he'd pushed him onto the bed to trigger the trap that killed him?"

I paused for perhaps half a second before explaining, "That was a rhetorical question. It doesn't require an answer." Another spate of muttering followed, and I caught a "Talk about stuck up!" and perhaps a faint "Who's she to tell us we can't shout out random nonsense in a theatre?" With my mic in hand, I got off the stool and walked closer to the audience. That was too much exercise, so I sat down beyond the lights at the edge of the stage to see them more clearly.

One seat in the front row was still empty, and my legs dangled in front of it as I finished my point. "I told you this story to show that, despite it going against all my wishes, I came to the right conclusion. But I wasn't the one to find the final piece of evidence. The police searched the room where David was supposed to sleep if the evening had followed its predicted route. Hidden in the wardrobe were various tools that the killer had used, along with the poison that was put into Mr Powell's food in order to kill him."

I had to stop then. It was all too much. I'd been on plenty of stages in my career and was no longer afraid of public speaking as I'd once been, but this time, the emotion was overwhelming. There were tears in my eyes as I forced myself to speak.

"David Hughes is a killer. He was the obvious suspect, and I should have realised it from the very beginning."

Chapter Thirty-One

I imagine that the resounding feeling in the room at that moment was one of pity. *Look at that idiot girl with her overly long limbs and penchant for murderers,* the audience must have been thinking. *Talk about pathetic.* Or perhaps people are kinder than I usually imagine, and they genuinely felt sorry for me.

I got back on my feet, wiped away the wee tiny tears from my eyes and walked towards the side of the stage. "I told you that I came here for two reasons tonight, and to finish off my support slot before my mother takes her turn, I need the help of a lovely assistant."

I walked into the wings and had to physically drag the person in question back on with me. David Hughes was a killer. He was also a heavy chap to pull about the place, and he had a shy grin on his face as I did so.

The audience were suitably horrified, but I didn't really care what they thought. I wasn't there for them. I was there to talk to the man I loved.

I held the microphone to his mouth and asked a question. That didn't work, as no one could hear it, so I reversed the arrangement and tried again. "David Hughes," I kept my eyes on him and paused for ten long seconds to savour the moment that had taken far too long to arrive, "will you marry me one day eventually?"

I couldn't exactly get down on one knee for it. He was six foot two, and no one would have heard his reply from down there. Thinking back, I should have asked for two microphones, but hindsight is a brilliant thing… in hindsight.

His eyes dropped to the floor, and he looked like he wanted to punch me – though not in a murdery way, I hasten to add. When he didn't answer, I poked him in the chin with the mic.

"Fine, yes. Of course I will."

There was a cheer from the balcony and some boos from lower down, but I didn't mind in the least.

"And did you kill Jack Campbell, Marco Romanelli, Eddie Vanguard, Mr I-Don't-Know-His-First-Name… Powell or Edmund Porter?"

He was really laughing now.

Inappropriate.

"No, of course I didn't."

Mic back to me. "Do you know who did?"

Mic back to him. "I haven't a clue. Are you going to tell us?"

Back to me. "Not quite yet." I dropped the mic to the floor. It made a truly horrendous noise. The audience complained en masse and, as we've already established, I really didn't care. I was too busy kissing my fiancé.

Miaow! Grrrr! Hubba hubba.

Would you please shut— Oh fine, think what you like.

I kissed him, and fireworks exploded overhead. Dogs in the surrounding streets howled at the moon, and the audience really got into it this time. The thunder of feet from the balcony was deafening. There were cheers and applause, and perhaps I'm not so different from my mother after all, as I loved every minute of it.

Kiss number seventeen (of course, I'd kept counting) is the best so far.

"Did you really think that I was the killer?" he asked when we finally pulled apart.

"I had to consider it. It would have made the best twist."

He kissed me again, and I bet in his head he was thinking, *Come here, dummy.*

The point at which the audience realised there was something a bit creepy about watching a newly engaged couple make out on stage came a lot sooner than I was expecting. The chants soon turned from, "Kiss him! Kiss him! Kiss him!" whenever we separated to "Identify the real killer! Identify the real killer! Identify the real killer!" It was really very moving.

"Okay, I will!" I shouted from the bottom of my lungs to get them to stop and then picked up the mic so that I didn't strain my voice. "Actually, can whoever's in charge of the lights turn them down a bit? It's like staring into BAT99-98 in the Tarantula Nebula." To pre-empt any questions from the audience, I explained. "BAT99-98 is the most luminous star yet discovered. And, yes, I briefly dated a guy who was really into astronomy."

My request was fulfilled, and, still holding David's hand, I started the story again. "I'm very happy to tell you that the man I have loved since for what feels like forever is not responsible for any murders (this year). The real killer wanted me to believe it was David because, with the evidence we found and his past record, any court in the land would have found him guilty."

Some warmer lights were cast onto the stage at this moment, so I guess that the tech guys were trying to help things along.

"I've already revealed the major spoiler that no one particularly hates me." I paused then, as I expected at least one heckle. But, nope, I am not as eminently detestable as I'd always thought. "This realisation forced me to question what had really been going on over the last month. It was undeniable that the four main victims were linked through my cases. I could think of no other way to connect a shamed Italian politician, an heir to a financial dynasty, a part-time weed dealer and one of London's most ruthless talent agents. Well, there was one thing; they were all men, and even one of the traps that my unfortunate uncle triggered was in the gents' toilet.

"Of course, nearly half of all people share that characteristic, but it made me wonder about the killer's motive and cast into doubt the idea that I was the ultimate target. Soon after I heard of the evidence that the police had discovered on David, I went to the front of the hotel and, as I watched the various suspects packing their cars, I finally began to ask the right questions.

"If I wasn't the killer's target, who was? Why murder three men before dragging all those people to a secluded house? And, for that matter, why come up with such an elaborate plan in the first place? I stood outside the mansion and looked at the killer's black car that was still parked where it had been when I arrived. Closer to the house was my own ugly box on wheels, Edmund's sports car, my stepfather's Audi and a space where there had once been a small Skoda. I only noticed it because three of the cars were arranged like a French flag. And I later assumed that the little red car belonged to Eilish, as she was the only other person who arrived before me. But when we left yesterday morning, I noticed that her yellow car was parked some distance away on the other side of the porch."

The audience was silent, but I liked this bit, so I took my time. "There were twelve cars at the house but only eleven people including the caretaker. Or at least, that's how it seemed. The killer didn't need to be there after our brakes had been cut. They took the caretaker's car and drove away as fast as possible. That isn't just conjecture. I told the police my theory, and they found the Skoda, burnt to char on a South London housing estate. People often accuse me of being excessively bound by the plots of mystery novels, and perhaps they are right. But I wasn't so beholden this time. I looked beyond the closed group of suspects to find the real culprit."

There was a stirring in the front rows of the theatre just then. My fellow guests from the Bron-Yr-Aur Hotel were happy that they weren't about to be accused of some terrible crime.

"The killer got away, but not without making a major mistake. For the story that David was the bloodthirsty maniac to make sense, I had to die, but that couldn't happen because I was supposed to read the clues that had been left for me just as I would a whodunit.

"It would certainly have been easy enough to kill me if that was the killer's intention. A trap set in the library would have been the obvious choice, but there wasn't even one in the ladies' toilet or the room where I was supposed to sleep. Such mistakes told me that the real victim – the only victim that mattered in all of this – was one of the two men who died in that house.

"It seemed unlikely that anyone would work so hard to link me to the killing of a caretaker I'd never met, which only left Edmund Porter. Edmund was the inordinately wealthy head of a major company. He was the brother of a killer, the son of a slain millionaire, and he'd once asked me out on a date."

I think I heard a murmur of, "Alright, show-off," from somewhere in the crowd.

"His sister in prison told me how fragile he was after a calamitous break-up, and that I should be careful how I treated him because of his feelings for me. Not many people would have known that about him, but it was the second time I'd heard it in the space of a few days."

I was still holding on to David, and his hand was warm and comforting. I didn't plan to let go for some time. "As I told you, I came here for two reasons. I've already bagged myself a one-day, at-some-point-in-the-future husband, but I'd also like to respond to the allegations that were made about me in a national newspaper. I was accused of all sorts of terrible things, and over the course of our interview, it was evident that the journalist had a problem with me. She mentioned my non-existent relationship with Edmund Porter, though I'd never told anyone about it.

"I don't know a great deal about Ella, the woman Edmund was supposed to marry until he realised how cruel and controlling she was. I know that she comes from a rich family called the Jamesons, has a job in the media and was furious when Edmund dumped her, but I had no way of linking her to the murders and no reason to think that she could be involved, especially as I was surrounded by people with well-reported grudges against me.

"The journalist who came to my house to gather facts that she would ultimately ignore for her article was called Janet Ellison, but sadly, she couldn't make it tonight. I'd hoped to bring her up on stage, as I promised her the story of the events in Bron-Yr-Aur in exchange for a few key pieces of information. I asked her to find out who the house belonged to, and though she informed me of its history, she neglected to give the name of the family that owned it. Meanwhile, all she could tell me about the car the killer used was that it had been written off and sold for scrap.

"She did do one very helpful thing, though. At eleven o'clock on Thursday night – which was around the time that Edmund fell for the only deadly trap in Bron-Yr-Aur in the very room that was reserved for him – she went in person to my house in South London to tell my parents that she couldn't get in touch with me and was worried that something bad had happened. She didn't tell them exactly where I was, but at least she put in an appearance.

"If you're lucky and there isn't too much traffic, you can drive from the Brecon Beacons to my home in West Wickham in about four and a half hours. The brakes on our cars were cut after the last of us arrived at five o'clock. Six hours would have given the killer plenty of time to complete the journey, set fire to the car that she'd taken and make her way to my Mother's house to provide herself with an alibi. It really wasn't so different from the scheme that Edmund's sister had conceived in order to kill their father. Both women made the mistake of inviting me along to follow the breadcrumbs they'd scattered, and both women were found out. Ella Jameson, or Janet Ellison as she goes by in her career, believed she could do a better job than the woman who would have been her sister-in-law. She thought she was cleverer than Audrey Porter, Izzy Palmer and the police."

David didn't know the whole story until then and looked a little impressed. My heart was racing, but I was determined to finish. "I wanted her with us tonight to hear the explanation I just gave you. I wanted her to think that I had fallen for her scheme and that this caring, blue-eyed, surprisingly muscly under his shirt, gorgeous…"

Oooookay, that's enough.

"…man would be arrested for her crimes. I wanted to see her face when she realised she'd been beaten, but apparently, that's not something that the police allow anymore." I looked at D.I. Irons and mouthed an awkward, *Sorry*. "So, instead, there's an empty seat in amongst the journalists who've come here to watch my mother's incredible show, and there's a newly occupied cell in central London tonight. My friends in the police have spent the last day compiling evidence against Ella Jameson to prove the part she played in five men's deaths. She was more than just a crazy ex. She treated Edmund as her possession and hated him so much after he broke off their engagement that she didn't care who had to suffer for her to get even."

I took a moment to gaze across the audience who were clearly stunned by the story I'd just told them. Well, it was either that, or they were wishing I'd get on with it so that the main event could start. "It's a terrible story, and so before the inimitable Bu-Bu La Mer takes to the stage, I just want to say thank you for listening, and tell you how happy I am that a truly despicable person will be punished for her crimes."

David leaned towards the microphone, to say, "Thank you, everyone," then he put one arm around my back so that we could leave the stage together. "There's one thing I don't understand," he whispered as we turned away. "Who wrote the note saying that you'd ruined their life?"

I kissed that sweet, kind-hearted man before answering. "I figure that was Arthur. He really would have said anything to win the game we never got around to playing."

I hadn't been expecting applause, but it was at this moment that the audience rose to their feet. The roar was immense, not just from the balcony this time, but right through the auditorium as hands clapped together and people shouted our names.

"Ladies and gentlemen," my mother stepped from the wings to declare, "I present my daughter, Izzy Palmer. The most brilliant detective I know."

I stopped to acknowledge the ovation, and my grin was no doubt just as goofy as David's. We stood there and let the sound wash over us, and I was just so happy that it was all done… until the next case, of course.

"And if we ask very nicely," my mother continued, "she might just join me in a song."

"Nope. Not going to happen. Bye bye."

Epilogue

A DAY IN THE LIFE OF IZZY PALMER AND DAVID HUGHES

A look inside the home of the noted detective and her ex-convict husband.

From a glimpse at their stylish terraced house on the border between Kent and the Capital, one might think that newlyweds Izzy and David have got life well and truly sorted.

"David is the house-proud one," Izzy confesses. "He'll normally run a feather duster over the place before I've fallen out of bed." She laughs at the sight of her husband's blushes, and I get a real sense of the love that the two share.

"A normal morning for us involves a lie-in," David explains, "and then we might have a quick practice on our accordions before Izzy's sidekick, press manager and official dresser, Ramesh, comes around with his wife and their two beautiful children, Pacino and Chris-Tina."

"Excuse me for interrupting," the debonair assistant interrupts, "but I'd just like to point out that my daughter's name isn't simply *Christina.* It's made up of the first part of Christina Aguilera's Christian name and the whole of Tina Turner's. The stress is on the first syllable."

"I don't know where we'd be without Ramesh," Izzy pipes up. "Not only does he choose our clothes each morning, he reads the papers in our presence to make sure there's nothing we need to know that might affect one of our cases."

"Of course, life is very different if Izzy and Ramesh are busy with an investigation," David explains.

"In what way?" I ask as I sit at their cosy kitchen nook enjoying a cup of Izzy's beverage of choice.

"Well, I drink a lot more hot chocolate," she candidly replies.

"There is that," the convicted killer and former manager of a major financial services firm confirms, "but it's more that her cases can take them far afield or just next door. We never know when someone might get murdered in Izzy's vicinity."

"That's right," his wife agrees. "At the rate that people are killed off around me, I couldn't quit this business if I wanted to."
"Scientists have named a syndrome after her." David looks proudly at the woman who once put him behind bars. "It's strange, but it appears that she's not the only one affected by the condition. There are quirky young women across the globe who find themselves compelled to investigate curious deaths. It's particularly prevalent around cupcake bakeries and coffee shops for some reason."
"And also on cruise ships and in cat cafes." Palmer looks serious for the first time since I stepped through the front door. "Izzyitis is a serious problem. We just have to hope that, with all the incredible breakthroughs that modern science unlocks, doctors will be able to find a cure."
"After breakfast," David says to get us back on track, and I have a sense of his role in the relationship, guiding his brilliant but flighty wife, "if Izzy hasn't got one of her biweekly dentist appointments, we'll normally go for a stroll in the park or up to the Addington Hills viewpoint. Then, if no one has been murdered, our friends will come around and Ramesh will cook us all lunch."
"Again, I'm sorry to interrupt," Ramesh interrupts, "but I'd just like to say that I tried to convince Izzy and David to go for a triple wedding with Dr Danny Fields and billionaire Dean Shipman of X-Tec Spyware, but they all refused. I did get to design their wedding clothes at least, and everyone thought that the Inspector-Morse-inspired suit looked just beautiful on the bride."
"And I would like to say," David interrupted the interruption. "That I was very happy to finish the wedding with the same number of guests as when we started."
Izzy laughs her gentle laugh as she looks at her two favourite men. "Though we weren't quite so lucky on the honeymoon."
"Yes, that was a pity." David glances down dreamily at the mug in front of him. "Who would have thought that the idyllic Greek island of Santorini could be a hotbed for such violent and complex murders?"
The details of that case have, of course, now been immortalised on film. 'The Honeymoon Mystery', starring Elizabeth Debicki as Izzy and supermodel David Gandy – in his first acting role – as her new husband, received rave reviews when it was released earlier this year.

"And what about you, David?" I ask in a tentative tone. Hughes has been notably reticent about his future since his early release from prison. "Are you happy playing the house husband, or do you have other plans?"

"I wouldn't call it playing," he chides me softly, "but the most important thing for me at the moment is to spend as much time as I can with the woman I love."

"What my dear husband isn't telling you is that he's actually a brilliant writer. He's been working on a book about his life in prison and his volunteer work with first-time offenders."

David doesn't say anything then, he just looks across at his accomplished wife and smiles. It's a very sweet moment, and I can tell how strong the bond is that the two of them share, especially after all they had to go through to find one another.

"If I may ask one final question," I begin, having finished the last sip of my hot chocolate. "Why do you think you work so well together? It can't be too common for a detective to marry one of the criminals she has sent to prison."

The room falls silent for a moment, and neither of them breaks eye contact as Izzy finds an answer. "We fit together perfectly. No one quite knows the reason, but we do."

The End

Find out how Izzy's adventure began...

Check out the complete Izzy Palmer Collection in ebook, paperback and Kindle Unlimited at Amazon.

The next **Izzy Palmer Mystery** will be available in **2044**

Izzy, David, Ramesh, his seven children with ridiculous names, Bu-Bu La Mer, some of her husbands, that guy who collects trolleys at the supermarket, Mrs Dominski from the newsagents, (not really a) Princess Penelope, Dean the secret billionaire, Danny the TV doctor, Auntie Val and Father Christmas will be back in 2044 for the 25th anniversary of **"A Corpse Called Bob"** in...

About this Book

This is a spoiler-filled final chapter in a massively spoiler-filled book. Please stop here if you haven't read what comes before.

So there we have it. My first series is complete… until someone can offer me enough money to continue it, Netflix picks it up for a series or I reach the ripe old age of 62 and find the inspiration to do credit to the imagined sequel above (which, for the ninety-nine per cent of people who don't get it, is a "Princess Bride" reference. And, yes, the best jokes are the ones you have to explain).

Before editing this book for the first time, I went back to the first novel in the series to prepare it for the audiobook. It is still one of my favourite things I've written and it's also my worst-reviewed book. Why is that? You may not ask, though if you're still reading book number ten, you must have some affection for it. Well, I think there's a mismatch between what I thought people wanted to read and the demands of mystery fans. The Izzy books are neither full-on saccharine, as so many cupcake/pet-based cozy mysteries are, nor are they quite so clean and innocent as most novels in the genre.

It was my idea to break the mould by mashing my love of murder mysteries with my love of rom-coms to create something totally new. If there's one thing that I've learnt since then is that there's a reason that books in clear genres tend to do well and mould-breaking books only succeed on rare occasions. A lot of readers, myself included, tend to stick to a few specific genres, and it makes it a lot more difficult for a publisher to market a book if you have to go to some length to explain what it is.

My Edgington books look like 1920s mysteries. You can see it from the cover already and, even if I've tried to do something a little bit different by writing them from the perspective of a young apprentice rather than the aging sleuth, you wouldn't necessarily know that from the blurb. I'm very grateful for the people who enjoy both of these series, but it's understandable that plenty of readers who found me through Edgington might not enjoy "A Corpse Called Bob" and give up on the series there.

Despite this seemingly negative precis, the Izzy books were essential for my career as they did well enough to make me believe that I could make it as an author, and I wouldn't have kept writing them if I didn't love them. I said from the beginning that I intended to write ten novels, and I'm glad to have fulfilled my promise and not let down those of you who have stuck with me.

I can also now tell you that this was the ending – and especially the final situation – I had always planned. David was always meant to reappear, and it is also the desired ending that many readers (including my mum) have hoped for since. When I was just starting out, a French friend of mine translated the first couple of books and was never surprised by my twists because, in his words, "Izzy isn't allowed nice things". I hope that I've proven him wrong this time around. To be honest, I did consider making David the killer a second time, but I'm not that mean. I had a funny e-mail from one of my regular readers complaining that I'd made the killer to obvious as there was simply so much evidence against Izzy's future husband, at which point I realised that she'd accidentally stopped reading before Chapter Thirty.

Around the time I published the first book, I wrote a list of potential settings and scenarios in which Izzy could find a corpse, but I also imagined a coming together of her various suspects – inspired in some part by the scene in the fairly disappointing James Bond film "Spectre", when Bond is confronted with images of his past failures and nemeses.

Of course, the difference between wee Izzy Palmer and tough old James Bond is that the people Izzy comes up against tend to display at least some level of humanity. Even the most cartoonish or despicable characters in these books present a more sympathetic side to their personalities. So, rather than Izzy coming face to face with a parade of horrors, I realised that I had to allow their goodness through (with the possible exception of her uncle and first stepfather). I liked the idea that former suspects had grown because of their involvement in Izzy's cases, as we see with Wendy and Noémi.

There's an argument to be made that this is not the story of Izzy and David, but Eilish Hart. She's the only other character to feature heavily in both the first book chronologically and the last, and she goes on a similar journey to Izzy. I'm not saying it would be a very convincing argument, but it was fun to maintain and even rehabilitate the seemingly awful people like her who keep popping up in Izzy's life.

I also wanted this book to be something of a greatest hits compilation. They have always been self-referential, and I love in-jokes and callbacks in books and TV shows, so this was a great deal of fun to write. I was forever flicking back and forth between the books, looking for information and, invariably, laughing at past jokes. To get all the references and even understand what on earth is going on, you need a good memory. I'm sorry if that means I've made you work too hard, but I love the idea that so many people wanted to make that effort to get the most out of these characters.

As in "Lost", "Game of Thrones" and plenty of other TV shows, there's always the danger of holding off an ending for too long and spoiling the story by adding in unnecessary plots and stringing out storylines beyond their natural life. I'm happy to say that I think I avoided such a fate with these books. I believe that every entry in this series has its place in the overarching story, and if I were to return to this group of characters in future, they would be at another stage in their lives and require a different approach.

Of course, now that they are going away, I will miss these loveable maniacs more than I can tell you. Since I started my other series, I have viewed writing the Izzy books as a bit of a holiday. It is very relaxing not to have to check the OED to see whether a word I'm using is anachronistic, and there's a freedom to my writing here that I don't have when I'm adopting a voice from a century ago. There are parts of me in all my main characters, but I feel a special affinity for Izzy, and I think it's fair to say that the voice in my head is somewhere in between hers and Chrissy's.

A reader once asked me whether I thought that Izzy suffers from a particular mental health condition or is perhaps even mildly autistic, but I don't believe that's the case. I've always thought of her as an anxious person who is learning to control her emotions in order to function in a world that is ultimately crazier than whatever is going on in her own head. My brother Daniel, to whom, in many ways, this series belongs, is a psychiatric nurse, and has had some very strong views on the characters. Despite being my big brother, he's complimented me on how I've dealt with the issue in my books, and I'm happy that Izzy's unusual outlook has resonated with people.

Daniel has been going through a very difficult time over the last few years. He was cured of cancer in one part of his body, only for its subsequent development in the liver to go undetected for almost two years. He started chemotherapy last November and, since then, the cancer has spread to his blood. We've had some incredibly difficult moments over the last couple of months as bad news compacted bad news, and my whole family has been affected by it. And yet, except for one call I had with him at the darkest moment, Daniel has been a fount of positivity. He has amazed me with his ability to keep believing in the cure and I'd really like to ask of you my (going by the fact you're hanging around after the story is over) most dedicated readers to do the same thing that he has asked of me.

He feels that the more intensive treatment he is currently having is his best chance of surviving and he's asked everyone he knows to focus on and hear in our minds the news that he has responded well to the treatment and is winning the fight against the terrible sickness that has invaded his body. I dedicated this book to him, not just because of all he's been through, nor his truly inspirational strength, but because he is one of Izzy's biggest fans and has shaped this series in any number of ways.

Izzy and David finish this part of their story surrounded by friends and family who love them. They also enjoy a shared appreciation of amateur accordion playing and walks up to the viewpoint where Bob staged his cringeworthy memorial service. I hope they'll be very happy together, and I hope these books have brought some sunshine into your lives, too.

Thank you so much for reading.

Some Final Bits That Don't Fit into the More Serious Section Above

I was slightly disappointed when I discovered that what I thought was a hilarious name for a website selling dog and cat accessories actually exists. Pet-à-porter.com is fictional, but there really is a pet-a-porter.co.uk. Similarly, there is also a Jack the Ripper musical!

Though I don't have to check quite so many facts in these books as I do in my historical ones, I did look up some confectionary items. I discovered that Maltesers were once sold as a weight-loss product, as it was believed that the malty filling really was lighter than ordinary chocolate. I also learnt that the inventor of M&Ms (and Mars, Maltesers, 3 Musketeers etc) was allergic to peanuts. The son of the original Mr Mars broke off from his family business and invented some of their most famous products – not to mention branching off into the pet food market, which they still dominate – before finally being tempted back to the main company.

My international readers might not know Jammie Dodgers, but they are two round biscuits filled with jam, like a miniature version of a Linzer cake. I assumed that they would have been around for a century or more, but they're actually only from 1960 and were named after a character called Roger the Dodger from the classic British comic, "The Beano", which still exists today and gave the world Dennis the Menace. The British Dennis the Menace is different from the American character of the same name. Extremely weirdly, both comics debuted on the very same date in 1951 but have no other connection to one another.

You probably know what mysteries have influenced me and Izzy, but I've been thinking a lot about the comedies that inspired me in writing this series. As I mentioned before, I do like romantic comedies. The nineties, when I was growing up, was a great period for the genre. I described the first book as Agatha Christie meets Bridget Jones, but before that seminal rom-com, I loved tacky nonsense like "10 Things I Hate About You", "Sleepless in Seattle" and "While You

Were Sleeping". More significant to the tone of these books, though, were bizarre British TV sitcoms like "Father Ted", "The I.T. Crowd", "Green Wing", "The Vicar of Dibley" and "Spaced", not to mention the brilliant stand-up James Acaster. I think that we do surreal humour pretty well in Britain, but I also love a lot of American stuff and especially the high-speed, non-stop gags of shows like "30 Rock" and "The Unbreakable Kimmy Schmidt" from Tina Fey. Give them a go if you're looking for a laugh.

The three countries I'm sure that I know best in this world are Spain, England, and Wales, possibly in that order. I've always wanted to set a book in my mother's home country, where I lived for six years after leaving home, and I'm not sure that this one really counts. We do get a glimpse of the beautiful countryside in the Brecon Beacons – and there really is an enormous hotel which once belonged to an opera singer up there – but David and his family, and the inspector at the end, are the only Welsh characters, so I will definitely have to revisit the Land of Song and its kind, generous, outgoing inhabitants in another book before too long.

And last, but not least, let me tell you about my brothers and me bickering. The biggest schism between Izzy and Arthur – and perhaps the reason that his marriage to her mother ended – surrounds arguments over board games. My brothers and I were well known in our family for being a touch too competitive. There was a famous game of Pictionary when I was about twelve that left Daniel and me wanting to murder each other, much to the enjoyment of our cousins. Suffice it to say, we patched things up afterwards, but for everyone's safety, we have not played again since.

Read More Lord Edgington Mysteries Today...

- **Murder at the Spring Ball**
- **Death From High Places** (free e-novella available exclusively at benedictbrown.net. Paperback and audiobook are available at Amazon)
- **A Body at a Boarding School**
- **Death on a Summer's Day**
- **The Mystery of Mistletoe Hall**
- **The Tangled Treasure Trail**
- **The Curious Case of the Templeton-Swifts**
- **The Crimes of Clearwell Castle**
- **The Snows of Weston Moor**
- **What the Vicar Saw**
- **Blood on the Banister**
- **A Killer in the Wings**
- **The Christmas Bell Mystery**
- **The Puzzle of Parham House**
- **Death at Silent Pool** (Autumn 2024)

Check out the complete Lord Edgington Collection at Amazon.

The first ten Lord Edgington audiobooks, narrated by the actor George Blagden, are available now on all major audiobook platforms. There will be more coming soon.

Get your **Free** Izzy Palmer Novellas...

If you'd like to hear about forthcoming releases and download my free novellas, sign up to the Izzy Palmer readers' club via my website. I'll never spam you or inundate you with stuff you're not interested in, but I'd love to keep in contact.

www.benedictbrown.net

Acknowledgements

To keep things simple, I'm going to focus on one group of people this time around; thank you to everyone who has fallen in love with these characters and (still to this day) begged me to write more about Izzy and her friends. Without you, I would not have had the desire or commitment to finish this series, so you're very much a part of the writing process.

A final thank you must go to my crack team of experts – my cousin, Dr Heather Elliott (medicine), Paul Bickley (policing), Karen Baugh Menuhin (marketing) and Mar Pérez (dead people) for knowing far more than me. Thanks to all my fellow writers too, especially Pete, Suzanne, Rose and (the real Izzy Palmer) Lucy Middlemass. Please keep leaving positive **reviews on Amazon**. They really help!

And last but not least to my ARC team... Rebecca Brooks, Ferne Miller, Melinda Kimlinger, Emma James, Mindy Denkin, Namoi Lamont, Katharine Reibig, Linsey Neale, Karen Davis, Taylor Rain, Terri Roller, Margaret Liddle, Esther Lamin, Lori Willis, Anja Peerdeman, Kate Newnham, Marion Davis, Sarah Turner, Mary Nickell, Vanessa Rivington, Helena George, Anne Kavcic, Nancy Roberts, Pat Hathaway, Peggy Craddock, Sonya Elizabeth Richards, John Presler, Mary Harmon, Beth Weldon, Karen Quinn, Karen Alexander, Mindy Wygonik, Jacquie Erwin, Janet Rutherford, M.P. Smith, Robin Coots, Molly Bailey, Nancy Vieth, Ila Patlogan, Lisa Bjornstad, Randy Hartselle and Keryn De Maria.

About Me

Writing has always been my passion. It was my favourite half-an-hour a week at primary school, and I started on my first, truly abysmal book as a teenager. So it wasn't a difficult decision to study literature at university which led to a masters in Creative Writing.

I'm a Welsh-Irish-Englishman originally from **South London** but now living with my French/Spanish wife and presumably quite confused infant daughter in **Burgos**, a beautiful medieval city in the north of Spain. I write overlooking the Castilian countryside, trying not to be distracted by the vultures, hawks and red kites that fly past my window each day.

I previously spent years focussing on kids' books and wrote everything from fairy tales to environmental dystopian fantasies right through to issue-based teen fiction. My book **"The Princess and The Peach"** was long-listed for the Chicken House prize in The Times and an American producer even talked about adapting it into a film. I'll be slowly publishing those books over the next year on Amazon.

If you feel like telling me what you think about Izzy, my writing or the world at large, I'd love to hear from you, so feel free to get in touch via...

www.benedictbrown.net

A Comprehensive Character List

(Including Countless Spoilers from Previous Books)

Izzy's Former Colleagues from Porter & Porter in "A Corpse Called Bob"...

Bob Thomas – the corpse in question. Izzy's monstrous boss who she found dead on the first page.

Jack Campbell – The security guard who was found to be running a semi-ethical marijuana dealing business on the dark web.

Amara Donovan – one of the managers at P&P. She's really lovely… no, really.

Wendy (she may have a surname, she may not) – Izzy's easily outraged nemesis who has a collection of interesting skirts and slept with, then got robbed by, Bob.

Suzie Hawkes – Izzy's near-mute deskmate.

Will Gibbons – Bob's apprentice who appreciated the way that Izzy and Ramesh avoided revealing details of his life and turned a page to be a better person.

David Hughes – Izzy's boyfriend who turned out to be Bob's killer – though he did it for really very reasonable reasons.

Izzy's Main Friendship Group...

Ramesh Khatri – If you don't know who this guy is yet, this book is not for you.

Patricia Khatri – his ever so patient wife.

Pacino Khatri – their bouncing baby boy.

Elton John, Kiki Dee, and Tammy Wynette – their cats.

Dr Danny Fields – Izzy's childhood crush, former boyfriend and newly minted TV doctor.

Shandy Duchamp – Izzy's schoolfriend (from A Corpse at a School Reunion and Birthday Party) who got together with Danny in the last book.

Dean Shipman from Bromley – a secret tech millionaire… or is it billionaire? He and Izzy once went on two dates back when he didn't know how to talk to other people. He's one of the good ones.

Fiona… (if she had a surname at any point, I can't find it!) – Dean's lovely red-haired lawyer girlfriend, now fiancée.

Izzy's Family…

Mum – Rosemarie Palmer / Bu-Bu La Mer – Mother and viral video star turned sweetheart of the British stage.

Dad – Ted Palmer – just a sweet, well-meaning man – kind of based on my dad, Kevin.

(Nice) Stepdad Greg – Rosemarie's third husband and the right man for her. He is generally serious and formal but goes along with the madness of the Palmer clan.

(Meanie) Stepdad Arthur – he makes his first full appearance in this book but has been mentioned many times and had a cameo in the first novella (A Corpse in a Freezer).

Noémi Castleton – Izzy's rich, stuck-up cousin. She was horrible when they first met, and only pretended to be nice at the family reunion in "A Corpse in A Locked Room" She was swindling her mother out of her money by getting her French boyfriend to pretend to be her boyfriend.

Elizabeth Castleton – Noémi's mother who realised what her daughter was doing and (big spoiler alert!) staged her suicide to look like a murder in order to incriminate her children.

Uncle Bradley – Izzy's old-fashioned, outspoken uncle who clearly hasn't learnt humility from his appearance in "A Corpse in a Locked Room".

Old Suspects Who Don't Fit in Anywhere Else...

Marco Romanelli – As Izzy explains, "a popular guru in Italy who threw his hat into the political ring only for his violent, pseudo-Nazi movement to falter when it turned out that his wife had murdered her way to fame and success." In "A Corpse on the Beach".

Eddie Vanguard – Izzy's mum's theatrical agent, featured in "A Corpse in London" and "A Corpse on the Beach".

Edmund Porter – the son of Izzy's former employer who was murdered in "A Corpse in the Country" by (big spoiler alert) his sister Audrey.

Audrey Porter – I literally just explained who she is.

Nicholas (Father Christmas) – a department-store Santa who Izzy dated in "A Corpse Wrapped in Tinsel".

Eilish Hart – Izzy's sort-of nemesis. She once stole some meat from our heroine in "A Corpse in the Freezer", and Izzy has never quite forgiven her, even after she appeared to have seen the error of her ways in "A Corpse Beside the Seaside".

New Characters in this Book Who Make Brief Appearances...

Janet Ellison – a serious journalist who interviews Izzy at her home and then writes a nasty (let's be honest, it's probably libellous) exposé about her.

Tom from Accounting – He... is in one scene for a bit.

Mr Powell – the caretaker of the now closed Bron-Yr-Aur hotel.

Inspector Narberth – a cherubic Welsh police officer

Made in the USA
Monee, IL
01 August 2024

63112688R00152